**Lady Tregowan's Will**

*An unexpected inheritance. A year to wed.*

When Lady Tregowan dies, she leaves an unexpected will. Her estate is to be divided between the three illegitimate, penniless daughters of her late husband—complete strangers until now. The terms? They must live together in London for a year and find themselves husbands or forfeit their inheritance!

*The Rags-to-Riches Governess*

Available now

And coming soon from Janice Preston:

*The Cinderella Heiress*

Beatrice Fothergill is determined to make a marriage of convenience on her own terms—she doesn't expect to fall for her suitor's brother!

*The Penniless Debutante*

Left destitute when her parents die, Aurelia Croome doesn't trust men—especially aristocratic ones. Until she meets James, Lord Tregowan...

## Author Note

Sometimes an idea comes to you as a writer and you dismiss it as too complicated to write. And so it was with Lady Tregowan's Will. I loved the idea of three young women—all strangers and down on their luck—who inherit a share in a fortune out of the blue, and who discover at the same time that they are half sisters. But I couldn't quite see how it would work, given that—inevitably—the three women's stories would be closely intertwined.

But the idea wouldn't go away, and so I explored how I could make it work without too many overlaps, given that each book must be able to be read as a stand-alone story. And I'm pleased I persevered, as I've thoroughly enjoyed writing this first book in the trilogy, all the while with one eye on the other two stories to come.

I hope you'll enjoy this first part of the trilogy as governess Leah earns her happy-ever-after with Lord Dolphinstone. Watch out for Beatrice's story next (*The Cinderella Heiress*) followed by Aurelia's tale (*The Penniless Debutante*).

# JANICE PRESTON

---

## The Rags-to-Riches Governess

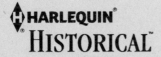

# HARLEQUIN®
## HISTORICAL™

ISBN-13: 978-1-335-50601-6

The Rags-to-Riches Governess

Copyright © 2021 by Janice Preston

This edition published by arrangement with Harlequin Books S.A.

For questions and comments about the quality of this book, please contact us at CustomerService@Harlequin.com.

Harlequin Enterprises ULC
22 Adelaide St. West, 40th Floor
Toronto, Ontario M5H 4E3, Canada
www.Harlequin.com

**Printed in U.S.A.**

**Janice Preston** grew up in Wembley, North London, with a love of reading, writing stories and animals. In the past she has worked as a farmer, a police call handler and a university administrator. She now lives in the West Midlands with her husband and two cats and has a part-time job with a weight-management counselor—vainly trying to control her own weight despite her love of chocolate!

## Books by Janice Preston

### Harlequin Historical

*Regency Christmas Wishes*
*"Awakening His Sleeping Beauty"*
*The Earl with the Secret Past*

### Lady Tregowan's Will

*The Rags-to-Riches Governess*

### The Lochmore Legacy

*His Convenient Highland Wedding*

### The Beauchamp Heirs

*Lady Olivia and the Infamous Rake*
*Daring to Love the Duke's Heir*
*Christmas with His Wallflower Wife*

### The Beauchamp Betrothals

*Cinderella and the Duke*
*Scandal and Miss Markham*
*Lady Cecily and the Mysterious Mr. Gray*

Visit the Author Profile page
at Harlequin.com for more titles.

With grateful thanks to my good friends and fellow authors Lynn Forth and Elizabeth Hanbury, who gave up a morning of their time to brainstorm the Lady Tregowan's Will trilogy.

## Chapter One

Miss Leah Thame stepped down from the post-chaise sent to convey her from Dolphin Court on the Somerset coast into the centre of Bristol and peered up at the office of Henshaw and Dent. The letter she'd received two days ago had been most insistent she attend a meeting here today, hinting she would miss out on the opportunity of a lifetime if she ignored its summons. Leah did not entirely believe in the idea that good fortune might strike one out of the blue, but even she, with her practical nature, could not quite bring herself to ignore the possibility of good news.

She surveyed the building in front of her—no different from the neighbouring houses in this terrace, except for the brass wall plaque next to the door—and bit her lip. Henshaw and Dent, Solicitors. Her hand slipped inside her cloak and she traced the shape of Mama's wedding ring, which she always wore suspended from a ribbon around her neck. Normally it remained hidden beneath the serviceable brown or grey gowns she wore day-to-day in her post as a governess at Dolphin Court, but today both ribbon and ring were on display, adding a touch of decoration to her old royal-blue carriage gown.

She rummaged in her reticule for Papa's pocket watch and opened the cover. Twelve minutes still to noon, the time of her appointment. It had been fifteen years since Mama's death and seven since Papa's, but the ring and the watch still conjured their memories and left Leah feeling slightly less alone in this world. A sudden, craven impulse to flee was quashed. She had come this far and, besides, she must rely upon Mr Henshaw for her transport home to Dolphin Court, for she had little money of her own to squander upon luxuries such as the hire of a post-chaise-and-four.

The clip-clop of hooves and the rattle of a carriage down the street behind her shook her from her thoughts, and she shivered as the brisk chill of the air on this, the last day of January, fingered beneath her cloak. It was time to find out why she had been summoned; she set her jaw, straightened her shoulders and rapped on the door.

'Miss Leah Thame,' she said to the sallow-faced, stooped clerk who opened it. 'I have been summoned to a meeting with Mr Arthur Henshaw at noon.'

'Follow me, miss.'

Leah stepped past the clerk, who closed the door, plunging the hallway into gloom. The building smelled of damp and dust, and her throat itched as she followed the clerk up a steep flight of stairs to the first floor. He knocked on a door and waited. Not once did he look at her or catch her eye, and although she was not a nervous type of woman—governesses could not indulge themselves in a surfeit of sensibility—Leah nevertheless identified the subtle tightening of her stomach muscles as being caused by unease.

'Enter.'

The clerk flung open the door and gestured for Leah to enter.

'Miss Thame, sir.' The door clicked shut behind her.

The office was lined with shelves crammed with books. A fire smouldered sullenly in the fireplace, emitting little warmth, and an ornate bracket clock sat on the mantel shelf above. Seated at the far side of a large mahogany desk was a middle-aged, bespectacled man with a receding hairline, who now rose to his feet and rounded the desk to bow.

'Arthur Henshaw, at your service, Miss Thame. May I take your cloak?'

Leah removed it, and he hung it on a coat stand in the corner of the room.

'Please, take a seat.' He indicated a row of three wooden chairs facing the desk. 'I am sure the others will arrive very soon.'

Leah frowned. 'Others?'

'All will soon be revealed.'

Henshaw returned to his chair at the far side of the desk, which was bare apart from a low stack of legal-looking documents, a silver and cut-glass inkstand and a silver wax jack, and immediately selected one of the documents and began to read, his high, narrow forehead furrowing. Leah chose the middle of the three chairs and sat down. The ticking of the clock was loud in the silence.

Her thoughts touched upon her employer, the Earl of Dolphinstone, and the news he was back in England after more than sixteen months away. He was expected back in Somerset soon—although he had not yet confirmed the date of his arrival—and Leah quailed as she imagined his reaction if he were to discover she had left his two young sons in the care of the local vicar's daughter, even though this was the first time she had left them, despite being entitled to one day off per month.

Leah adored both her job and her charges, but she

was apprehensive about His Lordship's return. Since being forced to earn her living as a governess—following her father's death when she was nineteen—this was the first time she had felt settled, happy and at home. She couldn't help but worry her employer's return would herald change.

A mental image of His Lordship—appealingly masculine and ruggedly handsome—materialised in her mind's eye. She had met him just the once, at her interview for the post of governess, and he had seemed harsh and remote but she'd made allowances at the time, knowing he had been recently widowed. By the time she took up her post, however, Lord Dolphinstone had already left for the continent and had been away ever since. For him to leave his children so soon after the death of their mother, and to stay away so long, beggared belief, and she still struggled to understand such a lack of fatherly concern. Leah had since done everything in her power to give the boys the stability they needed.

The clock suddenly chimed the hour, jolting Leah from her worries about the Earl's return. Henshaw looked expectantly at the door. Within seconds, a knock sounded.

'Enter.'

'Miss Fothergill, sir.'

Henshaw, once again, rounded the desk and greeted the newcomer before taking her coat. Leah fought the urge to peer over her shoulder at Miss Fothergill—she would see the other woman when Henshaw introduced them. The newcomer sat to Leah's right, but Henshaw remained out of sight behind them, tapping his foot on the polished floorboards and emitting the occasional sigh rather than perform any introduction.

Leah succumbed to her curiosity and glanced sideways. Miss Fothergill's eyes were downcast as she chewed her bottom lip. Light brown curls peeped from beneath her brown bonnet and her fingers fidgeted in her lap, prompting the governess in Leah to want to reach out and cover her hand to conceal both her restlessness and her emotions, as befitted a lady.

Before long there was another knock at the door and the previous performance was repeated as someone called Miss Croome arrived. This time, Leah did not look sideways at the newcomer but directed her attention onto the solicitor as he returned to his chair.

'Allow me to make the introductions,' he said. 'Miss Aurelia Croome.'

Leah inclined her head to acknowledge the woman to her left, summing her up with a sweeping glance—petite, and pretty enough, although she looked a little gaunt, as though a square meal wouldn't go amiss. Her dove-grey gown was well made but ill-fitting and shabby, much the same as the bonnet covering her hair, which was fair, if her eyebrows and lashes were any indication.

'Miss Leah Thame.' Leah became the object of attention from the other two women, and she acknowledged each of them with a nod.

'And Miss Beatrice Fothergill.'

Miss Fothergill—also petite and pretty but pleasantly plump—looked nervous, her smile hesitant. That knot of unease inside Leah tightened. Should she be anxious too? She glanced again at Miss Croome, who looked irritated, if anything, and she felt reassured.

'Well,' said Henshaw, leaning back in his chair. 'This is quite unprecedented.'

He removed his spectacles and peered down his nose at each of them in turn, then removed a handkerchief from his pocket and wiped his brow, the only sound in the room the ticking of the clock. Henshaw stuffed his handkerchief back in his pocket.

'Yes.' He shook his head as his gaze once again passed from woman to woman. '*Quite* unprecedented, not to mention perplexing. You ladies must appreciate it has given me a real dilemma as to how best to proceed.'

Miss Croome stirred. 'Perhaps if you enlightened us as to the purpose of this meeting, Mr Henshaw, we might shed some light on your...er...dilemma.'

She was well spoken; clearly a gentlewoman down on her luck.

'Yes. Well...'

The solicitor again paused, and again he fished his handkerchief out of his pocket, polished his spectacles and placed them back on his nose.

'Yes...the terms of the will are quite clear, of course. I just... I simply...' He looked at each woman in turn, his eyes, magnified through the lenses, perplexed. 'Lord Tregowan—the *current* Lord Tregowan—will be unhappy, you may be sure of that. I have written to him again, to clarify matters. Bad tidings for him, but *I* did not draw up *this* will, you understand. I thought I had her latest will and testament—drawn up by me and signed and witnessed three years ago in this very office.'

A will? Leah frowned. She had no family left to lose, unless one counted Papa's Weston connections on his mother's side, and she doubted any of them even knew of her existence. They had never shown the slightest interest in Papa, the connection far too distant. And what did it have to do with Lord Tregowan?

'This...' Mr Henshaw picked up a document, pinching one corner of it between his forefinger and thumb as though it might contaminate him, his nose wrinkling in unconscious distaste '...*this* arrived last week. And yet I cannot refute its authenticity. I'd recognise Her Ladyship's signature anywhere, and it is witnessed by the partners of a legal firm in Bath, although quite why she went to them I have no notion. No. I am afraid it is authentic. There can be no doubt of it.'

The dratted man was talking in riddles.

'*Mis*ter Henshaw. *If* you would be good enough to proceed…?'

'Patience, Miss Thame. Patience.'

*Patronising wretch.* Leah glared at the solicitor. 'The three of us have been sitting in this office for twelve minutes now, and in my case, considerably longer, and all we have learned is that the reason for this meeting—which *you* arranged, requiring the presence, I presume, of all three of us—meets with your disapproval. I have taken leave from my post to attend here today, and I should appreciate your expedition of the matter in order that I may return to my duties as soon as possible.'

Henshaw straightened, looking affronted. '*Miss* Thame—'

'You spoke of a will, Mr Henshaw?' Miss Croome interjected.

'Indeed, Miss Croome,' the solicitor said. 'The will of Lady Tregowan, late of Falconfield Hall, near Keynsham in the County of Somersetshire.'

Miss Fothergill stirred. 'My…my mother worked at Falconfield Hall.' Her voice quavered, as though it had taken courage to speak. 'She was companion to Lady Tregowan. Before I was born.'

'Quite.' Mr Henshaw levelled a censorious look at each of the three in turn. 'Your mothers each had a connection with Falconfield. And with Lord Tregowan.' His upper lip curled.

Leah elevated her chin. '*My* mother did not work there.

She and her parents were neighbours of the Earl and Countess.'

She would not have this shoddy little lawyer look down his nose at her. She might be forced to earn her living as a governess, but her mother—who had died of consumption when Leah was eleven—had been born to the gentry and her father came from aristocratic bloodlines, descended from the Fifth Earl of Baverstock.

Henshaw levelled a disdainful, but pitying look at her. Leah's teeth clenched, her pulse picking up a beat. She looked at Miss Croome, who had yet to react.

'I know of no connection between my mother and Falconfield Hall,' she said, 'but Lady Tregowan did once visit my mother's milliner's shop in Bath.'

Mr Henshaw consulted the will again. 'Miss Aurelia Croome, born October the fourth 1792 to Mr Augustus Croome and Mrs Amelia Croome?'

Pink tinged Miss Croome's cheeks. 'Yes.'

'Then there is no mistake. I am convinced it is the three of you who are to benefit from Her Ladyship's largesse.'

'What is the connection between the three of us?' The other women looked as confused as Leah felt. 'It is clearly through our mothers, but how?'

Henshaw's lip again curled. 'The connection is not through your mother, but through your sire. You are half-sisters.'

# *Chapter Two*

Leah stiffened, staring at Mr Henshaw. 'But...that is not possible. Papa...he would never... He was a man of the Church! He would *never*...'

Words failed her. She did not dare look at either of the other two, although she had heard their gasps at his pronouncement.

*Sisters?* No! It was impossible.

Mr Henshaw's lips pursed, and Leah's courage surged at his clear disdain for the three of them.

'My father,' she said, enunciating clearly and precisely, 'would *never* have played my mother false.'

'Well, I would believe almost anything of *my* father.' Miss Croome shot a sideways look at Leah. 'And, as for yours, I believe what Mr Henshaw is implying is that Lord Tregowan fathered each of us—presumably, in your case, before your mother married Mr Thame.'

'That is correct,' said Henshaw. 'It was Lord Tregowan who arranged the marriage of each of your parents, once your mothers'...errr...*conditions* were made known to him. And, from what I gather, each marriage was to a gentleman in need of funds, and none of your mothers suffered a lowering in their status after their indecorous behaviour.'

Shock sizzled through Leah. No wonder Henshaw viewed the three of them with condescension. She knew enough about the law, however, to understand that Mama's marriage to Papa before Leah was born meant she was not illegitimate. A shudder racked her at the thought—at least she did not have that stigma to blight her life.

'This…' Miss Fothergill sucked in an audible breath, and when she spoke again, she sounded close to tears. 'If this is true, it changes everything. I do not know what I shall do.' Her distress was palpable and, again, Leah resisted the urge to pat her hand.

'You mentioned the *current* Lord Tregowan earlier,' said Miss Croome. 'Does that mean our father is dead?'

'He died eight years ago, and the title and the Tregowan estates—which were entailed—passed to his heir. Falconfield and the London house were brought to the marriage by Lady Tregowan and he left them to her. He'd fallen out with the current Lord Tregowan's father years before, and so refused to leave his heir any more property than he was forced to under the entail.'

'Have you proof of this?' Every principle she held dear urged Leah to reject the solicitor's words. Her darling mama, fallen from grace? Her beloved papa, not even her true father? Nausea rose to block her throat.

'I have had copies made of Her Ladyship's will, which you may take with you when you leave,' Henshaw said. 'It confirms your paternity.'

'Would you kindly get to the point swiftly, Mr Henshaw?' Miss Croome's eyes narrowed as she stared at the solicitor. 'Clearly you are unhappy, and I, for one, will be pleased to leave this fusty old office behind. You mentioned bequests, so please say why you have summoned us and be done.'

'Very well. Lady Tregowan of Falconfield Hall has passed away, and it is my duty to advise you that she left the three of you her entire estate, to be divided equally between you, subject to certain conditions.'

Leah froze, barely able to comprehend his words. *Her entire estate?*

Miss Croome leaned forward. 'How much is it worth?'

'It is substantial. It comprises Falconfield Hall and its land, which, as I said, is near to the village of Keynsham on the Bath Road, plus a town house in London, and various funds, the income from which, in the past year, amounted to over fifteen thousand pounds. You are now three very wealthy young ladies.'

Miss Fothergill gasped and swayed in her seat. Leah, still reeling herself, opened her reticule and handed her smelling salts to Miss Fothergill. Beatrice. Her *half-sister*.

Excitement exploded through her. She had family. She would be wealthy. She would no longer have to earn her living as a put-upon governess. Except…as quickly as it had risen, her elation subsided. Her current post was not drudgery—she loved her life at Dolphin Court, and she adored Steven and Nicholas, as well as baby Matilda, and the boys adored and relied upon her in their turn. How could she turn her back on them? The very thought dismayed her.

And what about Papa? Her stomach churned. He wasn't her father. Worse, he had known it. But he had been the best, most loving father she could ever have wished for—to take pleasure in this news of unexpected riches seemed disloyal, almost as though she would be rejecting Papa in favour of a man who had seduced her beloved mama.

A sharp prickling in her nose warned of imminent tears and she surreptitiously pinched the bridge between thumb and forefinger.

*Oh, God! I have sisters!* How often as a child had she prayed for a sister or a brother, prayers that had gone unanswered? Until now. And, of a sudden, she had two of them. But they were complete strangers. Her mind whirled as violently as her stomach, but she strove to keep her inner turmoil hidden.

Beatrice handed back the smelling salts, smiling shyly. As Leah tucked the bottle back into her reticule she wondered where the other two women lived and if they would ever meet again. That thought triggered another. She frowned.

'You mentioned conditions?'

'Ah. Yes. They are quite straightforward. For a full twelve months from today the three of you will have the joint use of the two properties, and your living expenses will be met out of the income from the funds as mentioned. After that year, providing you have met the further conditions of the will, you will inherit your share of Her Ladyship's estate outright.'

'What further conditions?' Miss Croome… Aurelia… demanded.

'I am getting to that, Miss Croome. The conditions specified in the will are that you will reside in London for the entirety of the coming Season and you will remain under the chaperonage of Mrs Butterby, who was Lady Tregowan's live-in companion, until you marry. After the Season ends you will have the choice of whether to reside in London or at Falconfield Hall, but you must each of you marry within the year.'

*'Marry?'* Miss Croome's upper lip curled. 'Why?'

'As Lady Tregowan failed to consult me in drawing

up this final will, I am not privy to her reasoning.' Henshaw's lips thinned. 'I dare say Mrs Butterby will be able to enlighten you.'

Leah raised her brows, exchanging mystified looks with the other two—her half-sisters. 'And if we do not marry within the year?'

'If you fail to wed, Miss Thame, you will forfeit the major portion of your share of the inheritance, which will then be divided between the other two sisters. You will be required to return any purchases made during the twelve-month period, other than purely personal items such as clothing. So, jewellery, for instance, or carriages, or even houses, will be forfeit. A cottage on the Falconfield estate will be provided for you to live in, and you will receive a lifetime annual allowance of two hundred pounds so you are not left entirely destitute. Plus, there are two final stipulations. If any of you wish to sell your share of Falconfield Hall, the others—or, strictly, their husbands—will get first refusal. And, finally, you must not marry your father's—that is, the late Lord Tregowan's—successor, the current Lord Tregowan, who is a distant cousin.'

Leah frowned at the final condition. The aristocracy were usually keen to keep their land and estates together. 'Why?'

'As I said, Lady Tregowan sought neither my services nor my advice.'

An uneasy silence fell in the room and Leah used the time to attempt to collect her thoughts. Uppermost was the news she would have to marry, but she had long ago dismissed any likelihood of marriage. If she ever wed, she would want…*need*…a marriage like that of her parents: warm, loving, respectful, happy. She would never settle for putting her life and now her fortune—*how strange that sounds*—in the hands of a husband who did not love her. She had seen too many examples of such unions in her time as a governess, and she had no desire to be trapped in such a marriage herself.

She harboured no illusions about her prospects—she was already six-and-twenty, and she saw herself in the mirror every day, with her sharp nose, high cheekbones and pointed chin; her tall, lanky figure; her red hair and freckles. She had learned from bitter experience she was not a woman to stir romantic feelings in any man. The only two men who had ever shown any interest in her had both seen her merely as a means to an end.

Her father's curate, Peter Bennett, had courted her, but she'd learned too late he'd only done so in order to curry favour with Papa. When Papa died and Leah—with no prospects other than having to earn her own living—was forced to vacate the vicarage, Peter quickly revealed his true colours by turning his back on their informal understanding. Instead, he'd immediately set out to win the favour of the new vicar, who possessed two daughters.

And then there had been that dreadful Christmas when she had been working for Lord and Lady Petherton. Their eldest son and heir, Viscount Usk, had come home with two friends for the festive season and had promptly set out to charm Leah. She had been wary and had resisted him until, on Christmas Eve, he had captured her under the mistletoe and pleaded for a kiss. His single-minded pursuit of her had lulled her instincts… She had fallen for his protests that he adored red hair and freckles, and she had allowed the kiss. Even returned it. Whereupon Usk had pushed her aside and crowed to his friends, 'Got her! Told you I'd do it. Five pounds from each of you!'

She would never forget that humiliation, nor the shock of being turned away before the New Year after Usk's parents had learned of that wager. They had been painful lessons, and she had learned to be cautious where gentlemen were concerned. She had little doubt her half-sisters—both of them younger and far prettier than Leah—would have more chance of finding husbands.

'Ahem!' Henshaw broke the silence with a cough, then shuffled through the stack of papers on his desk. He handed one document to each woman. 'As I said, I have had copies made of the will—' he rummaged in his desk drawer and withdrew three small leather pouches '—and here is a purse of money for each of you, to offset any interim expenses before you arrive in London. You will no doubt need a little time to prepare for the change in your circumstances and to leave your old lives in good order, but I would urge you to allow time in London for your new wardrobes to be made before the Season proper begins after Eastertide.'

Leah stowed her copy of the will and the purse in her reticule, her mouth dry as uncertainty flooded her all over again. What would this mean for her future? She'd become accustomed to changes in her life since Papa's death, but each change had become harder and her soul yearned for safety and stability. Her chest squeezed with pain. *Papa.* He wasn't even her real father, but he'd been all that was kind and loving, all that she could have wanted in a father.

'All I require is your signatures to this declaration, confirming you have been advised as to the contents of the will and the conditions attached to your inheritance, and then you may leave,' Henshaw said.

Each woman signed the document in turn and Leah was appalled to find her hand was shaking. Surreptitiously eyeing both Aurelia and Beatrice, she identified signs of their own stress as they avoided making eye contact.

'Three post-chaises will be waiting outside to transport you home,' Henshaw continued. 'You must arrive at the London house—the address is in the will—at the very latest on the day after Easter Sunday, that is, by the fifteenth of April, or your share will be forfeit. Mrs Butterby is already in residence and preparations to accommodate you are under way. Do you have any questions before you leave?'

'I do.' Aurelia's voice faltered, her face bright red. Leah was alarmed to see her eyes sheen with tears. 'Might I...*may* I go to London immediately? Will I be allowed to live in the town house straight away?'

For the first time Leah spotted a glimpse of compassion in Henshaw's expression.

'Yes, Miss Croome, you may.' He scribbled a note. 'Here is a note for Mrs Butterby. Shall you need to return to Bath first?' Aurelia shook her head. 'Then I advise you to travel on the mail coach. It leaves the Bush Tavern on Corn Street at four every afternoon. It is not far from here; I shall send my clerk to purchase a ticket on your behalf and instruct him to dismiss your post-chaise.' He looked at Leah and Beatrice. 'Would either of you care to go immediately to London with Miss Croome?'

'Oh, no! My brother... I will be expected home,' said Beatrice breathlessly.

'No, thank you,' said Leah.

Henshaw crossed to the door and opened it, and she could hear the murmur of voices.

On his return, he said, 'I shall bid you all good day now. Miss Croome, you may wait downstairs in the general office until my clerk returns with your ticket.'

As Henshaw assisted Aurelia with her coat, Leah frowned, realising it made no sense.

'Why would Lady Tregowan concern herself with us?'

'I know nothing more than I have told you, but I dare say Mrs Butterby will provide you with more detail. She was Her Ladyship's companion for the last twenty years or so. I suggest you ask her when you convene at the town house.'

*If I go to the town house. I need not accept the terms of the will.*

The idea of a London Season—filled with beautiful, elegant young ladies, all vying for a husband—filled Leah with horror.

*But two hundred pounds per annum is a substantial sum, and I would have a roof over my head.*

True independence, even on a limited income, was enticing. But…how lonely it would be. For that, she would have to leave the boys—the very thought wrenched at her heartstrings and reminded her she must get back to them. Of a sudden, Leah could not wait to be in the solitude of the post-chaise with the chance to get her thoughts in order. She led the way down the dingy staircase and out into the fresh air, where two post-chaises waited at the kerb, each with a post boy stationed by its door. The third vehicle was driving away.

She turned to the other women. Her sisters. And had no idea what to say.

'We cannot discuss this here on the pavement,' Aurelia said. 'But… I am happy to meet you both. I always wanted a sister.'

Her smile glowed, and Leah could see the potential for beauty, once her skin bloomed with health, her hair shone and her face filled out. There was no doubt this news made Aurelia happy.

'As have I,' said Leah.

'And I,' said Beatrice, 'and now I have two.'

'Well, I hope you will both join me in London very soon, and we can get to know one another properly.'

'Ladies?' The nearest post boy interrupted them. 'Transport for Miss Thame? We must be leaving, or we won't get back before dark.'

'Thank you. I will come now.' Leah smiled at her sisters. 'If you wish to write to me, I live at Dolphin Court, Westcliff, Somerset. I know where you will be, Aurelia. And you, Beatrice?'

'Oh.' Beatrice appeared to shrink away from the others. 'I am not sure… That is…my brother…he will disapprove. I *shall* come to London, though, no matter what he—' She bit off her words with a gasp. 'I shall see you both then.' She hurried to the second post-chaise. 'Is this one for Miss Fothergill?'

The post boy nodded, and she stepped up into the vehicle. As the chaise pulled away from the kerb, she lowered the window and waved, her smile doing nothing to alleviate the anxiety of her expression.

'Well,' said Aurelia. 'I already dislike her brother intensely.'

'As do I.' Leah looked at her sister, mentally scrabbling for a friendly comment. 'Aurelia is such a pretty name.' She stepped up into her waiting post-chaise. 'I hope I shall see you soon. Have a safe journey.'

The horses moved off sharply, jolting her off balance. She sat down with a bump, and by the time she looked through the window, the post-chaise was turning out of the street and Aurelia was lost to sight.

## *Chapter Three*

Piers Duval, Lord Dolphinstone—Dolph to his friends—
leaned his head against the glass of the carriage window,
straining to catch his first glimpse of Dolphin Court.
Home. As the familiar building came into view across
the valley, his throat thickened with a mix of guilt, dread
and joy.

He had missed home and his three children more than
he'd ever thought possible during the long months away.
Within that churning mix of emotions, guilt gained the
upper hand—he should never have stayed away so long,
not when the children had just lost their mother. The
guilt intensified. When the request had come for him to
join Lord Castlereagh, the Foreign Secretary, in Vienna,
he had grabbed the excuse of duty with both hands and
had rushed off to Europe rather than face the bewilderment of two young boys whose mother was there one
day and gone the next. Matilda had thankfully been too
young to grasp the catastrophic change in all their lives.
Dolph had selfishly fled his own guilt and grief, unable
to cope with reliving each and every day that had led up
to Rebecca's death, wondering in despair what he could

have said or done differently. Wondering what signals he overlooked. Wondering how he could have stopped her.

He'd thought Rebecca was content with her life. Theirs had been an arranged marriage—they'd rubbed along together well enough, but they'd never been in love. Whatever that meant. Maybe he was incapable of loving anyone? After they'd wed, Dolph's life had continued much as before, with extended stays in London due to his interest in politics and government, and, when he *was* home, with the estates. Rebecca disliked London and had seemed happy to remain in Somerset. Looking back, he realised they had never really talked in depth about their lives or their feelings or their expectations of the other.

And his wife had been more unhappy than he had ever imagined.

Swamped by guilt, he'd been incapable of comforting his children after Rebecca died. Hell, he'd barely been able to look at them, knowing how badly he'd let down his entire family. So, he'd appointed a governess for the boys and he had left, convinced they'd all be better off without him.

'You're quiet, old fellow.'

Dolph straightened, pushing away from the window and from his inner turmoil, and eyed his travelling companion, George, Lord Hinckley, in whose carriage they travelled and who had been quick to accept Dolph's invitation to convalesce at the Court after a duel left him fighting a life-threatening infection.

'You must be eager to see the children again after all this time,' George continued. 'I can only apologise once more for further delaying your return.'

Dolph huffed a laugh. 'It was not entirely your fault— Tamworth has always been a hothead, but it was lunacy for him to challenge you over one waltz with Miss Andrews.'

'And lunacy for me to accept his challenge?' George's left arm rested in a sling to protect the shoulder pierced by Tamworth's sword. 'I did attempt to appease him, but he was spoiling for a fight and there's only so many insults a fellow can take.'

Dolph refrained from pointing out Tamworth would not have taken such exception had George refrained from flirting quite so outrageously with Miss Andrews. That comment would achieve nothing. George was a known flirt who fell in and out of love with alarming regularity, but his flirtations were never serious, and Tamworth, had he been thinking straight, knew it. Dolph had arrived back in London in time to act as George's second and had then felt obliged to remain with his old friend until his life was out of danger.

'I wonder if the children will recognise you,' George continued, reviving Dolph's fear the boys would never forgive him for abandoning them. 'How long is it since you've seen them?'

*Too long.* 'Sixteen months.'

It had been a long haul. Dolph had joined the British delegation in Vienna in October. He had been just one member of the delegation assisting firstly Castlereagh and then the Duke of Wellington in their endeavours to negotiate a long-term peace plan for Europe after twenty-three years of almost continuous war. And then had come the news of Napoleon's escape, and the appalling carnage at Waterloo, followed by weeks and months in Paris to negotiate a definitive peace treaty between France and the four Allied powers of Great Britain, Austria, Prussia and Russia.

'The boys will recognise me, but Matilda was only

three months old when—' He swallowed down the pain. *When Rebecca died.* 'When I left.'

Guilt stabbed him again. If only he had noticed the depths her moods had sunk to…the implications of her state of mind…he might have been able to stop her. To save her. He thrust that thought away. Officially, it had been an accident, and she had lost her footing as she walked on Dolphin Point.

Only Dolph knew the truth that Rebecca had taken her own life just three short months after giving birth to the daughter she had always longed for. He had destroyed the incoherent, rambling letter she had left him, aghast at how low she had sunk without him even noticing, her words seared into his brain. She had not blamed him. She had, heartbreakingly, blamed herself. Convinced herself he and the children would all be better off without her.

But he *was* to blame. If he had spent much less time away in London and more time with his young family when at home—and less time preoccupied with estate business—then surely he *would* have noticed. He *could* have stopped her. And it seemed he had learned nothing, for, rather than stay at home with the children after Rebecca's suicide, he had run away like a coward.

The call to go to Vienna had appeared to come at exactly the right time, allowing him to escape the tragedy. He now saw, however, that it had come at the very worst time, giving him the perfect excuse—patriotic duty— to avoid the difficult and painful aftermath of Rebecca's death.

He had, eventually, dealt with his grief, but his guilt at abandoning his children remained—hence the mix of joy at the prospect of seeing them again and the dread they would never forgive him. But at least—according to Mr Pople, his estate steward, who wrote regularly to update

Dolph on all matters pertaining to Dolphin Court—the boys were thriving in the care of Miss Thame, the governess he'd appointed before he left. So at least he'd got that right.

After the Paris Treaty had been signed in November, Dolph had hoped to be home for Christmastide, but a bout of influenza had delayed his journey, and then bad weather—with winds whipping up such a fury that ships lay hunkered in port rather than risk the English Channel—had delayed it some more. Once he'd reached London, George's escapade had delayed him still further, and here they were, already at the end of January.

Now was his chance to make amends, however. He intended to sacrifice his interest in politics and stay in Somerset for the sake of the children. Henceforth, they and they alone would be his priority.

He turned to George. 'We're almost there. How's your shoulder?'

'Still a bit stiff and sore, but I should soon be able to discard this sling. It has helped cushion my shoulder during the journey, however; the roads down here are shockingly full of potholes, my friend. I wonder you don't repair 'em.'

Dolph laughed. 'You cannot hold me responsible for the state of the entire road from Bristol to Westcliff.'

His laugh disturbed the third occupant of the carriage. Wolf lifted his great, shaggy head and gazed worshipfully at Dolph while his tail thumped gently on the floor. Dolph scratched Wolf's ear, and the dog's head lowered back to his paws as he heaved a sigh. He'd first met Wolf—full name Wolfgang—in the Augarten in Vienna, where his owner, Herr Friedrich Lueger, walked him every day.

The two men had struck up a friendship, enjoying many and varied discussions about the world, life and their place in it. It had been Herr Lueger who helped Dolph understand that burying his emotions beneath the business of the day was merely delaying the time when he must come to terms with Rebecca's suicide. By then, however, he had been fully embroiled in the Congress, and his patriotic urge to do his duty for his country had prevented him leaving until he was no longer needed to help navigate a diplomatic route through the turmoil Napoleon had left through vast swathes of the continent.

His heart ached at the memory of Herr Lueger, who, one day, had missed his daily constitutional in the park. After he'd failed to turn up for several days running, Dolph had gone to the building where Herr Lueger had rooms to discover he had died. The landlady had informed him, tersely, that the dog wasn't her responsibility, and she had turned him out. Several hours' searching had found Wolf, and Dolph had adopted him as his own.

The carriage rocked to a halt and Dolph yawned and stretched, thankful to reach the end of the journey. He gazed up at the Court. Home. He flung the door wide and leapt down onto the gravelled forecourt, followed by Wolf, before lowering the carriage steps for George, and then turned again to the house, the front door still firmly shut. Maybe he should have written to inform them of the exact day of his arrival, but he had wanted to surprise the children. All was quiet and still—hardly surprising at four o'clock when the light was fading... The children were no doubt indoors with their governess, maybe listening to a story by the fire.

Then a whoop split the air, and a young lad hurtled around the far corner of the house, closely followed by a younger boy shouting, 'Wait, Stevie. Wait for me.'

Dolph's heart leapt. Steven and Nicholas. His sons.

*Dear God, how they have grown.*

Dolph watched, enthralled, as his eldest son turned at his brother's plea and waited for him to catch up. He grabbed Nicholas's hand, and then, without looking up, he set off at a run, tugging Nicholas behind him, straight towards Dolph, who dropped his hand to Wolf's collar in case the dog should become too excited.

It was Nicholas who noticed the carriage, men and dog first, and he stopped, pulling Steven to a halt, pointing ahead, his eyes big with wonder. At that moment, a woman carrying another child puffed around the corner. Matilda. Love exploded through Dolph. His three children. Safe and well. He frowned. The woman...she looked familiar, but she was not Miss Thame and neither was she one of his servants. He could not fully recall the governess's features—they had only met the once, at her interview—but she had been uncommonly tall for a woman, and slender. The woman carrying Matilda was short and plump, and as she spotted Dolph, she jerked to a halt, her expression a picture of dismay. Dolph's eyes narrowed in recognition of Philippa Strong, daughter of the local vicar.

*What the Devil is she doing here, and where is Miss Thame? And why does she have Matilda as well as the boys?*

He employed a nursemaid to care for the baby so the governess could concentrate on Steven and Nicholas. Perhaps she was ill?

Dolph released Wolf and strode forward. 'Hold him, will you, George?' he snapped over his shoulder. But almost at once, he slowed. To reach Miss Strong and demand answers, he must pass his sons, who clung together, their eyes wide.

He reined in his exasperation and paused next to them.

'Well, Steven? Well, Nicholas? Do you recognise your papa?'

'Yes, F-Father. W-welcome home.' Steven, trying to be grown up at seven years of age. Let down by the quiver of his lower lip.

The urge to drop to his knees and to gather his sons to him in a hug was constrained by a surge of awkwardness. He'd been a somewhat distant father before he'd gone away, in the same way he'd been a distant husband. Uncertainty wound through him. What if he scared them? What if they didn't want to be hugged? What if he made them cry? Instead of following his instinct, he patted each boy on the head.

'Thank you, Steven. I am happy to be here.' His heart ached at the wariness in both boys' expressions. Miss Strong reached them at that moment.

'Lord Dolphinstone,' she puffed. 'Good afternoon. And welcome home. Leah…that is, Miss Thame…did not say you would arrive home today.'

Dolph bowed. This was not Miss Strong's fault. At least *she* was looking after his children, unlike the women he paid to care for them.

'Good afternoon, Miss Strong. I do not deny I am surprised to find you here. Would you care to explain?'

As he spoke, he reached out a tentative hand to touch Matilda's cheek with his forefinger. So soft. So pretty, with a mop of fair curls just like her mother's. Matilda jerked away from Dolph's touch and hid her face against Miss Strong's shoulder. She was a year and seven months now, and he was a stranger to her. He did not even know if she was walking yet. He glanced back at the boys, still clutching one another where they had stopped.

'I…um…well…'

Miss Strong's voice faded as a yellow bounder bowled

up the carriageway at a reckless pace and swung into the forecourt. The postilions reined their mounts to a steaming halt. Dolph frowned. A glance at Miss Strong revealed her relief. Before either of the postilions dismounted, Dolph strode to the door of the post-chaise and flung it wide. He recognised Miss Thame in an instant, with her scraped-back red hair, her pale, freckled skin and her large, wide-set eyes, although he recalled neither the brilliance of those same eyes nor the soft curve of her lips, parted in a gasp of surprise before they firmed. In that first moment their gazes collided, her eyes darkened until her pupils were ringed by the narrowest band of turquoise and Dolph's breath caught in his lungs.

'My Lord! I... I did not know you were expected home today.' Guilt danced across her expression as her cheeks flushed.

'That, Miss Thame, is patently obvious.' He held out his hand to assist her from the vehicle, ruthlessly quashing an inexplicable urge to close his fingers around hers. 'We will discuss this inside.'

By the time he closed the door and turned, Miss Thame had crouched down and Steven and Nicholas had run to her, clinging to her. Pain pierced Dolph as he took in the tableau—the scene he had wanted to create with his sons played out before his eyes with their governess.

'We *missed* you, Miss Thame,' Steven said. 'Miss Strong made me read the Bible!'

'Stevie...you know very well we study the Bible every Wednesday morning.'

*Morning? She's been gone all day?*

Dolph frowned. How often did she leave the boys like this? And why?

'Miss Strong was following *my* instructions,' Miss Thame said, before addressing the vicar's daughter. 'Miss

Strong… I have arranged with the post boys to drop you at the vicarage on their way back to Bristol, as they pass through the village.'

She rose gracefully to her feet. She was as tall and as slender as Dolph remembered, even clad in that dull cloak, which parted at the front to reveal a gown in a becoming shade of blue. Willowy, that was how he would describe her if ever called upon to do so. He tore his gaze from her, confused. What the Devil was wrong with him, noticing such things about his sons' governess?

*I'm weary from the journey. I'm confused…seeing the children again… I am not myself.*

'Thank you so much for standing in my stead,' Miss Thame was saying as she took Matilda from Miss Strong. 'I shall see you at church on Sunday.'

She took charge effortlessly, while he stood there, mute, like a visitor to his own home. Dolph shook himself, mentally, and stepped forward.

'Thank you, Miss Strong.' He handed her into the post-chaise.

'Thank you, my lord. And welcome home again.' She smiled shyly, and her gaze slid past him. 'I do hope your friend's arm is soon better.'

George! He'd forgotten all about him. Dolph glanced around, to find George—his hand still on Wolf's collar—smiling engagingly at Miss Strong, his eyes bright. Dolph's heart sank, knowing it only took a shapely ankle, a pair of fine eyes or a tinkling laugh to turn George's head, and he made a mental note to warn George off Miss Strong—a country vicar's daughter would be unprepared for the kind of flirtations a more worldly girl would take in her stride.

He turned again to Miss Thame, who stood quietly waiting for his attention, Matilda hugged close and the boys clinging to her cloak. Irritation that he understood none of this made him brusque.

'I suggest you resume your duties by taking charge of the children, Miss Thame, and allow my guest and I the chance to go indoors and recover from our journey. We will talk later about where you have been and why you saw fit to leave my children with a woman not in my employ.'

Her cheeks flushed. 'As you wish, my lord. Come, boys.'

He watched her walk to the front door and stop to speak to Palmer, the butler, who was now waiting at the open front door. A groom, alerted by the arrivals, had appeared to direct George's coachman, Winters, to the stables.

'Well!' George broke the silence. 'I am exceedingly happy I accepted your invitation, Dolph. Miss Strong is a gem, is she not? No chance of me getting bored now.'

He grinned happily and Dolph heaved an inner sigh; George was truly irrepressible.

'Come. Let us go inside.'

He shivered, suddenly aware of how the temperature had dropped while they had been standing there. The wind had picked up, bringing with it the salty tang of the nearby Bristol Channel, and he shivered again. Not, this time, at the cold but at the memories. He thrust them aside, greeting Palmer as they went indoors. The butler closed the front door behind them.

The entrance hall looked the same. Palmer looked and sounded the same. Everything was familiar, and yet unfamiliar because Rebecca was not there. The reality of her loss rose closer to the surface than at any time during the past sixteen months—his grief might have eased, but guilt still hovered like a black spectre at the edges of his mind. He still woke up in a cold sweat some nights, haunted by how unhappy and confused Rebecca had been and tormented by his own failure to see it.

The sound of Palmer clearing his throat interrupted his thoughts, and Dolph realised he had omitted to inform his household, not only of his arrival today, but also that George would be accompanying him.

'Please prepare a bedchamber for Lord Hinckley, Palmer. He will be staying with us until he returns to London for the start of the Season.'

George would be fully recovered by then and would be loath to miss the balls and parties and other entertainments. Dolph, however, had no interest in such frivolity and had barely looked at a woman since Rebecca's death. Indeed, the very notion of marrying again made him shudder. How could he face that responsibility? Look how he had neglected Rebecca. What if he was incapable of making any woman happy? Guilt continued to haunt him. Had he driven her to such a drastic solution? Had life with him been such a trial?

It was too late now to compensate for his inadequacy as a husband, other than to vow never to risk destroying any other woman's life. All that mattered now was his determination to redress his failings as a father.

Palmer bowed. 'Mrs Frampton is already preparing the guest room with the maids, my lord. We saw you arrive. And there is hot water upstairs already for you both.'

'Thank you, Palmer.'

'And the dog, my lord?' Palmer's tone made his opinion of Wolf absolutely clear.

Dolph bit back a grin as he ruffled Wolf's head. 'Get used to him, Palmer. He is here to stay.'

'Very well, my lord.'

Dolph could feel peace and contentment hovering.

Tentative feelings as yet, maybe—he might feel awkward with his children and he might still have his guilt to cope with, but it was good to be home.

## Chapter Four

An hour later, having bathed and changed his travel-soiled clothes, Dolph made his way downstairs, Wolf close behind him. Palmer greeted him in the hallway.

'Lord Hinckley is resting,' he said, 'and Mr Pople is waiting in your study, as he wanted a word before he leaves.'

Roger Pople had been steward at Dolphin Court since Dolph's father's time.

'Thank you, Palmer. Be so good as to advise Miss Thame I wish to speak to her in the drawing room in half an hour.'

No need to be formal, with an interview in his study— he would listen to the reason for the governess's absence before judging her.

'Very good, my lord.'

Thirty minutes later Dolph—Wolf padding at his heels—headed for the drawing room after Mr Pople had updated him on the latest news about the estate. Now to face Miss Thame and find out what on earth she had been playing at. He deliberately hadn't questioned either Palmer or Mr Pople about her absence, and neither had he asked how frequently she left his sons in the care of others. He was interested to hear what she had to say for herself first.

He strode into the room and slammed to a halt, a peculiar hollow feeling in his chest among the emotions that erupted at the sight before him—Miss Thame sitting on the sofa with a sleepy-looking Matilda on her lap as she read aloud to Steven and Nicholas, who were snuggled either side of her. The governess fell silent and her impassive appraisal of Dolph swiftly dispersed that odd flood of nostalgic nonsense as well as the lingering memory of his visceral response to her as he handed her down from the post-chaise. No longer did he attribute a magnetic quality to those wide-set eyes, which now considered him coolly and somewhat haughtily. Her lips were far from luscious, as he'd earlier thought, but were now firmly pursed above her surprisingly delicate chin. And she found him wanting, he realised, with a start of temper that very quickly morphed into amusement. If one look had that effect on *him*, what effect must it have upon two small impressionable lads?

Relief spread through him as he realised that earlier inexplicable tug of attraction had been an illusion, born out of a combination of his own weariness and a trick of the late afternoon light. Her features looked almost severe, with her high, sharp cheekbones and her compressed lips and her red hair severely scraped back from her face with the aid of numerous hairpins. She had changed out of the blue gown he had glimpsed beneath her cloak and was now attired in a plain, dull brown gown. *This* was the woman he had hired. A governess with enough backbone to raise two boys without accepting any nonsense from them.

'Good evening, my lord. I brought the children down to say goodnight, as you did not have much time with them earlier. I make no doubt you will be happy to see them before they go to bed.'

He detected a note of warning in her tone but, although he would take heed and do nothing to upset the children, Miss Thame need not imagine the children's presence would do anything other than delay his questioning her over her absence and neglect of duty.

'I am. Thank you for the thought.' He advanced into the room. 'What book are you reading?'

Her smile was cool. '*The History of Little Goody Two-Shoes* by John Newbery. Have you read it?'

He frowned. 'No.'

'It was in your library,' she said. 'The only children's book I could find. The boys enjoy it, although I do not believe they fully understand it all.'

'What is it about?'

She glanced down, and he saw her suck in one cheek before releasing it again as her lips twitched. But when she looked up at him again, that hint of amusement in her expression had smoothed away.

'It is the story of Margery, a poor orphan who makes a career for herself as a teacher before she marries the local landowner, having won his heart through her honesty, hard work and good sense.'

Her gaze held a hint of challenge, as if daring him to object, and he could hardly fail to see the irony even though there was no chance of fiction turning to real life in their case, despite that ridiculous emotional reaction to seeing her there, on his sofa, with his children surrounding her. Two could play at blanking expressions, however. He'd developed that trick during his diplomatic role in Europe, as well as the ability to understand people beyond what their words might reveal, by observing their unconscious mannerisms and behaviour.

'I see. It sounds an innocent enough fairy story. Now, Miss Thame, I still wish to speak with you about today. I suggest, therefore, it is time the children went to bed.'

'Of course.'

Steven clutched Miss Thame's sleeve and whispered urgently in her ear.

'I am sure he won't harm you, Stevie. My lord...is your dog safe?'

'You cannot think I would bring a dangerous beast into the house where my children live?'

'I know not what to think, my lord, as I barely know you.'

Dolph narrowed his eyes, suspecting her of insolence, but her open expression and slightly raised eyebrows belied that thought, and when he examined her words, he could not fault them.

'*I* am not afraid of it,' announced Nicholas, with a slightly scornful look at his brother.

Steven leaned across Miss Thame's lap and punched Nicholas on his arm. 'Nor am I! Don't you say I'm scared!'

'Boys! Enough!' Miss Thame stopped any further physical contact by the simple expedient of standing up, still holding Matilda, and taking Steven by the arm, obliging him to stand too. She kept her own body between the brothers as Nicholas, too, scrambled off the sofa. 'What *will* your father think of such behaviour?'

Dolph hesitated and then knelt down on the Aubusson carpet. Wolf immediately sat on his haunches next to him. 'Their father thinks they should come here and meet Wolf and then go up to bed.'

He caught Miss Thame's flash of approval, but he felt absurdly awkward considering they were his own children. He was more nervous facing them than he ever felt while negotiating between high-powered military men and politicians. If only he'd made more effort to spend time with them when they were younger, but it had never occurred to him. During his own childhood, he and his sister had been brought up by servants, his parents remaining remote for much of the time.

Miss Thame urged the boys towards Dolph and Wolf, whose head reached as high as Steven's waist.

'Lie down,' Dolph ordered, and Wolf shuffled his front paws forward. He laid his head on his outstretched legs and sighed.

The boys crept closer. Nicholas appeared the bolder of the two, even though he was the younger. He was the first to touch Wolf's head, and then he stroked, getting braver as the great dog just lay there and suffered his attention. Steven, after hanging back looking worried, finally followed suit. He then beamed with delight as he patted Wolf. Miss Thame crouched down to show Wolf to Matilda, but Dolph's daughter was having none of the dog, or of Dolph, as she clung to the governess like a little monkey, hiding her face.

'She is tired,' said Miss Thame. 'She will be better in the morning if you visit the nursery. The boys will be at their lessons, too, if you care to come to the schoolroom?'

'I shall try,' said Dolph.

He reached out to stroke Matilda's soft curls. He ached to hold her in his arms, but he feared making her cry, so he made no attempt to take her from Miss Thame. He stared hungrily at Steven and Nicholas but, as with earlier, he could not quite bring himself to hug them. Partly because he did not want to frighten them but mostly, he realised with a lurch of sudden understanding, because he was afraid of rejection.

*But I am their father and they are just children. And
so young. It is my responsibility to bridge this divide.*

'Steven? Nicholas? Will you hug your papa goodnight?'

The boys came to him, eyes downcast, and allowed
Dolph to enfold their stiff little bodies in his embrace.
Dolph closed his eyes, lowering his face to their hair,
breathing in their scents as his heart cracked. He had felt
it his duty to stay in Europe all these months, but now...
oh, how he regretted it. He'd missed over a year of their
lives, a year he could never get back. How abandoned
they must have felt, so soon after losing their mother.
How on earth had he made such a colossal error in judgement in leaving as he did?

Remorse swirled through him and he silently swore he
would make it up to his family, whatever it took.

Leah watched Lord Dolphinstone with Stevie and
Nicky, her throat tight with emotion. How many times
had she cursed this man for leaving the boys when they
were already hurt and bewildered by their mother's sudden disappearance? Every day of the sixteen months she
had lived here at Dolphin Court, that was how many
times. Although the other servants had spoken well of
His Lordship, Leah's opinion had been formed by the
brusque—albeit handsome—man who had interviewed
her. She had been shocked he would leave his sons immediately after their mother's funeral and disgusted by
his prolonged absence, and she'd worked hard to give the
boys the love and approval they needed in their lives to
try to compensate them for the loss of *both* their parents.

And yet, seeing him now with his sons, he seemed
truly remorseful. She knew from working as a governess in other households how little love many gentlemen

showed towards their own children. She did not doubt they loved their children but, somehow, they appeared unable or unwilling to show it. She had been so fortunate with her own papa… She dragged her thoughts from the man she had called Papa. The news was too recent and the emotions it aroused still too agonisingly raw.

She crossed to the door. Cassie, the nursemaid who cared for Tilly, was waiting in the hall to take all three children up to bed—Leah had not wished to further anger His Lordship by taking them upstairs herself while he kicked his heels waiting for her in the drawing room.

It had been a calculated risk, bringing the children down to say goodnight to their father after he had ordered Leah to wait for him in the drawing room. She no doubt faced a reprimand for her absence that day, but the boys were already wary of their father. She had noticed Dolphinstone's discomfort in that short first meeting with his sons, and so she had followed her instinct that the sooner they began to rebuild their relationship, the better.

After Cassie left with the children, Leah remained standing while Dolphinstone paced the room. She had already decided to tell no one about Lady Tregowan's will and her unexpected inheritance. Not yet. The journey home had given her time to think, and she had not only decided she must, for her own sake, accept this opportunity, but she had also decided to delay leaving Dolphin Court for as long as possible. Partly for selfish reasons—just the thought of leaving the children shredded her heart—but also because the boys were already so unsettled by their father's imminent return.

And now Dolphinstone was here, and the boys' reaction to his arrival confirmed she had made the right decision. Both father and children needed time to overcome their understandable awkwardness, and it would surely be easier if they were unaware Leah would be gone before Eastertide.

Her initial reaction that to accept the inheritance would be disloyal to Papa had soon been dismissed by her usual logic. A woman in her circumstances had little choice but to be practical, and she could almost hear Papa's voice in her head saying, *'Leah. Will you really cut off your nose to spite your face? Accept this chance to improve your life, and I will be looking down on you and cheering you on.'*

Only a fool would reject such a change in fortune, and she was not a fool, but…marriage? Nerves coiled in her stomach. Her parents' marriage had always been her ideal. She had been wrong to believe it was a love match from the start, but the truth—that it had been arranged, and her parents' love had developed *after* they wed—gave her hope that, even if she didn't marry for love, she might at least meet a decent man she could respect.

And if not, at least she would have somewhere to call home and a guaranteed income of two hundred pounds per annum. No longer would she fear losing her job or falling ill and being unable to work. She might be lonely, of course, but one could also be lonely in the wrong marriage, and she loathed the idea of putting her life in the hands of a man who was only interested in her for her money. If only she could meet a good man, as Mama had done. A man like Papa.

*Oh, Papa…* The grief she had suffered when he died now reared up to engulf her anew. She had lost him all over again, for he was not her father at all.

*'Miss Thame!'*

Lord Dolphinstone's exasperation dragged Leah from her thoughts. Her cheeks burned as he glared down at her, his dark brows bunched. He was so close she noticed his newly shaved cheeks and the glint of silver hairs at his temples. His close-cropped dark brown hair curled a little at his hairline, softening his male ruggedness, and she once again felt that unwelcome flare of attraction she'd experienced earlier when he had wrenched open the door of the post-chaise and their eyes had met.

His gaze pierced her again now, and she lowered her eyes. 'My apologies, my lord. I'm afraid I was wool-gathering.'

'Still dreaming up excuses for your absence?'

Leah stiffened, her emotions on a tight rein as grief over Papa still simmered.

'I have no need to dream up excuses, my lord. Today is the very first day I have left the boys for more than an hour since you employed me sixteen months ago. Employed me with the promise, might I add, of one day off per month. A day off I have *never* taken.'

His eyes narrowed. 'Until today.'

'Until today.' She dug deep inside herself for a measure of calm. 'I am sorry I left the children, but they are already familiar with Miss Strong, which is why I asked her to come and look after them, knowing the rest of the staff have been busy preparing for your return. Cassie would have been run ragged had she been required to watch the boys as well as care for Tilly for the entire day.'

'Tilly? Her name is Matilda.'

*Petty...inconsequential...*

'She is a little girl. Let her be Matilda when she grows up. Which she will...faster than you can possibly imagine.'

'I am aware of it.'

She barely heard his muttered words. Might they signify regret at how much of his children's lives he had missed? The sigh that sounded next, however, was loud. And still exasperated.

'Sit down, Miss Thame.'

Leah perched on the sofa, plaited her fingers together on her lap and braced herself for his questions, for the first time realising her plans might be in jeopardy. Her nerves fluttered as she watched Dolphinstone cross to the fireplace and lean down to poke the fire into life.

The decision was in this man's hands. This *stranger's* hands.

Although she had decided to leave, she needed time to grow used to this change in her life. Dolphin Court was her fifth post since she had been forced to earn her own living, and it was the only one where she had felt loved and valued. She liked the rest of the staff, without exception; in Philippa she had a close friend who lived nearby, but, above all, she adored the children and she was not yet ready for the wrench of leaving them. Besides, after all they had suffered, she was determined to help them adjust to their father's return before she went.

His Lordship threw a log onto the fire and, despite her preoccupation, she was struck by his powerful frame as he filled the shoulders of his coat. His features were somewhat harsh in repose, as though he smiled seldom—frown lines rather than laughter lines were etched into his face—but he'd had little to smile about after losing his wife in such a tragic accident. He sat opposite Leah, on the matching sofa, and leaned back, crossing one leg over the other and folding his arms across his chest. In his evening clothes and meticulously tied neckcloth, he looked every inch the wealthy aristocrat as his penetrating grey gaze raked Leah.

*Like my real father: entitled; powerful; privileged.*

Leah's unease faded to be replaced by icy control at the thought of her real father and his despicable actions.

'Well, Miss Thame? Would you care to enlighten me as to your whereabouts today?'

'It was a personal matter requiring my presence in Bristol, my lord.'

His brows lowered. 'And is that your entire explanation?'

What would he do if she told him the truth—that the man she thought to be her father was not? That, technically if not legally, she was illegitimate? That she was some dissolute nobleman's by-blow? Would he turn her off immediately?

She could not risk it. She would keep her secret for a few weeks, at least, before going to London and getting to know her new half-sisters. Her heart leapt with anticipation. Would Aurelia and Beatrice become friends as well as sisters? Leaving Dolphin Court would be a dreadful wrench, but knowing she was no longer entirely alone in the world, that she now had a family… That thought was a huge comfort, like being wrapped in a warm blanket.

'Wool-gathering again, Miss Thame?'

Her gaze flew to his and, again, her cheeks heated.

'This meeting you attended today… Forgive me if I have misread you, but it appears to have left you with a dilemma of sorts.'

She stared at him. 'What makes you say that?'

His eyebrows flicked high. 'Reading people is a skill I have developed over many months of complex negotiations in Europe. You are undoubtedly distracted, and it is reasonable to assume your preoccupation stems from your meeting.'

She swallowed. 'I do not deny there is some truth in both of those statements.' She would stick as close to the truth as possible. 'And I have been wondering how much I must reveal, for, as I said, it was a *private* matter. I received a letter from a firm of solicitors in Bristol requesting I attend a meeting today. I did so and I am sure you will understand my reluctance to reveal the details of that meeting.'

He frowned and she sensed his desire to probe further, so she elaborated, 'The meeting involved other individuals and therefore I am not at liberty to divulge any further information.'

His jaw bunched, before he said, 'I do not like secrets, Miss Thame. Do you anticipate further attendance at such meetings?'

'I do not.'

'And will any of this affect your employment here?'

'Not at this present time,' she said, carefully.

He held her gaze, his own expression revealing nothing. 'I do not appreciate such a veiled threat hanging over me, Miss Thame.'

'Threat?'

'The possibility you may—for whatever reason connected to this clandestine meeting with your solicitor— leave your post here. That *is* what I am to gather from your answer, is it not?'

Leah considered her clasped hands. 'Lord Dolphinstone,' she said when she looked up again. 'Do you concede my employment in your household is by mutual agreement?'

His brows shot up again, but this time a smile hovered around his mouth. His assessing gaze elicited a strange tingling sensation deep in the pit of her stomach.

'I cannot deny it.' His voice deepened and he sounded warmer, somehow. Or, maybe, amused.

'Then you must also concede that I—or, indeed, you—

have the right to terminate my employment whenever we might choose. My comment was not a threat, my lord. It was a simple statement of fact. All I am in a position to say is that I intend to remain in my post in the immediate future. More than that, I am unable to promise.'

## Chapter Five

Dolphinstone stood up and strode to the window. As he tweaked the curtains aside and peered out into the darkness, Leah stared at the fire. A log settled into place with a soft sound, followed by the hiss of sap evaporating, and a cold, wet nudge at her hand brought her gaze back into the room. The dog—Wolf—stood by her, looking at her with his yellowish-brown eyes. When he saw he had her attention, he waved his tail and nudged first his broad muzzle and then his domed head under her hand. Remembering his gentleness and patience with the children, Leah stroked his thick, soft, black-tipped, tawny fur in a soothing rhythm. He leaned into her leg, his body solid and warm.

'Wolf! Where are your manners?'

Leah's head snapped up. She had been lulled by the repetitive action of stroking…the sense of peace it induced…and had failed to notice Dolphinstone's return. He towered over both her and Wolf, who turned his head to gaze up at his master adoringly, his tongue lolling from the side of his mouth. Leah shivered as she glimpsed his teeth—if she had noticed them earlier she doubted she would have drifted into that state of unawareness while stroking him. But she was glad she had not. He seemed sweet-natured, despite his size.

'Please do not reprimand him. I do not mind.'

Dolphinstone's smile relieved the harshness of his face. 'Most ladies are too afraid to be anywhere near him,' he said. 'And plenty of gentlemen too. But he really is a gentle giant.'

'Then why do you call him Wolf? Is it *meant* to give people a fear of him?'

'No. Of course it is not.'

Dolphinstone flung himself down on the opposite sofa, surprising Leah, as this was the first time he had appeared relaxed.

'Wolf is short for Wolfgang.'

'Oh! That is an unusual name for a dog. Is he named for Mozart?'

'He was, yes. But not by me. His former owner died, and I adopted him. In Vienna. Wolfgang—or *Volfgang*, as Herr Lueger pronounced it—is, in my opinion, too much the mouthful for a dog. So I shortened it. Didn't I, old lad?'

Wolf padded across to Dolphinstone and laid his head on his knee, grunting his pleasure as his master fondled his ears. Dolphinstone appeared much more at his ease with the dog than with his own children and he appeared to forget Leah's presence as he stroked. A frown marred his brow, and the urge to soothe it—to soothe *him*—crept over Leah as she watched and waited. Finally, his hypnotic stroking, the silence and that inexplicable urge became too much, and Leah cleared her throat. His gaze snapped to her face.

'My apologies, Miss Thame. I am afraid it was my turn for wool-gathering.' His frown deepened. 'I admit I am uncomfortable with the idea of someone in my employ who is keeping secrets from me, but I cannot fault you when you declare it is your private business that also involves other people.' He smiled at her, and her heart gave a funny little leap. 'Your point of view was cleverly argued, by the way… I suspect you would make a good solicitor yourself!' He sobered again. 'I cannot force you to confide in me but…' He paused, his gaze roaming her face, and she felt her colour rise, yet again, under his scrutiny. 'If I am correct that what you learned today has left you with a conflict of emotions, and if you wish to discuss the matter—in general terms, without compromising the others involved—please know I shall be happy to oblige.'

*A conflict of emotions.* That perfectly described her feelings. But she would not confide in anyone until she had helped Dolphinstone rebuild his relationship with his children.

'Thank you. I shall bear that in mind.'

'Very well. You may go.' He stood, and Leah did likewise. 'Miss Thame…' He hesitated, and she sensed a tussle going on inside him, although he gave little outward sign. 'I wonder…would you care to join myself and Lord Hinckley for dinner? I am aware in some households the governess dines *en famille* and, due to my absence, that is a custom we have yet to establish.'

Leah could think of nothing worse, especially tonight when she had so much on her mind and she craved time and peace and quiet to think. On the other hand, it would be foolish to miss this opportunity to practise her social skills when she would no doubt be invited out to dine when she moved to London.

'Thank you, my lord. I appreciate your thoughtfulness and I shall be delighted to accept, although I should prefer to dine in my parlour tonight, as usual. I am weary after today and I fear I might nod off over the soup.' She smiled at him, hoping not to sound too ungrateful.

'As you wish. I shall bid you goodnight, Miss Thame.'

Leah bobbed a curtsy. 'Goodnight, my lord.'

Dolph scratched his jaw as the door closed quietly behind Miss Thame. That final smile was strained, and he did not believe it was solely due to weariness. She might believe herself to be unreadable but, as they had talked, he had picked up on her unconscious signals that she was troubled. Her reluctance to confide in him was understandable but, although he had accepted her silence, he had an instinctive dislike of secrets and mysteries, especially within his own household. If Rebecca had not so successfully concealed her inner torment, he felt certain she would not have reached the stage where she could see no solution other than to take her own life.

*Why could she not confide in me?*

Guilt and regret swelled yet again. He sat down, fondling Wolf's ears when the great head again settled on his lap, and his tension slowly seeped away as his mind cleared. The sound of the door opening eventually interrupted what had slipped perilously close to a doze.

'Dolph! This house is amazing!' George strode into the room, waving his good arm. 'Palmer has been telling me all about the secret passages and hidden doorways.'

Dolph straightened, his friend's enthusiasm jerking him fully awake. George was only four years younger than Dolph but, at times, it seemed more like a fourteen-year age gap. 'I know… I did grow up here, after all.'

George's excitement was undaunted. 'Well, of course you did. But why did you never tell me you live in such an intriguing place? My country estate is modern and utterly boring—but now I plan to build a folly in the park, and to have a secret passage dug.'

'A passage leading to where?'

George waved his hand dismissively. 'Does it matter? Just think, when I have sons, we will have such fun.'

Dolph flinched at his words. When had he ever considered simply *having fun* with his sons, even before Rebecca died? His family had been a copy of the family he had grown up in and he had modelled himself on his father—stern and remote, his word law. Rebecca had been raised in a similar family, although she had been closer to the children. Dolph's experience of childhood fun had come from his sister and, later, from his school friends.

'I was fortunate, I suppose.' He was referring to the house rather than his family life. 'You can imagine the thrill of exploring it as a young boy. My sister and I loved to play tricks on our governess when we were young.'

'I am thrilled enough as a grown man—I'd have been in my element as a schoolboy. Have I your permission to explore tomorrow?'

'Of course. There are no secrets here. There is even a tunnel that supposedly once led to the church. I suspect it was used to transport smuggled goods in days gone by, but no one knows for certain.'

'The church, you say?' George said, with a telling smile. 'Now, *that* will be worth exploring.'

'Well, you will be out of luck, George, for that tunnel has been blocked up for as long as I can remember.'

'That is a pity. How far is the church from here, did you say?'

Dolph eyed his friend. 'George…'

George raised an innocent brow at Dolph's warning tone. 'Dolph?'

'Miss Strong is the vicar's daughter. She has lived in the village her entire life. Do not, I beg of you, raise expectations with one of your flirtations—she is far too innocent to understand *that* sort of game.'

'What do you take me for?' George laughed. 'I shall be as discreet as…well, as discreet as I can possibly be.'

'That,' said Dolph, 'is what I am afraid of.'

It was late when the two men retired for the night after a few hands of speculation and a game of billiards. Dolph bid goodnight to George on the first landing and, with Wolf at his heels, he headed to his bedchamber, where his valet awaited. After settling in bed, however, he found sleep elusive and, after a good half-hour of tossing and turning, he threw aside the bedcovers and reached for his banyan and slippers. He paced to the window and pulled back the curtain, but there was only a black void beyond the windowpanes. He leaned his forehead against the cold glass and closed his eyes, a jumble of images and snatches of conversation whirling through his thoughts. He made no attempt to pluck any one of those fragments from the spinning mass to examine it more closely but allowed them to come and go as they pleased.

A distant noise tweaked his attention. A noise from *inside* the house—the creak of a floorboard and the click of a latch. He turned and saw Wolf, too, had been alerted. The dog still lay on the rug before the hearth, but his head was up, his ears pricked. All the occupants of the house *ought* to be asleep. Even George had been yawning widely as they came upstairs. So, who was awake, and what were they doing creeping around in the dead of night?

Dolph lit his bedside candle with a taper from the smouldering remains of the fire before walking softly to the door and easing it open. He strained his ears. He could hear nothing and see nothing, the landing and stairs swallowed by the dark shadows beyond the halo of light cast by his candle. Wolf pushed past him and trotted across the landing to stand, head cocked, at the foot of the upper staircase, which led up to the second floor, where there were a couple of smaller guest rooms and the children's rooms.

*The children!*

He ought to have thought of them first, not last. Dolph strode to the stairs, protecting the flickering flame with his cupped hand, and ran up them, before pausing to listen. Again, he could hear nothing, but Wolf did. His attention was fixed on the boys' bedchamber door, standing slightly ajar, his ears pricked as he whined low. Dolph trod quietly now. If the boys were asleep, he had no wish to frighten them by startling them awake. He put his ear to the door. Silence. And it was dark within. He reached to push the door open but, as he touched it, it suddenly opened.

To give her credit, Miss Thame quickly stifled her squeak of alarm, her hand clapped around her mouth. Her eyes, though…they were huge, his candle flame glittering in those dark, dark pupils, the irises a deep green-blue, like the sea on a bright day. Dolph felt his heart turn over in his chest as his breath caught. He tore his gaze from hers. And his pulse rocketed. Her hair was no longer severely scraped back, but lightly caught in a thick plait draping over one shoulder. Loose, glimmering strands—russet and gold, the colours of autumn—framed her freckled face.

Her gaze dropped to his chest and then snapped up again, a telltale blush washing her pale cheeks and her forehead puckering, jolting Dolph out of his sudden paralysis.

'I—'

His jaw snapped shut as Miss Thame sucked in a breath, placed one hand squarely on his chest and pushed him, gently but firmly, back. She exited the bedchamber and turned to quietly ease the door shut.

'What—?'

'Shhh.'

Her long, slim forefinger pressed to her lips in a hushing motion, and his mouth watered as he focussed on her full lips. No longer pursed in disapproval, they were lush and tempting.

*For God's sake, man. She is your sons' governess. You're lusting after her as though she were a comely barmaid.*

Not that he had lusted after any woman, let alone a barmaid, for more years than he cared to recall. He beckoned to her to follow him, pivoted on his heel and strode for the stairs.

'Wait!'

He halted mid-stride at her command and pivoted to face her. He raised his brows, remaining silent as she glided towards him. A blue and gold paisley shawl enveloped her from neck to…almost…foot. Both shawl and nightgown fell a few inches short of her feet, which were bare and thrust into embroidered slippers that had seen better days. Her ankles were as fine and as well turned as any he had ever seen. Again, he wrenched his gaze away, but there was nowhere to look other than at her, and every part of her enticed and intrigued. He fought to keep any hint of his feelings from his face as she halted in front of him, telling himself he was simply unsettled by his return to his marital home.

'We will not wake Stevie if we talk in my sitting room. Nicky—' her smile flashed '—will sleep through almost anything. No fear of waking him.'

*Stevie! Nicky! As if Tilly is not bad enough.*

Poking at his irritation as though it were a fire in need of rekindling, Dolph strode to the door she indicated, thrust it open and stood aside as she preceded him into the room. He noticed her shiver and draw her shawl tighter around her shoulders, but a glance at the grate revealed a bed of cold grey ashes. He closed the door—after Wolf padded in—and took a stance by the fireplace, one elbow resting on the mantelshelf. Miss Thame sat on a wooden chair next to a table by the window, ignoring the solitary wingback chair next to the hearth. He noticed she avoided looking directly at him.

He came straight to the point. 'What happened? I heard movement and thought we had an intruder.'

Rattled by his visceral reaction to the governess, he knew he must control this conversation, get the business done and remove himself from her presence before the unthinkable happened. She was not even particularly beautiful but, somehow, he found it hard to tear his eyes from her as his body responded in entirely inappropriate ways.

'Stevie…that is, Steven—' she spoke to the fireplace, flags of colour still highlighting her sculpted cheekbones '—suffers from occasional nightmares. If I hear him cry out, I go to him. I can usually soothe him straight back to sleep, but if he awakens fully he becomes distressed, and it's much harder to settle him back down. And then Nicky is more likely to wake as well.'

Her voice and her expression were exactly those of a governess reporting to her employer, but her failure to meet his eyes suggested she was embarrassed, or maybe

even offended, by his state of undress. Shame washed
through him as he accepted his earlier irritation with her
was totally unfair. Any anger ought to be directed at the
person he was actually angry with—himself, for his inappropriate response to her.

*And Rebecca.*

The whispered thought rocked him to his core. *Was* he
angry with Rebecca? The thought had never occurred to
him. It seemed heartless but, yes…there was anger there.
Deep inside. He would think about that later.

'I see. Yes, of course,' he said to Miss Thame. 'I understand now.' He tried a smile. 'I dare say I must accustom
myself to having children in my life again.'

'Indeed.' She finally looked at him, her voice frosty.

'You disapprove of my having been away all this
time?'

Her chin tilted. 'I believe it was not the wisest…' She
hesitated, her fine eyes narrowing. She shook her head
slightly, and her chest rose as she inhaled. 'I believe it
was neither the wisest nor the kindest decision for your
children's sake.'

The fact she was right hurt more than if she'd accused
him unfairly. 'What about for *my* sake?'

She eyed him in silence, before shaking her head
again. 'It is not for me to say.'

'Oh, come, Miss Thame. You have given your opinion most freely. Do not hesitate to speak your mind now.'

He read the doubt in her eyes before she bent her head.
He softened his voice. 'Do not think I shall hold it against
you. I am not so petty as to dismiss an employee because
they dare to voice a criticism of me. Please believe me
when I say that, from now on, my sole purpose is to do
what is best for my children. If my absence has injured

them, then I need to know before I can begin to make amends.'

'Very well. Since you ask, I shall tell you my opinion. I make no doubt your wife's death was painful and shocking for you and I understand your need to get away from the place where painful memories dwell. But you were not only a husband. You are a father, too. And the children were—and still are—too young to fully comprehend death. All they knew was their mother left them, and then their father disappeared, leaving them with a houseful of servants and a new governess. A stranger to them. I could have been a dreadful governess—and a monstrous person—for all you knew. You did not even wait to find out.' Her voice rose, shaking with strength of feeling. 'You ran away and you did not return for sixteen months! Your daughter has already spoken her first words, and she has started to walk.'

Her words stung, even though they were no different from the words with which he had castigated himself. Many times.

'I had my duty to do for my country.'

'That, with the greatest respect, is a weak excuse. There are plenty of other men who could have taken over your role, and you must know that. There was no other man to fill your shoes here at Dolphin Court. Those children only have one f-f-father.'

Her voice cracked over her final word, her eyes sheening over.

'What is it, Miss Thame? What is wrong?'

She flicked her hand in a dismissive gesture.

'It is nothing. I am tired, that is all.'

She was lying but, as she'd pointed out earlier, everyone was entitled to a certain amount of privacy. As long as it did not interfere with his children's well-being, he would not pry.

Dolph pushed away from the mantelshelf. 'In that case, I shall bid you goodnight, Miss Thame. Come, Wolf.'

He went down the stairs to his bedchamber, shrugged out of his banyan, kicked off his slippers and climbed into his now cold bed. Shivering, he huddled under the covers, but sleep continued to elude him as he pondered Miss Thame.

When had he last experienced such a physical desire for a woman? Certainly not since long before Rebecca's death…in fact, since she had known she was with child again. Maybe that was his trouble—it had been over two years since he'd enjoyed intimacy, and returning to Dolphin Court had revived his natural male desire for a woman. His marriage to Rebecca might have been arranged—the result of a long understanding between both their families—but he had remained faithful to her throughout their marriage. Somehow, his subconscious linked home with lovemaking, and poor Miss Thame had become the unwitting object of his reawakened sexual urges.

Satisfied he had logically explained away his uncharacteristic and odd fascination with his sons' governess, Dolph rolled onto his side and slept.

## Chapter Six

'Not too close to the water, boys, or you will get wet feet.'

The following day Leah watched, smiling, as Stevie and Nicky played with Wolf on rock-strewn Dolphin Beach—a small, secluded cove on the Bristol Channel, sheltered by low sandstone cliffs with angled faces—the eastern cliff rising a touch higher towards Dolphin Point at its head. It was from here that poor Lady Dolphinstone had slipped to her death. The thought always made Leah shudder, but the boys—unaware of the location of their mother's tragic accident—loved to run around the beach and release their pent-up energy after suffering an entire morning of lessons.

At least here on the beach there was no danger of disturbing anyone, unlike if they ran whooping and shrieking around the house and gardens. Here, the breeze soon carried away the sounds of their exuberance, and Leah was a great believer in the efficacious effects of sea air. Today, the boys had the added bonus of Wolf to play with, and Leah's legs were saved from taking part in their game of chase.

It had been a frustrating morning. After their encounter last night, Leah had fully expected His Lordship to look in on the boys' lessons. Truthfully, she had eagerly anticipated his visit even as she assured herself she merely wished to show him how well the boys had progressed with their lessons.

Last night, upon opening Stevie's door to find Lord Dolphinstone looming there—clad in a deep red dressing gown, the neck of his nightshirt agape, revealing a tantalising glimpse of dark chest hair—heat had scorched her skin as she'd struggled to hide her instinctive response to the sight of him. He was so...*commanding*. Tall, upright and ruggedly handsome with penetrating grey eyes. She couldn't help but be physically attracted to him, even though she scolded herself for reacting like an infatuated schoolgirl.

But today, for all his fine words, he had not visited the schoolroom as promised. When she and the boys were preparing for their customary walk before luncheon, she had learned the reason for his absence—His Lordship was showing Lord Hinckley around the estate and the surrounding area.

*So much for making his children his priority.*

The boys had asked after their father, and Leah told herself any disappointment was purely on their behalf and nothing to do with her own wish to see him again. She knew words meant nothing, from past experience—it was a person's actions that revealed their true character. So far, Dolphinstone's actions had done nothing to persuade Leah of his worth as a man. Men such as he felt entitled to do as they pleased, concerned only with their own needs and pleasures without consideration of the consequences for others.

Men like her real father, Lord Tregowan. Men like Peter, Papa's curate. Men like Lord Usk.

His Lordship had left Wolf behind when he and Lord Hinckley had set off on their tour, and feeling sorry for the dog, Leah had suggested to the boys he might join them on their walk. Although both boys had been wary at first, Nicky had soon gained his confidence, and Stevie, determined not to be outdone by his little brother, had soon joined in and was now happily haring around the beach with Wolf, dodging the boulders that dotted the patches of shingle and sand.

Leah closed her eyes and tilted her head back, breathing in the bracing air, trying, without much success, to quiet her conflicting emotions: nervous excitement at the change and opportunity coming her way; eagerness at the prospect of getting to know Aurelia and Beatrice; anxiety as to what the future held; dread at the prospect of leaving this place and the children.

She spun around at the crunch of shingle behind her, her heart leaping into her throat, to see Lord Dolphinstone and his friend Lord Hinckley—both well wrapped up against the cold weather in greatcoats, scarves and gloves—approaching.

'Oh! You startled me.' She put her hand to her chest, which heaved as though she had run the length of the beach. 'I did not hear you approach.'

As her fear subsided she felt her cheeks scorch and a curious swooping pull deep in her belly as her gaze met that of Lord Dolphinstone, in spite of her earlier annoyance that he hadn't visited the schoolroom. Heavens! What a ridiculous state of affairs—a twenty-six-year-old spinster governess reacting like a breathless girl of eighteen at the mere sight of her employer. An earl, no less. But, surely, that had been an answering blaze in those hard grey eyes of his...just as there had been last night. Or had that been a trick of the candlelight?

*Or the product of a too-vivid imagination! You are seeing what you want to see. Did you learn nothing from that episode with Viscount Usk?*

One thing was certain—she could not put *this* reaction down to the magic of the night and their state of undress, as she had last night. Her face burned even hotter. She put her gloved hands to her face, praying Dolphinstone would attribute her flushed cheeks to the sea breeze. She never could blush a pretty pink, but always turned a fiery red that clashed with her hair.

'I am not surprised with all the racket the boys are making,' Dolphinstone said dryly as he turned his attention to the boys.

Lord Hinckley, however, grinned at Leah in a friendly manner. 'What a splendid place to grow up. I wish I'd had this when I was a lad. You don't know how lucky you are, Dolph. *My* place, Miss Thame, is in the Midlands—as far from the coast as it is possible to be in this country.'

Leah smiled back at him, grateful for any distraction from the brooding figure by his side.

'Dolph has been showing me around the place this morning, so I have my bearings,' Hinckley continued. 'Good of you, old man—' he slapped Lord Dolphinstone's back '—when I know you were eager to visit the children at their lessons. Do you know, Miss Thame, upon our return, Dolph was so disappointed he had missed them, he insisted on coming straight down here to find you all.'

Leah's earlier irritation with Dolphinstone faded. At least he'd been thinking about the boys...and Lord Hinckley *was* his guest, so he did have a duty as his host. Mayhap she'd been a bit harsh in her condemnation—it was only his first morning home, after all.

Hinckley continued, 'Look at your fine, healthy lads, Dolph. They're a sight for sore eyes, sure enough.'

'They are indeed.'

Leah noticed a touch of strain in Dolphinstone's voice, and she caught his sideways glance up towards Dolphin Point. A muscle bunched visibly in his jaw, and he looked away. Leah sympathised. This beach must revive tragic memories for him. The cliff might not be high, but the mounds of rock at its base would prove lethal to anyone who fell, even when the tide was high. She suppressed another shudder, thoughts of the late Lady Dolphinstone close to the surface.

'Anyway, I have my bearings now,' Hinckley went on, 'and I promise not to monopolise so much of your time in future. I am afraid you will have to bear my company for a few weeks yet, Miss Thame. I cannot face another long, bruising journey until this wretched shoulder heals, so I shall remain until it is time to return to London for the Season.'

Leah frowned. Did that mean Dolphinstone, too, would be leaving the children to go to London again? And how would these two aristocrats react if they saw her—Dolphinstone's former governess—at Society events? She thrust aside those questions for now.

'How did you come by your injury, my lord?'

Hinckley reddened. 'A misunderstanding, that is all. Nothing too serious, you understand, but I am grateful for the opportunity to rusticate.' He surveyed the beach and the surrounding cliffs. 'I wonder...do you see much of your friend Miss Strong? I was sorry she had to rush away yesterday.'

'You forget, my lord—I am here to work. My days are taken up with teaching the boys.'

'Teaching?' Dolphinstone dragged his attention from his sons and stared at Leah. 'What is it they are learning here, other than to run wild?'

Leah stiffened, wounded by such unfairness. 'They are hardly running wild, my lord.' She kept her tone even and polite, but the knowledge she would soon be leaving gave her the courage to defend the boys. 'They have worked diligently all morning, and they are now benefitting from much-needed fresh air and exercise. Young boys, in case you have forgotten, have a surfeit of energy that needs release on a daily basis.'

'You cannot argue with that, Dolph. You were one yourself, once. Allegedly.' Hinckley grinned at Leah, waggling his eyebrows. 'Now…where is that cave you told me about?' Dolphinstone, his lips tight, pointed to the western cliff. 'Ah, yes. I see it. I must take a closer look. Do either of you care to accompany me?'

'I must stay and watch the boys,' Leah said, when Dolphinstone remained silent, even though the question was clearly not meant for her.

'I will stay here too,' said Dolphinstone. 'I outgrew my fascination with caves long ago and that one is hardly worthy of the name. It is disappointingly shallow.'

'But I have never been inside a cave before. You cannot expect me to pass up such an opportunity, Dolph.'

Dolphinstone grinned, shaking his head at Hinckley. 'You never cease to amaze me, George.'

Hinckley strode away across the beach, leaving Dolphinstone with Leah, who wondered if he would deliver another reprimand following that jibe about the boys' noisiness and excitement. In the ensuing silence, she reflected that if Dolphinstone should prove a harsh father it would make leaving the boys even more distressing for her, although at least it would counteract any physical attraction she felt for him.

It had been many years since that part of her nature had stirred, not since she had fallen for Viscount Usk's silver-tongued compliments and cajolery. That, as well as Peter Bennett's false courtship to gain favour with Papa, had been a harsh lesson to learn, but she had learned it well.

'I apologise for my earlier remark, about Steven and Nicholas running wild.' Dolphinstone's voice broke into her thoughts, sounding strained, his expression, in profile, somewhat grim. A gust of wind caught his hat, and as he grabbed it, one end of his scarf was blown from around his neck. He rammed his hat back on his head and held it secure with one gloved hand. 'I can see they are not. They have clearly thrived under your care.'

'There is no need to apologise to me, my lord.'

'There is. I… I do not care for this place, but that is no reason to take it out on you.'

Leah gripped her hands together against her natural instinct to touch him in sympathy. To offer comfort. As she would do for anyone, male or female, in distress. But she had already succumbed to an inexplicable urge to touch him, last night…so tempted by that glimpse of hair at the open neck of his nightshirt that she had laid her hand against his chest to propel him away from the boys' door. Her fingertips tingled at the memory. That was a boundary she would not cross again.

She would be leaving here within the next few weeks, however, and she was emboldened to touch upon subjects she might otherwise avoid.

'I understand,' she said. 'It must bring back painful memories.'

His gaze raked her, his expression inscrutable. 'It does. Tell me, do the boys ever talk about their mother?'

'They do. Especially Stevie. Being that bit older, he remembers more, and he still misses her a great deal.'

'Remembers…? He does not know about…about… what happened?'

'He knows she had an accident, but he knows no details. That is why this beach is still a happy place for the boys to come and play—I did not think there would be any benefit in them knowing the location.'

'No. That is true. I should have thought…' He folded his arms across his chest as his words faded. He stared out across the water. Then he visibly swallowed. 'I was not thinking rationally when I left. But I should have thought of that and left instructions. You made the right choice in not telling them more. Thank you. I count myself fortunate it was you who answered my advertisement—Mr Pople has told me how good you have been. As you said last night, I did not even wait to ensure you were capable, let alone kind. I should never have left as I did.'

He fell silent. His claim of not thinking rationally echoed what Philippa had said to Leah several times, in defence of Dolphinstone's abandonment of his children. Leah had still found his behaviour hard to excuse, however. The wind had dropped a little, and Dolphinstone used the lull to wrap his scarf securely around his neck again. 'This wind is chilly. But, then, it *is* the first day of February. It is to be expected.'

Leah deduced from the change of subject that the confidences—and the apology—were over.

'Do not blame yourself too much, my lord. You were distraught. But it is in the past now. They—' she gestured to Steven and Nicholas, who were trudging back up the beach, while Wolf investigated the rocks at the base of the cliff '—are what is important now. Them and Matilda.'

Dolphinstone's lips quirked. 'You may continue to call her Tilly. And I shall even endure Stevie and Nicky for

my sons. For the time being. I have no doubt they will be
called far worse things when they go to school.'

The thought of either boy being sent away to school
was unbearable, even though Leah would be long gone by
then. The fact of her imminent departure from this place
and from the children she loved hit her all over again, as
it had done at unexpected times throughout the morning
even though she tried to ignore any thoughts about her
future while she was with the boys. At those times she
felt herself gripped by the fear and uncertainty of giving
up her life here, and the worry she would fail to find a
man who might fall in love with her…a man with whom
she could be happy. Whenever she thought of the Season to come, her stomach tied into knots, for she would
be competing in the marriage stakes not only against
all the young ladies making their debuts this year, but
also against Aurelia and Beatrice, both of whom would
match her fortune and both of whom were far prettier,
and younger, than Leah.

And now she had the worry of meeting Lord Hinckley—let alone, God forbid, Lord Dolphinstone—in London to add to her fear of seeing that rat Lord Usk again.

'Miss Thame?'

Leah came to with a start.

'Wool-gathering again?' His Lordship asked, dryly.
'Is this a habit of yours…a quirk I must become accustomed to?'

She was spared from reply by Nicky, who reached
them ahead of Stevie and now held out his hand to show
them something.

'Miss Thame! Look what I found. It's sea glass like
you showed us before. The sea's made it all smooth.
Here.' He handed it to Leah. 'It is a present.'

'Why, thank you, Nicky. It is beautiful. I shall treasure it.' Her throat thickened with emotion.

'Good afternoon, Father.' Stevie halted about three paces from Dolphinstone and bowed.

So solemn and correct… Leah's heart went out to him. He'd taken his position as the oldest—he was now seven, to Nicky's five—so seriously in the time she had been here, and now he stood before his father, unsmiling, like a little soldier presenting himself for inspection. She willed Dolphinstone to do, or say, something to help the boy relax, but a glance at the man revealed his indecision, and she recalled his awkwardness with his sons yesterday. But how could she help them when this was a moment strictly between father and son?

As it happened, she was saved from having to intervene by Wolf, who, unlike Stevie, was absolutely convinced of his welcome. He barrelled up to them, tongue lolling, tail wagging furiously. He stopped midway between Stevie and Dolphinstone and shook himself vigorously.

Dolph flinched as ice-cold drops of sea water showered over him. Stevie and Nicky both shrieked with laughter, dancing away from Wolf, and the strained atmosphere eased. Suddenly, it seemed easier to know how to act with his sons. He knew what he didn't want—he didn't want his son to bow to him or to be stiffly formal. Despite his jibe at Miss Thame earlier, he preferred to see them as they had been on his arrival at the beach. Running around, playing, having fun. She was right—they had worked hard, and they deserved a chance to run off their excess energy. And he wanted them both to feel as relaxed with him as they were with their governess, who, at this moment, was laughing with the boys as she attempted to restrain an overexcited Wolf. Her unfettered laugh was musical. The joy on her face warmed him. And that she could have fun with the boys as well as teach them effectively was a definite bonus. The affection between them all was clear to see.

'Here. Allow me.' Dolph reached around Miss Thame to take hold of the dog's collar. His gloved hand closed over hers. He heard her sharp intake of breath, and he loosened his grip. 'Sorry,' he muttered. 'I hope I didn't hurt you. I know how strong Wolf is… I have difficulty in holding him myself if he is determined to go.'

She turned her face to him. She was close. Too close. Her deep turquoise eyes fathomless like the ocean, framed by thick, auburn lashes and straight, no-nonsense eyebrows. Countless light brown freckles danced across her nose. Freckles that seemed far too frivolous for such a straight nose and for a prim, proper and practical governess. Her scent mingled with the sea breeze—soap, with the merest hint of lavender. Her lips were parted in surprise, and the urge to kiss her grabbed him. It took hold of him deep inside, squeezing until he felt breathless.

## Chapter Seven

Dolph jerked back, noticing a fiery blush colouring Miss Thame's cheeks as her lashes swept low to conceal her innermost thoughts. The entire interlude had lasted a second…less than a second…but had seemed endless.

'You did not hurt me,' she said. Then her eyes opened, and she was visibly back in control of her feelings, once again the archetypal governess, any hint of a sensual being ruthlessly quashed. 'You are right. He is exceedingly strong. Thank you for your help. But…' She lowered her voice to a whisper and leaned closer. His breath seized all over again, with the anticipation of her touch, but that touch never came. 'Please…tell Stevie to call you Papa. He usually does when he speaks of you. He is unsure of himself, and of you, and he is desperate to please you.'

Then she moved away, leaving Dolph to silently rebuke himself for his uncharacteristic… He struggled to come up with a word. Lust? But, no, that did not fit. And when the word eventually came to him, it was need. Hardly flattering and not at all as he would normally view himself, but it perfectly described how he had been overcome with the sudden desire for someone to be close to…someone to share his innermost feelings.

Maybe returning to Dolphin Court had been a mistake? He'd had no choice, however. He must think of the children, which meant he must come to terms with his guilt over his failure as a husband, and he must get used to the ghostly reminders of Rebecca. Time might have helped him over the worst of his grief, but he was no closer to forgiving himself for his failure to recognise how mentally disturbed she had become in her final months.

But those feelings, unexpectedly awakened by his return to Dolphin Court, were no excuse for him not to maintain a proper professional relationship with his sons' governess, no matter his sudden craving for intimacy.

He wrenched his thoughts away from Rebecca and onto his sons and Miss Thame, who was saying in a laughing voice, 'Did Wolf get you all wet? Come…it is time we went home, and you can change out of your damp clothes.' She looked towards the cave and then back at Dolph. 'I see Lord Hinckley is returning—shall you wait here for him?'

Dolph read the unspoken plea on both boys' faces. 'No. George will soon catch us up, and I would prefer to walk with you three, if you have no objection?'

Nicky whooped and ran ahead. Stevie, on the other hand, smiled—a touch hesitantly—and said, 'Of course we do not object, Father.'

'I do have one condition, though, Steven… Stevie.'

The small solemn face tugged at his heartstrings. 'Yes, Father?'

'My condition is that you call me Papa, as you used to. When you call me Father it feels as though you are cross with me.'

Those grey eyes…so like his own…searched Dolph's face. He smiled encouragingly, noticing Miss Thame put her hand on Stevie's shoulder and give him a gentle squeeze. Then Stevie smiled and the solemn little man transformed into the small boy he should be.

'Very well. Papa.' He gave a little skip, then shouted, 'Come on, Wolf, let's catch Nicky,' and hared off after his brother.

Dolph watched his son scamper away with a smile and a sigh. 'Thank you,' he said to Miss Thame. 'That was a timely reminder.'

He waved to George and pointed up the beach before he and Miss Thame started to stroll in the direction of home. Off to their left, George altered his direction to intersect with them at the top of the beach.

'You are welcome, my lord. And I am pleased you do not object to my…um…*interference*, some might say.'

He was pleased to note she seemed to have put that instant of… What had it been? A frisson of awareness? A spark of some current between them? Well, she appeared to have put it behind her, and he would do likewise. No good could come of him lusting after a governess. Or even needing her. She was a gently bred lady in his employ and his own honour would not allow him to take advantage of her.

'Interference? Have you been accused of such in previous posts?'

He knew Miss Thame had been governess to other families before she came to Dolphin Court.

'Once or twice.' She was unsmiling, but her voice revealed hidden amusement. 'I cannot help myself, it seems. It is often easier for an outsider to detect strains within a family and how they…er…mismanage those strains, thus worsening them. And, in those circumstances, I confess I find it difficult to keep my opinion to myself. Not everybody is open to advice, however, and previous employers have raised objections to my *getting above my station.* Understandably, perhaps, for we none of us enjoy criticism, do we? Even if, deep down, we know it to be justified.'

'That is true. At least I am forewarned, and I shall now brace myself for more of your *interference.*'

'Oh, I try to keep my advice to a maximum of once per day, so you are quite safe until this time tomorrow.'

Dolph roared with laughter. George joined them at that moment and said, 'What is the joke? Do share.'

'Miss Thame is managing my expectations about our future working relationship,' Dolph said, still chuckling. 'She has just warned me she will have no compunction in educating me, should she deem it necessary.'

'Oh. I say…that *is* a bold manoeuvre, Miss Thame, if I might say so. And what sort of education did you—?'

*'George…'* Dolph put as much warning as he could into his tone, realising his guest had mistaken his meaning. 'Miss Thame has promised to help me rebuild my relationship with the children and will tell me if I make mistakes. *That* is all I meant.'

'Ah. Yes. I see.' George executed a bow to the governess. 'My apologies—I assumed you were to teach Dolph decent penmanship at long last, Miss Thame. His handwriting is quite abysmal, you know.'

*Smoothly recovered, my friend.* Fortunately, Miss Thame appeared innocently oblivious of the end of the stick George had initially grasped, much to Dolph's relief after that earlier frisson between them.

'Now, then.' George rubbed his gloved hands briskly together. 'I understand from Dolph you are to dine with us tonight, Miss Thame?'

'Oh! I...' Her gaze flew to Dolph's. 'I was unsure if that was something of a spur-of-the-moment suggestion, my lord? If you would rather—'

'Nonsense!' George grinned at Dolph. 'No offence, Dolph, but a third to vary the conversation would be welcome, would it not?'

'Yes, without a doubt. And no offence taken, George. Your presence, Miss Thame, will hopefully lead to more civilised subjects of discussion at the table.'

George guffawed. 'Are you suggesting my conversation is uncivilised, old fellow?'

Dolph bit back a grin. 'I cast no such aspersion, *old fellow*. I was merely expressing a general desire. Well, Miss Thame? What do you say? Are you prepared to lend your calming influence at the dining table each night?'

'As you put it like that, my lord, the answer is yes.' A smile curved Miss Thame's lips, her eyes crinkling with silent laughter. 'After all, I have garnered plenty of experience in directing and diverting the attention and conversation of small boys, and that skill will no doubt prove valuable.'

They had reached the track that led to the Court. Steven, Nicholas and Wolf had ranged far ahead of the adults and were currently tussling over a fallen branch in a tug of war, the boys at one end and Wolf at the other. Shrieks of laughter rent the air.

'Evidently,' said Dolph.

'My lord...one of the most important lessons with children is to learn which battles to fight.'

Miss Thame's smile turned wistful as she watched the boys, and Dolph once again realised how lucky he had been it was she who had replied to his advertisement. Her fondness for his sons was clear, and she had undoubtedly helped them to recover from their mother's death.

'I do have one request, though, as we are on the subject of evenings,' said Miss Thame, her attention still on the boys. 'During your absence, I have been accustomed to play the piano for a short time after the boys are asleep. I wonder if I might continue the practice—mayhap while you gentlemen indulge in your after-dinner port?'

'Of course, Miss Thame, and we would also be delighted if you would play for us on the occasional evening as well.'

'I should say so,' exclaimed George. 'Unfortunate there are no ladies with whom to dance, though, eh, Dolph?'

Dolph just smiled. He, for one, had no desire to dance with anyone. But some light piano music to soothe the soul? That would be most welcome.

Dolph spent the afternoon visiting his tenants with Roger Pople, followed by catching up with his correspondence while George—claiming to be in need of exercise—set out to walk the half-mile to the village. He returned two hours later with a smug smile on his face and a twinkle in his eyes that put Dolph immediately upon the alert.

'And what delights did you discover in the village?' he asked his friend, somewhat dryly. 'I am surprised you were away so long, unless you dawdled at a snail's pace all the way there and back.'

'I called at the church and the Reverend Strong told me all about its fascinating history and showed me its interesting architectural features.'

'Such as?'

'Eh?'

'I wondered which architectural features in particular?'

'Oh…you know…columns and stained-glass windows.

The altar. The bell tower—you know, Dolph. The usual churchy type stuff.'

'It must have been a thorough examination of the building. As I recall, it is not that extensive.'

'Oh, well, we got chatting and he very kindly invited me to the vicarage for a glass of Madeira. Well, I could hardly refuse, could I? Not after he had been so attentive.'

'And was Miss Strong at home, perchance?'

'Why, yes. She was. I was delighted to be properly introduced to her. A charming girl.'

'George…please do not forget these people are my neighbours. And Miss Strong is an innocent.'

George's eyes opened wide. 'Dolph! You wound me! I am not Bluebeard, you know. And what is a little harmless flirtation? Miss Strong blushes most delightfully— she reminds me of a plump little chicken.'

He sighed, his expression dreamy.

'I have never yet seen a chicken blush, George. Do, please, take care. Miss Strong is young and not at all worldly-wise. You ought not to raise her expectations.'

'So you said before, old chap. And I shall watch my words, believe me. I have no wish to be sued for breach of promise.' He winked. '*I* am too worldly-wise to fall into *that* trap.'

Later, Leah stared at her reflection in her mirror. It had taken no time to choose a gown to wear to dinner, as she only had two suitable dresses from which to choose—a green sprigged muslin round gown, more suited to day wear, and an evening dress of light blue net over a white satin slip that she used to wear on the odd occasion Papa invited guests to the vicarage to dine. Both were somewhat outmoded, but neither of the gentlemen would expect a governess to wear the latest fashions. Besides, she was not dressing to impress—although that did not stop her spending an inordinate length of time styling her hair. For once, rather than scraping it back from her face, she pinned it more loosely and teased out a few tendrils to frame her face. She hesitated over whether to wear the necklace she had made out of Mama's wedding ring but, in the end, she decided in favour of it, simply because her upper chest looked horribly bare without it and it detracted from the horrid freckles that marred her skin.

Finally, it was time to go downstairs. The boys had been in bed for a while—they were both early risers—and Cassie had agreed to listen out for them as well as for Tilly. Leah's nervousness had killed her appetite and, as she descended the staircase and heard male voices drifting from the drawing room, her hands grew clammy and her pulse raced. Never had she dined in such exalted company and she prayed she would do nothing to disgrace herself.

'Miss Thame!'

Lord Hinckley leapt to his feet as Leah entered the room while Lord Dolphinstone was already standing next to the fireplace in a similar pose to that he had struck in her sitting room last night. That memory did nothing to quell her nerves but sent more heat spiralling through her as her mind's eye conjured up that intriguing glimpse of dark chest hair and her hand twitched in memory of that solid wall of muscle beneath her palm. Her unruly imagination painted a picture of his entire chest and she felt another of her wretched blushes rise up her neck to flood her cheeks.

Hinckley ushered her across the room, while Dolphinstone looked on, his expression—as it often was—inscrutable as his gaze roved over her, appraising her. As their eyes met, without volition that moment on the beach sprang into her consciousness—the moment when they had been so close, and time appeared frozen, and he had looked deep into her eyes and she had seen…what? Heat? Desire?…flare in the depths of his, triggering that same tug of attraction she had experienced before.

Her mouth dried, and she licked her lips. His Lordship's grey gaze dropped to her mouth, causing her pulse to leap. She lowered her own gaze, resolutely quashing her growing fascination with her employer.

'Good evening, my lords.' She bobbed a curtsy.

'Welcome, Miss Thame.' Dolphinstone pushed away from the mantel and nodded to her. 'Might we dispense with the "my lord" appellation? Sir will be sufficient. If that is agreeable to you, George?'

'Yes, indeed. Or Hinckley, should you prefer, Miss Thame. After all, you're almost one of the family, ain't that right, Dolph?'

Her employer's grey eyes gleamed with amusement, and he bowed again—this time, Leah felt sure, somewhat ironically. 'Indeed. But Dolphinstone is such a mouthful, so perhaps you would prefer to stick to "sir"?' He clearly did not intend Leah to reply as he continued, 'Shall we make our way to the dining room?'

Leah was surprised when Hinckley proffered his arm—it was a courtesy she had not anticipated, with them both being earls and her a mere governess. She supposed gentlemanly behaviour came naturally to men of their ilk—although that had not been her experience in the past—but she still felt a fraud as she placed her hand on Hinckley's forearm. As they entered the dining room, however, she reminded herself this was an excellent opportunity for her to practise the etiquette expected in Society.

In the dining room, Dolphinstone himself held her chair as she sat, and she began to feel less of an interloper. A glass of wine served with the meal helped her relax, but she took little part in the conversation other than to reply when directly applied to for an opinion, which was seldom. Lord Hinckley proved to be an entertaining guest with a ready supply of stories, many of them self-deprecating. He clearly enjoyed being the centre of attention, and he recounted many anecdotes about London—in which Leah had no need to feign interest—before embarking on conjecture about the forthcoming Season.

'I hope I am not boring you, Miss Thame, with all this talk of people you have not met. I did not mean to rattle on so.'

'Not at all, sir. I am interested to hear about lives and places so far removed from my own experience.'

'Have you ever been to London?'

It was the first time Dolphinstone had directed a question to Leah, and she noticed his gaze lingered somewhere around the crown of her head as he avoided meeting her eyes.

'No. I have never visited, but I should like to.'

'Oh, you must! You would enjoy it. I have told Miss Strong the same thing.'

It was easy for Hinckley to say. He clearly had no clue how impossible it was for a woman in Leah's position to simply go to a big city like London upon a whim. Although now, of course, she had precisely that opportunity—but she could not admit it. Fortunately, Hinckley did not wait for her to answer.

'I am eager for the start of the Season. Are you not, Dolph?'

'No, I have no intention of going away again so soon, as I told you before we left London.'

'But...' Hinckley's brow puckered. 'I made sure you would change your mind. After all, you missed the Season last year when you were overseas. Although, come to think of it, last year would have been too soon after Rebecca's death, would it not?'

Leah cringed at Hinckley touching on such a personal subject in front of her, and a glance at Dolphinstone saw his brow darken. Hinckley, however, appeared not to notice as he forked roast beef into his mouth, chewed and swallowed before continuing.

'Really, Dolph...you must reconsider. You ought to marry again, for the children's sake if not your own.'

'George. I have no intention of marrying again. Ever.'

Dolphinstone's growled words brought Hinckley up short.

'Ah. Yes. Of course. I apologise. None of my business. I quite see that.'

A strained silence prevailed. Leah wished the ground could swallow her up, even though it was Hinckley who was at fault, with his glib chatter. She raised her wine glass and sipped as the two men applied themselves to their food, casting around for a subject to ease the strained atmosphere.

'My lord...sir...' Dolphinstone looked up, his grey eyes hard. Leah's spirit reared up in response—she would not be cowed by that look. 'Might you visit the boys at their lessons tomorrow? They would be delighted to show you what progress they have made. Stevie, in particular, has made great strides in his reading and writing. Although that is not to decry Nicky's ability but, being younger, he is, of course, behind.'

'Yes. I will come in the afternoon, if that will fit in with your plans, Miss Thame.'

Embarrassment that she'd witnessed his reprimand of his guest gave way to nervous but pleasurable anticipation of him visiting the schoolroom the next day. Dolphinstone continued to stare at her, his features rigid. Then his expression softened.

His chest inflated as he inhaled. 'I apologise for barking at you, George. I know you only meant well. And I am sorry you had to witness that lapse in manners, Miss Thame. I cannot excuse myself.'

Leah experienced a satisfying sense of accomplishment. *She* had successfully soothed Dolphinstone's temper and rescued a fraught situation. She eyed His Lordship surreptitiously as she sipped her wine. He looked so very splendid in his evening clothes, radiating masculinity. He drew her attention like a magnet and, before she could help herself, she found regret coursing through her that he was so far out of her reach. Not only due to his status in Society but also because he was clearly still in love with his dead wife.

*You fool! Did you learn nothing from Peter and Usk? Do not allow a handsome face to draw you in again. You will end up hurt.*

'It's quite all right, old chap,' Hinckley was saying. 'I didn't think… I know returning here has been something of a trial for you. You will settle in time, I'm sure.'

Dolphinstone's lips quirked in a brief smile. 'I know.'

Leah sat awkwardly for a few minutes before realising she was expected to withdraw now they had finished eating. That was one of the stories with which Papa used to regale her and Mama about life in Society, for, as the younger son of a gentleman, he had travelled well in his youth and had spent some time in London during the

Season, even though he had always been destined for the Church. She pushed back her chair and rose to her feet.

'If you will excuse me, I shall withdraw now. Is it still acceptable to you I practise on the pianoforte, sir?'

'It is. It will be a pleasure to hear music in the house again.'

# Chapter Eight

The next afternoon Dolph hesitated outside the school-room door. His palms, ridiculously, were damp, and his stomach roiled uneasily. He sucked in a calming breath. How absurd was this…a grown man nervous of talking to his own sons? They were only children. But maybe that was the trouble. If they were older, closer to man-hood, he would not be so anxious about saying or doing something to upset them. Or even frighten them. What did *he* know about how to talk to children?

He rubbed his palms down his coat and steeled him-self to push open the door.

The minute he was inside the room his nerves sub-sided when he saw the delight shining on the two little faces turned to him. He might still worry the boys would hate him for leaving them the way he did, but it seemed his sons were more forgiving than he deserved. A little of the guilt he had carried for the past sixteen months slipped from his shoulders.

'Greet your father, boys.'

Miss Thame's murmured instruction drew his atten-tion. She was once again clad in her governess garb, as he thought of it. Every inch the respectable governess. She had appeared a different woman last evening—alluring in a way that captured his interest—with her hair pinned in a much softer style and wearing a blue gown that accentuated her porcelain skin and revealed the upper slopes of her breasts. The only adornment had been a simple blue ribbon from which a gold ring was suspended. His gaze had returned to her décolletage time and again—drawn as though to a magnet—as he'd speculated about whose ring it was. Her mother's, perhaps? It was too small to fit a man's finger. A memory from last evening formed in his mind's eye, of Leah at the pianoforte, her slender, sensitive fingers dancing across the keys, the pale vulnerability of her nape and the long lines of her back... He jerked his thoughts away from those mental images before his body could respond.

'Good afternoon, Papa,' the boys chorused obediently across the width of the room.

'Good afternoon, Stevie. Good afternoon, Nicky.'

'Would you care to hear the boys read to you, sir?' Leah—as he had begun to think of her inside his head—approached him, and her fresh scent filled his senses. She lowered her voice, smiling a conspirator's smile. 'Would you ask Nicky to read first, as he is a little less sure of himself in the schoolroom than he is outside it? If Stevie reads first, it will make him more anxious.'

'Whatever you think best,' Dolph murmured, then raised his voice. 'Nicky, will you read to me first?'

His younger son's face fell, but he nodded stoically.

Miss Thame returned to sit with Stevie and redirected his attention to the map they had been studying when Dolph came in. As he listened to Nicky laboriously reading aloud the words chalked on his slate, Dolph also eavesdropped on the way Leah tested Stevie upon his understanding of the world. She teased out Stevie's knowledge, and his admiration and respect for her grew as she seemed instinctively to understand when the boy reached his limit, never pushing him too far beyond his capabilities, so he didn't get discouraged and give up. Dolph attempted to adopt the same tactic with Nicky, although he soon realised all his younger son needed was a huge amount of patient repetition to try to imprint the letters and the sounds they made into his brain.

He had vowed to concentrate solely on the boys during his visit to the schoolroom, but it proved impossible to completely ignore his growing fascination with Leah. That unexpected frisson between them on the beach when their gazes had locked, kindling the slow burn of desire deep inside him—for the first time in a very long time— had unsettled him enough. As a consequence, he had found himself uncharacteristically tongue-tied at the dining table, wary of revealing any hint of his inappropriate interest in her, and she, too, had been clearly ill at ease. He was glad she had agreed to dine with them, however, and she had impressed him with her skill in defusing the tension after George's crass remark about Rebecca.

When the time came to swap over, he was impressed with Stevie's quick mind and his confidence with reading—he was reading from a text rather than from a slate—and he noticed Leah completely changed her approach to help Nicky, who was clearly struggling with the concept of maps and countries.

But, still, only half his attention remained on his son and his schoolwork. Still, it proved impossible to keep his eyes from straying to Leah, eyeing her tightly pinned hair and imagining how it would look, and feel, if let loose to flow over her shoulders and down her back.

And those freckles… Where else did they dot her pale, translucent skin?

\* \* \*

As the days passed, such improper thoughts made him careful to avoid being alone with Leah. When they spoke, their conversation—as if by mutual, unspoken agreement—focussed on the children and their progress, and when Dolph visited the schoolroom, Leah's attention remained steadfastly on her pupils. Dolph would watch them with an aching hollow in his chest, envying their closeness, hoping he might soon achieve that same, easy relationship with his sons.

The evenings became less fraught, with George as entertaining a raconteur as ever and proving the perfect foil. It was then, at dinner and afterwards, that Dolph noticed more of those telltale signs Leah was still troubled. At odd moments her thoughts seemed to turn inward, and a vertical line would score the pale skin between her brows while her teeth worried at her lower lip, sending Dolph's pulse rocketing.

The relative intimacy of those evenings bothered him. What would happen when George left? He could hardly insult Leah by not dining with her, but what if this unexpected lustful interest continued? He had never before considered taking a mistress, but that might be the only solution if his physical needs continued to plague him… Surely there must be a local widow who would be happy to— That line of thought slammed to a halt as every fibre of his being rebelled against the very idea of a mistress.

The weather turned colder over the next few weeks, with brisk winds bringing daily showers of hail or sleet. Everyday life fell into a pattern: every afternoon, George rode or walked into the village—rendering Dolph uneasy as he wondered about George's intentions towards Miss Strong—and Dolph would visit the schoolroom for half an hour. The deteriorating weather increasingly confined the boys to the house and, on those days, instead of their daily brisk walk, they were set free to play as soon as morning lessons were over. The house would shake to the din of thundering feet, shrieks of laughter and excitable barks from Wolf, who, increasingly, had abandoned Dolph's company in favour of spending time with the boys. Later, after afternoon lessons, there would be more outdoor exercise or a quieter session of indoor play, when the boys would fight battles with their toy soldiers or play a game of hide-and-seek, with occasional bursts of excitement as someone was found.

On the first day Dolph had experienced the phenomenon of what Leah called *indoor play*, he had emerged from his study ready to restore the peace but, at that precise moment, the noise had suddenly abated and order had been restored. Later that afternoon, when Leah had brought the boys and Tilly to the drawing room to say goodnight—another habit that had become a routine—she had turned to him, saying with a smile that reached deep inside him and tweaked his heartstrings, 'Do you now appreciate why I take the boys outside for exercise whenever possible?'

It had taken him a moment or two to identify the emotion triggered by her smile. Loneliness. That was how he felt. And, without warning, resentment—aimed squarely at Rebecca—spiralled through him. How could she have left him…left her *children*…in such a cruel way? As quickly as it arose, his anger with his dead wife subsided and he was consumed once again with guilt.

*My fault. I should have noticed. I let her down.*

He had retreated to his study without answering Leah, headed straight for the decanter and poured himself a glass of claret, downing it in one, mentally shoving those feelings into a box and slamming the lid. He didn't *want* to feel, dammit. Nothing could change what had happened.

On the twenty-third day of February, which had so far lived up to its reputation as the worst winter month weather-wise, Dolph came downstairs dressed for dinner to discover a message from George had been delivered, along with a letter for Leah.

'Have that taken up to Miss Thame, Palmer,' he said to the butler as he opened the seal on George's note.

*My dear Dolph*
*Reverend Strong has kindly invited me to dine to-night. I know you will not object and, as it has been a rare dry day, I shall walk back later by the light of a lantern so you need have no fears for my safe return.*
*Your friend*
*Hinckley*

Dolph's first reaction was dread at the prospect of dining *à deux* with Leah, but he soon realised there was no point avoiding it—George would not be at the Court for ever, and Dolph must learn to behave normally around his sons' governess whether they were alone or not. He went to the drawing room to await Leah, positioning himself by the fireside and staring mindlessly into the flames until he heard her enter.

He turned. She was dressed tonight in her green muslin gown, her shawl around her shoulders, and that wedding ring around her neck, tonight suspended on a green ribbon. Her cheeks were flushed, and her eyes sparkled, prompting him to wonder who her letter had been from. She was clearly happy with the news it contained. For a split second his imagination conjured up an image of her dressed in a fashionable evening gown, with sapphires or pearls around her neck, but he batted that picture aside with a surge of self-loathing.

*I pay her wages. She is powerless. If I do not control these lustful urges for the poor woman, it will be her who suffers. Not me.*

'I'm afraid it is just the two of us for dinner this evening, Miss Thame.' He would make no big thing of them dining alone together. She, he knew, would follow his lead. 'George sent word that he is invited to dine at the vicarage.'

'The vicarage?' She frowned. 'He visits the Reverend Strong almost daily, does he not? Or is Miss Strong the magnet that draws him to the village so frequently?'

'George enjoys the Reverend's conversation, but I won't deny he also takes pleasure in Miss Strong's company—he is a man who enjoys the society of women probably more than that of other men.' Dolph resolved to warn George once again about not raising Miss Strong's expectations. 'He means nothing by it… He likes to flirt and pay compliments.'

Leah's eyes narrowed.

'It's just his way,' Dolph added. 'Now, shall we go to dinner?'

Once seated, with bowls of soup in front of them, Dolph said, 'I see you received a letter today.'

Her cheeks coloured. He adored the way she blushed so readily—an unexpected trait in a woman who was ordinarily so sensible and unemotional.

'I did.' She raised a spoonful of soup to her mouth.

'And…?' he prompted.

She fixed him with a steady look and a lift of her brows.

'Did you have time to read it before you came down to dinner?'

'I did, thank you.'

Dolph rubbed his jaw, stubble rasping his fingers. 'Will you tell me who it was from?'

He caught the twitch of her lips before she raised her wine glass and sipped.

'Am I obliged to?'

'Of course not.' Dolph sipped from his own glass. 'But I thought you might like to share your news. I recall from your interview you have no immediate family.' Her gaze slid from his and sought her plate. A thought struck him. 'Was it from your solicitor? Does that explain your reluctance to speak of it?'

'No.' She still studied her plate but had ceased to eat. 'It was from someone I met at that meeting, though.'

It was Dolph's turn to raise his brows. A man, perhaps? Did that account for her secrecy?

The servants came in with the main course and dessert then, and the conversation paused as they helped themselves to game pie, creamed leeks, boiled potatoes and carrots, and more wine was poured.

'It was not from a man,' Leah said when they were alone again. It was as though she'd read his mind. 'It was from another lady. But that is all I can say, I'm afraid.'

He could pry no further without being rude, but the exchange left him feeling unsettled. He truly did dislike the idea of her keeping secrets from him, not least because she was in charge of his sons, but he could not force the truth from her. Thinking of Stevie and Nicky, though...

'Do you think the boys have forgiven me yet?'

She shot him a puzzled look. 'Forgiven you?'

'Yes. For abandoning them.'

'Children are very forgiving… They will judge you on how you behave with them now and henceforth. They are not like adults, forever looking back and regretting this thing they said or that way they behaved.'

Her words comforted him. 'I hope you are right. When I returned, I feared they would never be able to forgive me, but they have never given me reason to believe they resent the way I left them. I am immensely proud of them…and I do thank you because I know that is due to you and your care for them. They are lucky to have you. As am I.'

Her gaze lowered again, and her hand rose to cover the ring suspended around her neck.

'Did that ring belong to someone special? I have noticed you wear it every evening, albeit with a change of ribbon.'

'It was my mother's wedding band.' She sipped more wine. 'I wear it all day, too, beneath my gown.'

Hidden beneath her awful, drab governess garb.

She shrugged, appearing almost embarrassed. 'It keeps the memory of my parents close. Mama's ring and Papa's fob watch.'

'Ah…the watch I have seen on your desk in the schoolroom?'

She nodded. 'I have Papa's old writing slope too. I always feel him near whenever I use it. I do not need wealth…' she appeared to have forgotten he was there; it was as though she was talking to herself '…not when I have such treasures and such precious memories. And I don't…' She paused, and he saw her throat ripple as she swallowed. Then she shook her head and sat a little straighter. When she looked at him her eyes were bright with emotion. 'I didn't feel as alone as long as I had them with me.'

'You must miss them very much, but it seems you have happy memories of your childhood.'

'Oh, indeed. My parents…they were very much in love. I always hoped—' Her cheeks turned fiery red.

'You hoped…?'

She shrugged and gave him a rueful smile. 'You will think me a fool. It was never more than a forlorn hope, really, but my ideal if I ever married was for a love match, like my parents. I should not talk like this, I know, but I fear the wine has loosened my tongue and I am feeling somewhat nostalgic.'

His heart went out to her. 'It must have been difficult for you—a woman alone—when your father died.' She had told him at interview that she'd been nineteen years old. 'You must have felt very alone.' Her words sounded again in his head. 'You changed from *you don't* to *you didn't*. May I hope that means you feel more at home here than you have in previous households?'

Her smile was sad. Reflective. 'Yes. Everyone here is so friendly. And the children are an absolute joy.'

Her voice cracked on her final words. Her hand trembled as she raised her wine glass once again, and without conscious thought, Dolph reached across and gently squeezed her shoulder. She started at his touch, and he snatched his hand away, his hand—his entire arm—tingling from the contact.

'My apologies,' he said. 'I did not mean to startle you.'

*Fool! What were you thinking?*

He had finished his meal, and to cover his dismay, he selected a large slice of apple pie from the dish on the table and poured custard over it.

'Would you care for dessert, Miss Thame?'

She nodded. 'Thank you.'

Trust something prosaic like food to restore the equilibrium. Dolph dished out a slice of pie for Leah and then handed her the jug of custard before tucking into his own dessert.

His instinct to reach out and comfort her had shaken him. He must take more care—she had revealed more of her heart than she realised, and that must act as a warning to him to ignore his desires. Leah was happy here at Dolphin Court. She considered it as her home. He would never forgive himself if she felt obliged to leave because he could not control himself. He was her employer; in a position of authority over her. His honour as a gentleman would not allow him to take advantage of such power.

If he were to follow his natural desire and seduce her, the only remedy would be to offer marriage and—quite apart from his own resolve to never wed again—how could he do that to a woman who had just confided in him her ideal marriage was a love match? He was incapable of love. Incapable of making any woman happy.

*I would drive her to despair, just as I did Rebecca.*

He picked up his glass and tipped the remaining contents down his throat as Leah set her spoon down and rose to her feet.

'If you will excuse me, I am very tired, sir, and so I shall say goodnight.'

He'd noticed dark circles around her eyes had formed over the past week, suggesting she was not sleeping well—was she still troubled over whatever she had discovered at that meeting in Bristol at the end of January? Maybe he would ask her again about it, but not this evening. He would choose a more suitable time and place.

'Of course. Goodnight, Miss Thame.'

## Chapter Nine

Leah's cheeks were still burning when she reached her bedchamber. She lit her candle, undressed swiftly, donned her nightgown and climbed into bed, shivering until her body warmed the chilly sheets. What had she been thinking, to reveal so much to Dolph? Her stomach churned and she felt tears scald her eyes. What on *earth* had she been thinking?

Of all the nights for Lord Hinckley to be absent, this must have been the very worst. She had already been unsettled by Aurelia's letter when she came downstairs. Sally, the housemaid, had delivered it to her just as she was leaving her bedchamber, having dressed for dinner, and she had returned to her room and read it quickly, her heart thumping with excitement and hope—and joy at having a sister...*two* sisters...in this world.

But the letter had also reminded her the day was fast approaching when she must leave the children and Dolphin Court. And leaving Dolph—she had found herself, in the weeks since his return, thinking of him by the nickname George used—would also be a wrench, despite knowing there could never be anything between them, for she already cared for him and she had, in recent days, found herself longing for the right to soothe away the grief that still shimmered in his eyes in unguarded moments.

So by the time she had gone downstairs, her emotions had already been in turmoil with that mixture of joy, excitement, dread and pure misery, and then Dolph had unsettled her further with his teasing questions about the letter and then utterly disarmed her when he had revealed his fear the children would never forgive him. Her heart had gone out to him, and the wine had lulled her, and he had been so kind, so understanding when she'd spoken of Mama and Papa, that she had almost forgotten she was talking to him. To Dolph. Her brooding, handsome, rugged employer. It wasn't until her emotions had threatened to overcome her, and she had felt his hand on her shoulder, offering comfort much as she would do for the boys, that she had come to her senses, eaten her pudding in record time, gabbled an excuse and escaped.

This evening had served as a warning, though. The spark of attraction she'd felt on that first night had not sputtered out but was now a steady flame. Her feelings for Dolph had grown, and she now dreaded saying goodbye.

A feeling of hopelessness washed through her. She had recognised the occasional gleam in his eyes when he looked at her. He desired her, strange as that was to believe. Although she had little experience of men, she did know they seldom found women like her—tall, redhaired and freckled—alluring. Peter and Usk had taught her that when they discarded her after she ceased to be of any use to them—Peter after Papa died, and Usk as soon as he won his wager.

Leah huddled deeper under the bedclothes. She closed her eyes, willing sleep to overtake her, but still her mind whirled with the many changes fast approaching, and her many worries about her future. If she met the conditions of Lady Tregowan's will, then by this time next year she would be wed. What if her husband turned out to be a scoundrel? Was her judgement of the true nature of men sound enough to protect her and keep her safe, and to sort the decent gentlemen from the rogues? Her record to date gave her little confidence—her experiences with both Peter and Usk proved her lack of good judgement.

One thing was certain... Once she was wed, everything—her life, her future, her inheritance—would depend upon that one man. Her husband.

But she had no choice but to go to London and to try.

Leaving Dolphin Court, and all the people she had grown to care about, was bad enough, but the other side of that coin was what awaited her in her future. How would the three half-sisters be received in Society? Their wealth would help to smooth their paths—money always proved an excellent lubricant—but, as Aurelia had already discovered, there would always be some to peer down their noses at three down-at-heel gentlewomen joining their ranks.

She almost wished she had never gone to that meeting... Then she could continue her life here in blissful ignorance and would not be plagued by this ceaseless uncertainty.

*Except...then I wouldn't have met Aurelia and Beatrice.*

Only the thought of her two half-sisters buoyed her spirits. For the most part. Because even that godsend was two-edged—what if they did not like one another? Or what if Aurelia and Beatrice became friends but disliked Leah? She had been so happy to receive the letter from Aurelia, but a pleasant letter did not guarantee an amicable relationship in person, and Aurelia had struck Leah as somewhat confrontational at that meeting with Mr Henshaw. Beatrice seemed more amenable, although mayhap a touch timid.

Leah could only pray the three of them would become friends because, if not, then her greatest fear might come to pass—that she would leave here and that she would end up alone.

The following day Dolph was in his study, reading a treatise on animal husbandry, when Nicky burst into his study from behind the secret panel that led to one of the secret passages with which Dolphin Court was blessed. Nicky slammed to a halt, his eyes wide with dismay as he saw his father. In his hand he clutched a carved wooden horse: a toy Dolph recalled from his own childhood.

'Nicky...' the breathless voice sounded from within the secret passage '...you *know* you are not meant to come this way.' Leah appeared in the opening in the panelled wall. 'Oh!' Her hand went to her hair, which had worked free from the hairpins that normally held every strand strictly in place, and her cheeks flamed. 'I am so sorry we disturbed you.'

'You are not disturbing me, Miss Thame.' But that was untrue. Loose tendrils of hair formed an auburn halo around her head, enticingly, and an image formed in his mind's eye of her hair tumbling loose around her pale, freckled, naked shoulders. He swallowed, thrusting that image away. 'This paper is so dull I am in danger of falling asleep. Nicho—Nicky...will you allow me to see your horse?' Nicky approached him and handed over his toy. 'I used to play with this when I was a boy.' Dolph examined the carving. 'The saddle and bridle were painted blue, and I called him Thunder. And there was another one, with red saddlery, called Lightning.'

'That is Stevie's pony.'

'Ah, of course; you would have one each. Have you given them names?'

Nicky nodded. 'Mine is Bullet and Stevie's is Peg'sus. He says that's what he will name his real pony when he gets one. But he says I can't have one yet 'cause I'm too little. But I can ride Billy as well as he can.'

'I noticed Old Billy is still around, but I should think he's a bit wide for your little legs, Nicky.' From the corner of his eye he saw a smile flicker around Leah's lips as she nodded approvingly. 'Well...' and he wondered why he had not thought of it before '... I should think it is time for both you and Stevie to have your own ponies—ones the right size for you. I shall make it my priority. After all, it is important for a gentleman to learn to ride from a young age, is it not, Miss Thame?'

'It is,' she said. 'Now, Nicky, let us leave your father in peace. Stevie is no doubt wondering where we can have hidden so successfully.'

She smiled at Dolph. No longer distracted by her hair, he realised the shadows under her eyes were even more pronounced than before.

'Stevie will not ignore my instructions to avoid that passage, unlike this little imp.'

She ruffled Nicky's hair and started to shepherd him from the study as Dolph pushed the secret panel shut with a click and wished he could behave half as naturally with his sons.

'Papa?'

'Yes, Nicky?'

'*I'm* going to be in the cavalry when I grow up. I'm

going to fight with the Duke of Wellington and beat Napoleon.'

'Now, Nicky.' Leah flashed a smile at Dolph. 'You know Napoleon has already been beaten, and I doubt the Duke will still be fighting battles when you are old enough to join the cavalry.'

'But I *want* to fight. Stevie doesn't even want to, and he'll only be an earl when he grows up and that's *boring*. Like lessons.'

Dolph bit back a laugh as his younger son's scornful gaze scanned his desk. 'Nicholas. Apologise to Miss Thame, if you please,' he said. 'It is impolite to call her lessons boring.'

Nicky hung his head. 'I'm sorry, Miss Thame.'

'I accept your apology, Nicky. Now come.'

They went out into the hall, but before Leah could close the study door, Nicky peered back around its edge.

'You will not forget about our ponies, Papa?'

'I won't forget.'

'Can I tell Stevie?'

'Yes, of course you may.'

'Hurrah!'

Dolph heard the scamper of feet as Nicky ran off. On the spur of the moment, he called, 'Miss Thame?'

She reappeared in the study, her eyes wary. 'Sir?'

'I should like to speak with you—a matter I cannot discuss in front of the children. Would you arrange for someone to watch the boys for a short while, and come back here?'

Better to quiz her about what was causing sleepless nights here, in the daylight, than risk another too-intimate conversation after dark.

An anxious frown creased her forehead. She inclined

her head. 'Of course. I will take the boys up to the nursery. Cassie will watch over them.'

Fifteen minutes later, having left the boys in Cassie's
care and scraped back her wayward hair, pinning it ruthlessly in place, Leah descended the stairs and crossed the
large entrance hall to the study door. She couldn't quell
her apprehension as she paused and smoothed her palms
over her hips. Had he noticed her infatuation with him
last night? She'd tried to hide it, but that proved trickier
without Lord Hinckley to provide a distraction.

Or was he unhappy with the way she cared for and
taught the boys? She believed she struck the right balance between work and play—and he'd seemed to take
their invasion of his study in good part—but many parents failed to recognise the necessity of physical activity
for boisterous lads.

What if he sent her away? She wasn't ready to leave.
Not yet. She pushed aside the sly inner voice that whispered maybe it would be for the best if he *did* send her
away—from him. He was part of the reason she was still
reluctant to leave, but she also hated the thought of leaving the children before she absolutely must, even though
they were already more relaxed around their father. That
excuse for delay was rapidly receding.

She sucked in a steadying breath, straightened her
shoulders, lifted her chin, knocked on the study door
and entered.

Dolph was at his desk, writing. He raised his head and
smiled briefly. 'Do take a seat.' He indicated the pair of
wingback chairs set either side of the fireplace. 'I shall
be with you in a minute.'

Feeling calmer, certain if he intended a reprimand he
would do it at his desk, Leah sat as bid. But that sense

of calm did not last, as her worries over the future once again scurried around inside her head.

'Have you discussed your dilemma with anyone yet, Miss Thame?'

His Lordship's quiet question interrupted her constantly circling thoughts. His grey eyes studied her, and she saw nothing other than kindness and concern in their depths. Appalled, she felt her throat thicken. Sympathy... She could cope with anything other than sympathy. She swallowed down her emotion and stretched her lips in a smile.

'You are mistaken, my lord. There is no dilemma.'

He raised one brow and indicated Leah's lap. Looking down, she saw her fingers busy pleating and repleating the wool of her gown. She released the fabric and smoothed her skirts, her face heating.

'Or perhaps it is my fault?'

Her gaze flew to his as her stomach turned a somersault. Had he indeed noticed she had developed a *tendre* for him?

'Do I make you nervous?'

'No!' Instinctively, she touched the hard shape of Mama's ring beneath her gown.

A smile played around his lips. 'I thought not, judging by the way you usually speak your mind. Look... Miss Thame... I do not suggest myself as confidant, but I hope you will take my earlier advice and confide in a friend—perhaps Miss Strong? You deny the existence of a dilemma, but my observations of you since my return tell me you are increasingly troubled.'

*His observations of me?*

Leah's breath seized at the thought he had taken such notice of her. She moistened her lips and swallowed again, this time to try to quell the fluttering in her stomach.

'I am surprised you would notice such a trivial matter when you have so many responsibilities.'

His smile was puzzled. 'Would you rather I remain oblivious when someone in my household is troubled? Allow me to help. Please. Miss Strong *is* your friend, is she not?'

'Yes, she is.'

'In that case, if you would like to confide in her, you only need to say the word and I shall arrange for one of the servants to care for the boys during your absence.' His grey eyes twinkled. 'I fear, Miss Thame, I shall have to allow you yet *another* half-day off.'

His words kindled a warmth inside her. He was so hard to resist. He was kind. He talked to her as another adult, not as a servant, and he cared. Oh, not in the way she longed for him to care about her, but he did care for those around him. He was a good man. She felt it deep in her soul.

'Thank you, sir. I shall think about it, and let you know what I decide.' She rose to her feet. 'If that is all, I must return to the children.'


After Sunday service the following day Leah noticed once again how Lord Hinckley danced attendance upon Philippa, paying her extravagant compliments, which, to be fair, she appeared to thoroughly enjoy. He also appeared on excellent terms with the Reverend Strong, who, in Leah's opinion, really ought to discourage His Lordship for his daughter's sake—could he really believe an earl would contemplate matrimony with a country vicar's daughter?

Worried Philippa would be hurt, Leah garnered her courage to broach the subject with Dolph.

'I know His Lordship is your friend and guest, but do

you see now why I was concerned about his behaviour?'
she said, low-voiced, as they stood shivering by the carriage with the boys, waiting for Hinckley to join them.

The temperature had fallen dramatically over the past
couple of days, the weather having turned cold and dry
with bright, sunny days and a sharp frost every night.
The village pond had already frozen over.

'I do, and I admit I share your concern to a certain extent. I fear Miss Strong is unaccustomed to such casual
flirtations as are normal within Society, and she might
believe George's attention to be genuine.'

Leah frowned. 'He *is* lying to her, then?'

'It's not that simple. Gentlemen in our world are expected to flirt with ladies, and they often pay extravagant
compliments that are without substance, but the ladies
of the *beau monde* are worldly enough not to attach too
much significance to such behaviour.'

The pitfalls ahead of Leah loomed large. She would
be seeking a husband among men of a similar character and outlook as Hinckley, and she had already proved
she was as unworldly as Philippa. Look at how she had
fallen for the lies of both Peter and of Usk.

She watched as Hinckley bowed to Philippa, clearly
saying farewell. They both looked rapt as they gazed at
one another, and Leah frowned, doubtful all of a sudden.
Could she be worrying over nothing?

'They do look smitten with one another.'

'Oh, I have no doubt George *is* smitten…for now. But
he is a man who regularly fancies himself in love—it's
in his nature—and I have seen this too often to trust his
adoration will endure this time. I *have* warned him to
take care, however, and reminded him of her inexperi-
ence in matters of the heart.'

Anger stirred on Philippa's behalf. In Leah's opin-

ion, Hinckley should take responsibility for his own behaviour. He was a grown man… What right did he have
to treat Philippa as a convenient way to pass the time,
leading her on? Leah liked Lord Hinckley, but this made
him appear as no better than Lord Usk when he had
fooled Leah into kissing him. Or, even worse, than Lord
Tregowan, who had seduced Mama, an innocent, and
then offloaded her onto another man like a second-hand
coat.

Hinckley finally joined them and, as they climbed
into the carriage for the journey home, Leah decided she
*would* accept Dolph's offer of time off to visit Philippa.
The need to unburden herself to a friend had become almost irresistible, and she could at the same time warn her
friend to treat Lord Hinckley with caution.

## Chapter Ten

That night sleep again evaded Leah as worries about her future tormented her. The minute she lay in her bed, they surged to the fore, keeping her mind active even as her body craved sleep. With a muttered oath, she threw aside the bedcovers and rose from the bed, pushing her feet into her slippers. She lit a candle, slipped her dressing gown on over her nightgown and left her bedchamber by the connecting door to her sitting room. The fire was not yet dead, so she stirred it with the poker and laid small sticks in a lattice over the hot ashes. In no time, the dry wood caught, allowing her to feed bigger sticks and lumps of coal onto the fire.

When it was burning steadily, she went to the table by the window and pulled her writing slope towards her, running her fingertips over the rosewood surface, her mind travelling back into the past with every familiar scratch and dent. It had belonged to Papa—her *real* father, not the man whose blood she shared—and she treasured it and the memories it evoked; happy memories, of Papa writing his sermons, his pen quietly scratching over the paper while Mama sewed, her head bent over her needle. A lump of pain formed in Leah's throat. She had been so very alone since Papa died…no one to really care if she lived or she died. Dolphin Court had given her a sense of belonging she had felt nowhere else, and now she must leave here and face an unknown future with two half-sisters who were virtual strangers. She must say goodbye to the three children she adored, and how she dreaded that prospect. How would she say those words without dissolving into tears and making her departure even more painful for them? Increasingly, too, the prospect of never seeing Dolph again played havoc with her emotions.

Her head might accept that going to London and attempting to fulfil the conditions of Lady Tregowan's will was the only sensible course of action, but her heart was still not convinced.

Cursing again beneath her breath, she opened the slope to form a writing surface and then took a sheet of paper from inside. She opened the inkwell, picked up her pen and began to reply to Aurelia's letter, hoping the activity would help quell the turmoil of her thoughts. It did not. She pushed her chair back, crossed to put more coal on the fire and then paced the room, her mind still hopelessly alert. After several turns up and down the room, a wail penetrated Leah's constantly circling inner monologue.

*Stevie!*

She did not take her candle, knowing from experience the light would rouse him more fully and make it much harder to settle him back down. She went out onto the landing and hurried along it to the boys' room. Stevie was thrashing around, whimpers escaping him from time to time. Leah sat on the mattress and stroked his clammy forehead as she murmured soothing words, her eyes growing accustomed to the dark.

'Hush. It's all right. There's nothing to fear, sweetie. Settle down now. I'm here.'

Gradually Stevie calmed, lying still. His thumb stole into his mouth—a habit she still could not break him of at night although he no longer sucked it during the day, long since cured of it by his little brother's scorn. Gradually, Stevie's breathing eased, and Leah stood to go. Stevie's eyes opened, looking right at her, and he mumbled something around his thumb. Gently she removed it from his mouth and asked him to repeat what he'd said.

'I dreamed you went away, like Mama did.'

Her heart cracked in her chest. She could not promise him she would not go. Oh, but how she wished she could give him that reassurance. She stroked his hair back from his forehead again.

'It was just a dream, Stevie. See? I am here.'

She bent to kiss his cheek, tormented even more by the dread of saying goodbye. His eyes fluttered closed and his thumb crept into his mouth once more. He sighed. Leah straightened, watching him; within minutes he was asleep, and Leah slipped out of the room, having left the door ajar. She frowned at a pool of light further along the landing, then gasped, her heart in her throat as a dark shape stirred and stepped away from the wall, resolving itself into the silhouette of a man.

'It's all right. It is me.' Dolph spoke in a whisper. 'I left the candle along there so the light wouldn't disturb Stevie. You did well to settle him down again so quickly.'

Her insides fluttered at the realisation he must have stood in the doorway, watching her. Listening to her.

'Thank you.' Leah stepped past him. 'Goodnight, sir.'

'Wait.'

His hand on her shoulder sent shock waves rippling through her as her breath caught. His fingers closed, not violently but more in a caress. She faced him and his hand dropped away. He was still dressed in his evening clothes, enticingly masculine in black coat and white neckcloth. An evocative mix of citrus, brandy and musky maleness wreathed through her senses, sending a pleasurable shiver racing through her, right to her tingling nerve endings. His breathing sounded ragged in the hush of the night but, rather than fearing him and the subtle tension that appeared to hold him in its grip—or even fearing the alarming leap of her pulse and those tingles sweeping her skin—Leah felt drawn to him, as a moth was tempted to a flame. Even though she knew, as a moth did not, that flames burned. She stood still and waited, hardly daring to breathe.

'I heard floorboards creaking.' His gaze raked her face, and she struggled to blank her expression. 'Footsteps…in your sitting room. Back and forth. For several minutes. Are you still struggling to sleep?'

'Evidently. But it was not I who disturbed Stevie.'

'I do not accuse you of it. It was one of his nightmares, I assume?'

Leah nodded.

'We cannot talk here, and I confess I, too, am not yet tired. Will you join me in a glass of brandy downstairs? It might help us both sleep, and I would welcome the chance to talk to you about Steven and these nightmares.'

Leah's mouth dried as her pulse beat erratically at the thought of being alone with him. She should refuse. But…

'Yes, of course.' She scanned the dark landing. 'No Wolf?'

The dog would at least have provided some distraction for her.

'No. I left him in my room.'

She forced a quiet chuckle, desperate to appear non-chalant. 'That was wise. I'm sure if Stevie caught sight of Wolf, it would thoroughly wake him up.'

From being wary of the dog, Stevie now worshipped him and they were all but inseparable during the day.

Dolph led the way downstairs to the library, where he lit candles on either end of the mantelshelf and poked the fire into life before pouring two glasses of brandy.

'I was reading in here before I came up, so I knew the fire was still warm.' He handed her a glass. 'Have you thought further about confiding in Miss Strong?'

'I have. I shall write and ask when I might visit her.'

His gaze did not waver from her face, and she felt the weight of it…read the concern in his grey eyes.

'I am relieved, and I hope it might set your mind at rest. You look tired, and I know the boys are early risers.'

'I shall cope.'

The urge to be honest with him, to tell him she must leave, rose up within her, but she could not possibly tell him now. Not here, in the dead of night, attired only in her nightgown, with her dressing gown clasped tightly around her and her hair casually plaited. She knew, without recourse to a mirror, her hair would be a mess—it had ever been unruly and required ruthless pinning during the day to tame it and render it suitable for a governess.

Dolphinstone stared at her frowningly before poking the fire again and feeding it with more coal. Then he faced her, nudging the candlestick out of the way to allow him to prop his elbow on the end of the mantelshelf.

'Come. Sit. I wish to discuss Steven.'

Dolph watched as Leah moved to a chair by the fire, her movements graceful and, somehow, measured. She had poise. She held herself in a way many a society lady could only dream of emulating, even though she was attired in plain nightclothes and her hair…her hair… His heart gave a funny little thump at the sight of those fiery tendrils floating around her crown. That fat rope of plaited hair, held loosely in place by a pale green ribbon, draped over her shoulder and her breast—a siren call to a man to tug the bow free and to plunge his fingers through the heavy, shining mass.

*For God's sake, man! Stop this fantasy. You told her you wanted to talk to her about Steven.*

It had been a lie. He would have said anything at that point, with the scent of warm woman filling his senses, to bask in her company for just a few more moments. Anything to avoid retiring to his cold lonely bedchamber. How had the simple act of returning to Dolphin Court awakened within him this urge for female company? The desire to be held? The drive to hold a warm, willing woman in his arms and to bury himself deep within her heat? He had told himself it was the memory of Rebecca and the echoes of married life, but could that be the only reason for this strange emptiness deep in his soul? He and Rebecca had never been that close. It had been a good enough marriage—they had each passed their time leading their own lives and doing more or less as they wished, no different from so many Society marriages. His political interests and the estates occupied his time and attention. Rebecca had disliked London and its frantic pace of life and had been content to spend her time in Somerset with the children.

*But she wasn't content, was she? And I did not even notice.*

He shivered as reality hit him, chilling him. He had failed her. He had not even seen the warning signs.

'You wished to speak to me about Steven, sir?'

Leah's quiet question brought his attention back to her.

'Yes. I am concerned about him.' And that was true, even though it had not been Steven in his thoughts when he had spoken. At times, his son and heir seemed so timid...too anxious for a child, far more so than the younger, more rambunctious Nicky. 'He is intelligent and has a quick understanding, but I do worry how he will cope when he goes to school. He is so nervous.' Her brows drew together, and he added, 'He will have to go away to school when he is older, you know that. I should like your opinion as to what we can do to toughen him up a bit. Is there anything we should do to—?' He fell silent at her disapproving expression before continuing, 'I am aware I still do not know the boys very well, but I wish to learn; to be guided by you.' He scrubbed his hand up the side of his face, feeling the rasp of stubble. 'I just want to help my son become the best man he can be.'

She smiled at that. 'You can do that by allowing him to be a little boy. He *is* still only seven, you know. And please do not mistake his sensitive nature for cowardice or timidity. Yes, he is sensitive, but in a good way. He is sensitive to others' feelings whereas Nicky lacks that awareness. *He* is more concerned with his own wants and needs.'

Dolph leapt to the defence of his younger son. 'Nicky does not have a nasty nature. He is just...lively.'

The weight of her luminous gaze settled on him, sending tingles down his spine. The illumination from the candles highlighted the blue-greenness of those beautiful, and intelligent, eyes.

'It was not a criticism of Nicky.' His ruffled feelings were instantly soothed by her gentle words. 'I was trying to illustrate—perhaps a little clumsily—that the two boys are quite different in character, and there is no need to force them to fit the same mould. They each have strengths and weaknesses and, in time, they will hopefully recognise and learn to compensate for the latter.'

'Much as we do for ourselves as adults?'

'Precisely. Although, regrettably, not all adults identify their own weaknesses or, if they do, are not prepared to remedy the flaws in their characters.'

Dolph's eyes narrowed. 'It sounds as though you speak from experience.' Having lived with guilt for so long, he worried her barb was aimed at him. It should not matter what she thought, but he couldn't bear her to think of him as the sort of man who could not—or would not—learn from his mistakes. 'Were you speaking of anyone in particular?'

Her lashes swept down, concealing her thoughts, and her teeth caught at her lower lip. His blood surged at that unconsciously erotic act even as he read her avoidance of eye contact as confirmation that the criticism had, indeed, been for him. His entire body tensed as he awaited her answer.

'Not necessarily,' she said, after a pause. Her tone became acerbic as she then added, 'Although perhaps Lord Hinckley would benefit from a dose of introspection as to *his* behaviour.'

His shoulders relaxed. 'George?'

'Yes. I apologise, because I know he is your friend, but I find it reprehensible he thinks it acceptable to trifle with women's feelings and then shrug off any responsibility. He must know how such behaviour might be misconstrued.'

'But… I explained this to you…' He cringed inwardly at his patronising tone but felt honour bound to defend his friend. 'And I *have* warned him, but these…games, if you will…are constantly played out in Society. It is expected. If a gentleman fails to compliment a lady, he is considered a very poor sort of fellow.'

'And is that how you behave in Society too, Lord Dolphinstone?'

'My behaviour is neither here nor there. We are not discussing me. And do not forget Miss Strong is a willing participant.'

'Willing only because she trusts Lord Hinckley, thinks him sincere and believes him to be a gentleman!'

Dolph straightened, pushing away from the mantelshelf. 'Or willing because she *wants* to believe him. May I remind you that George, as a wealthy earl, is regarded as quite a catch in the matrimonial stakes. The young ladies and their mamas fawn over him at Society events, each of them praying she will be the one to finally ensnare him. Can you categorically deny Miss Strong is any different?'

'Oh!' Leah sprang to her feet to confront him. 'How *dare* you imply Philippa is mercenary.' One finger poked him in the chest as her face tilted up and she glared at him, those extraordinary eyes blazing. 'Is it too hard for you to understand a woman might place the personal attributes of a man above any amount of wealth or status?'

*God, I want to kiss her.*

He could think of nothing else. She fell silent. Their gazes remained locked. The tip of her tongue emerged to moisten her lips, sending the blood rocketing through his veins. Without volition, he traced those full, lush lips with one finger. Her breathing hitched in the quiet of the room. He moved closer. She did not retreat. Rather, she swayed towards him, and then, before he had time to gather his thoughts, or to consider the consequences, his arms swept around her and their lips met in a searing kiss. She melted in his arms as his tongue penetrated her mouth and he deepened the kiss. Their tongues tangled, and his blood sang at her eager response. All too soon, however, she stiffened and pushed him away.

He reined in his rampaging lust, forcing his arms to release her, and stepped back, thrusting one hand through his hair as Leah stumbled back and covered her mouth with the back of her hand, her eyes huge and round.

'Is this how gentlemen such as Lord Hinckley and yourself treat unwary females?' She spoke from behind the shield of her hand. 'You all appear to believe you are entitled to act as you please, and that we are there for your pleasure: to be dallied with and cast aside at will.'

'What do you mean by *you all appear*? Has this happened before? Were you cast aside by some man?' Anger flared inside him.

She shook her head vehemently, her eyes stricken. The desire to protect her made him extend his hand, but he did not touch her and instead tried to soothe her with his words.

'I apologise. I had no intention….I did not mean for that to happen. It was entirely reprehensible.' What else could he say? There was no excuse to justify kissing her, not even when she appeared willing. He was her *employer*. He had a duty of care towards her. 'I have no intention of casting you aside for something that was my fault, but I shall understand if you wish to leave. I will supply you with a good reference, you need have no fear of that.'

'I…'

She heaved a sigh, her bosom rising and falling. Dolph forced his gaze higher. To her face. Her flushed cheeks. Her glittering eyes. Were they suppressed tears? He felt even more of a scoundrel.

Her voice trembled as she said, 'I must bear some of

the blame. I could have stopped you.' She subsided into the chair again. 'I *should* have stopped you.'

There was a sadness in her eyes, and a touch of shame that puzzled him. Again, he wondered if she had experienced something similar in her past, but the air between them seemed too brittle to broach the subject again, so he resisted the urge to bombard her with further questions.

'You bear none of the blame, Leah. I meant what I said—the fault was mine. But I had no intention of kissing you. It took me by surprise as well.'

Her eyes searched his face. 'So…if you did not mean to kiss me, why did you?'

*What to say? I couldn't not kiss you, at that moment, when you looked up at me with your eyes like deep, sunlit pools? I couldn't not kiss you because I find you irresistibly alluring, with your long, slender limbs and your red hair and your freckles, that entice me into wondering if—and where—they sprinkle your skin in places hidden from my gaze?*

'I cannot explain it.' He moved again to the fireplace to prop his elbow on the mantelshelf, his heart thundering in his chest. 'I have found it difficult, coming back here… The memories are unsettling. *I* am unsettled. Although that is no excuse for taking advantage of you. I do not know what came over me.'

'You must miss your wife dreadfully.'

Her sympathy penetrated deep inside his soul like a knife and twisted. He welcomed the pain. He didn't deserve her sympathy. Not when he was responsible for Rebecca's death. He had kissed Leah to satisfy his own needs without a thought as to how it might affect her— he was no better than George.

He liked Leah and he admired her courage in standing up to him when she deemed it necessary. But she was a respectable gentlewoman and *he*...he could offer her nothing apart from the loss of her virtue and the ruin of her reputation.

'Dolphin Court is very different without her.'

*But I do not miss her. Not like you mean.*

And that was yet another reason why he did not deserve to consider his own unhappiness. Why could he not have loved Rebecca as she deserved? If he had, she would still be here now. Was he even capable of love? He stepped away from the fireplace.

'I'm sure I will come to terms with her absence in time. I must bid you goodnight now but, please, stay and finish your brandy. I hope it will help you to sleep when you go back to bed. If you need time to recover in the morning, send word and I shall arrange for the boys to be cared for. Again...' he executed a small bow '... I apologise for my behaviour and I hope we may put it behind us.'

Her mouth twitched into a tentative half-smile that did not reach her eyes. 'Goodnight, my lord.'

## Chapter Eleven

As the library door closed softly behind Dolph, Leah allowed her forced smile to drop. She leaned back in the chair, one hand pressed to her bosom, feeling as though the weight of the world rested on her shoulders.

'Oh, dear God,' she whispered, closing her eyes. Warm moisture seeped from beneath her lids. 'Oh, dear God... what now?'

But the question was rhetorical. She knew very well *'what now'*. The luxury of staying at Dolphin Court until the last possible minute had been wrenched from her. She must now leave for London sooner rather than later because she knew neither she nor Dolph could move past this. That kiss would always lie between them—unspoken and unacknowledged, maybe, but it would be there, overshadowing everything. Muddying their relationship as employer and employee. Distracting them both from the most important thing—the happiness and welfare of Stevie and Nicky.

She relived that kiss, the entire surface of her skin tingling as she recalled his lips moving over hers and their tongues dancing together. Never had she dreamed of such a wonderful sensation, and she had—for several enchanting, sensual, *delusional* minutes—revelled in the fantasy that he had fallen in love with her. Her treacherous mind had conjured up a hopeless dream of her and Dolph and the children as a family, living together happily at Dolphin Court for the rest of their lives.

But reality had eventually intruded, thank goodness, although it had taken every ounce of her strength to push him away.

She'd been attracted to him from the first moment they met and, since his return, that attraction had strengthened, and she'd suspected—maybe even hoped—it was not entirely one-sided. But she could not and would not fool herself the glimpses of fire and longing she had seen in him had anything to do with feelings or love. She must face the truth. Those flashes of desire were merely the frustration of a widower with no outlet for his physical needs. He'd all but admitted it.

Dolph was still grieving, and she must not allow herself to become a convenient prop to help him get over his wife's death. She had been used by both Peter and Lord Usk for their own purposes before being cast aside, and she vowed that never again would she allow her foolish dreams to override her common sense in matters of the heart.

Her throat tightened, a painful lump lodged inside as she accepted she must say goodbye to the children and to Dolph within days. But how soon? Tomorrow? Impossible to walk away just like that. Would it really hurt to stay an extra week, or maybe two? But she knew, deep down, she was lying to herself if she tried to pretend the boys still needed her support to become more confident around their father. In truth, their relationship was strengthening every day.

There was no excuse not to go straight away but, for her own sake, she would wait a little longer, just to give her a little more time with the boys... A sob built up in her chest but she managed to gulp it back. She would spend that time storing up memories, and she would avoid being alone with Dolph, for that way lay temptation of a sort that would only give her more heartache. She would delay telling either the children or Dolph about her departure until she was ready to go. A selfish decision, perhaps, but she could not bear the thought of a long, drawn-out painful goodbye. A short, sharp pain would be better for all concerned, but especially for her.

But... Dolph would need time to find a suitable new governess. She pondered that dilemma—there must be a way to stay fair to everyone. Her thoughts flew to Philippa. Philippa...her level-headed friend who loved children and to whom she had already decided to unburden herself about Lady Tregowan's will and that amazing and unexpected change of fortune. Philippa would, surely, step in and bridge the gap between Leah leaving and a new governess being appointed?

So, she would say nothing to Dolph—or to anyone at the Court—until she'd spoken to Philippa and, in the meantime, she would work on creating happy memories for both herself and for the children. The minute she reached that decision, a feeling of calm descended despite the voice of warning in her head that her decision to stay for even one extra day was risking more heartbreak for herself.

She straightened in the chair and reached for her brandy, swallowing it in one huge gulp. She coughed, her eyes watering. It would take all of her strength, but she would behave as though that kiss had never happened.

\* \* \*

Leah had still not visited Miss Strong when, two days later, the door to the schoolroom burst open while Dolph—later than usual—was helping Stevie with his arithmetic and Leah patiently worked with Nicky on his writing skills on the far side of the room. It was as though that kiss had never happened. Leah gave no hint of discomfort in his presence, while Dolph studiously avoided being alone with her.

George—a hectic flush on his cheeks—rushed in with a panting Wolf at his heels.

'Oh! Apologies, et cetera. But, Dolph, really! Tell me you have skates.' George executed a hasty bow in Leah's direction. 'Apologies, Miss Thame, for the interruption to your lesson, but Palmer told me you were here, Dolph, and I could not wait.'

'Could not wait for what, George?'

'I have come from the village—the pond is covered in thick ice, and I've been ice skating with Phil—Miss Strong. Such fun! The whole village was out there, watching or taking part.'

'Skating?' Leah said. 'But... Lord Hinckley...your shoulder...'

George had only recently dispensed with using the sling to support his left arm. He laughed. 'Oh, I took care, never fear. I wasn't likely to fall, you know, Miss Thame—my balance is first rate, and there is nothing wrong with my other arm, so I took particular care to skate on Miss Strong's left so I could catch her if needs be. Not that I was needed, for she is an excessively talented skater—pirouettes and all sorts! She showed up everyone else on the ice, I can tell you.'

'And that is what you have come to tell us, George?' asked Dolph.

'Well, yes. I thought we might take the boys skating tomorrow—I am sure they will enjoy it and Miss Strong is very much looking forward to seeing us all. Tell me you have skates stashed away in an attic somewhere, Dolph. You *must* have.'

Dolph rubbed his jaw, conscious Nicky was looking at him pleadingly. Stevie sat quietly, head bent, making it hard to decipher whether he would enjoy such an excursion, and he noticed Leah give his hand a quick squeeze. But...ice skating. It would be good fun, and it would be an opportunity to spend time with the boys away from the schoolroom until they found suitable ponies, and they could ride out together.

Frinton—who presided over the stables—had asked around about suitable ponies for the boys, learning of two for sale at a farm some four miles away, but the weather had been too cold and the ground too hard and slippery to go and try them out. So, until then, any time spent with the boys involved lessons.

Leah and the boys still took their daily walk when the weather was dry, but Dolph had avoided going with them, fearing the boys would rush hither and thither and leave far too much time for he and Leah to talk privately. He had taken care to avoid being alone with her since the morning after that kiss, when they'd both agreed it had been a mistake and they would forget all about it. Easier said than done, he had found, for he'd been unable to banish it from his thoughts no matter how hard he tried. Leah, on the other hand, appeared to have shrugged off the incident with little effort.

'*Please*, Papa,' Nicky begged. 'I *love* to skate on the ice.'

'You do, Nicky?' Leah's lips pursed, holding back a smile, but her blue-green eyes laughed, and Dolph's

heart felt as though it were performing a slow somersault. 'When did you try ice skating?'

Nicky pouted. 'I skidded on a puddle yesterday. It is
*fun.*'

'It's not as easy as you might think, Nicky,' said Dolph.
'You have to balance on a thin metal blade strapped to
each shoe. People fall over. A lot.'

'*I* won't fall,' said Nicky. 'But I bet Stevie does. An'
he'll cry!'

'Will not!' Steven glared at his younger brother.

'Enough, boys. Yes, we will all go tomorrow. I know
there are skates around somewhere from when I was a
lad.' He found himself looking forward to it with an eagerness that surprised him and, before he could check
his words, he added, 'And I am fairly certain there is a
pair for you, too, Miss Thame.'

'Me?' She looked startled. 'I cannot skate.'

'Oh, come now, Miss Thame,' said George. 'Dolph
was just teasing the boys. It's not that hard. You will
enjoy it.'

'Nevertheless, I shall take even greater enjoyment in
standing on solid ground and watching the rest of you.'

'Now, come on, Miss Thame. George is right, you
know. It's not that difficult. I'm certain you will dem-
onstrate perfect balance. This is no time to be chicken-
hearted, when your charges will both be complete
beginners too.'

'Yes! Miss Thame is going to skate too.' Nicky jumped
around, waving his arms.

Stevie tugged at her sleeve. 'I will catch you if you
fall, miss. I promise.'

She smiled warmly at him. 'Thank you, Stevie. I
will think about it, but no promises.' She stood up and
smoothed her skirts. 'Lessons are over, boys. Would you

like to go now with your papa to find your skates while I tidy up the schoolroom?'

Her eyebrows flicked as she smiled jauntily at Dolph.

*There,* her smile seemed to say. *That is what to expect if you challenge me. You may have the boys all to yourself.*

Leah awoke the next morning with dread weighting her stomach. Stevie had whispered to her, as she was tucking him in last night, that Papa had found enough skates for them all, but it was to be a secret and the boys weren't to tell Miss Thame in case she refused to accompany them to the village. 'But,' Stevie had continued, 'you *will* still come, won't you, miss? We can help each other.' And, aware he was afraid his younger brother would show him up in front of his father—for there was no doubt Nicky was more proficient in most physical activities—Leah did not have the heart to let Stevie down.

Ice skating. She had never tried it, but she had slipped and fallen on ice before, and it was *hard.* It hurt. And she would fall, she just knew it. She would fall and make a fool of herself. And her fear was greater than Stevie's, for she was an adult. Nobody would turn a hair if a child fell over, but if she were to fall, it would be so undignified. She could already feel the heat of humiliation.

Unable to bear the suspense, she threw back her bedcovers and rushed to the window, tweaking the curtains apart to look at the weather outside. It was still dark, but the ice on the inside of the windowpanes told its own tale. There had been no miraculous thaw overnight.

*I can refuse. He cannot* force *me to do it.*

But Stevie's anxious expression materialised in her mind's eye. How could she let him down?

It had been agreed they would leave Dolphin Court

at eleven, and after skating, they were all invited to the Rectory for soup and sandwiches. Lord Hinckley had arranged it all with Philippa, making Leah wonder if he could possibly be serious about her after all.

*Don't be a fool! He is an earl, for goodness' sake... He will look much higher for a wife than a country vicar's daughter. We don't live between the pages of* Little Goody Two-Shoes.

Surely Philippa must realise it? Leah couldn't bear to think of her heart being broken or, even worse, that she might succumb to temptation and allow herself to be seduced by Lord Hinckley. After all, it did happen. It had happened to Mama. Leah vowed to warn her friend at the earliest opportunity.

*In two hours or so it will all be over. I can cope with that.*

But, despite her nerves, Leah could not quell the flutter of purely feminine satisfaction as she had gazed at her reflection in the mirror after dressing in her royal-blue velvet carriage gown, for this shade of blue had always suited her. She did not care that such thoughts were pure vanity and she thrust aside the question of whom she might be hoping to impress.

Eleven o'clock arrived all too soon. Leah donned her warm winter cloak, the blue velvet bonnet that matched her gown, a pair of fur-lined gloves, a woollen scarf and a pair of fur-lined half-boots before collecting the boys—already well-wrapped in warm clothes—from Cassie's care. Tilly, upon realising she was not included in the outing, set up a loud wailing as Leah ushered the two excited boys out of the nursery and followed them down the stairs, her insides heavy with the grim determination to see through the ordeal if it killed her.

'Miss Thame!' Hinckley laughed up at her from the hall. 'Look, Dolph! She looks for all the world as if she's facing the gallows!' Dolph's expression remained indecipherable.

'Cheer up!' Hinckley continued. 'You might find you enjoy skating.'

Dolph's brow furrowed. 'George…' he growled.

Hinckley reddened. 'Oops! Sorry, Dolph.'

Leah descended the final few stairs, striving to keep her expression blank, although she knew very well what they were talking about. Dolph's frown softened as she reached them and her stomach swooped as it always did when their eyes met.

'Well, George has let the cat out of the bag and, yes, there is a pair of skates for you too,' he said to Leah. 'But no one will force you to skate if you do not wish to—the option is simply there if you decide to try.'

Leah felt a hand nudge into hers. Stevie, looking up at her pleadingly.

'I have changed my mind already.' She firmed her grip on Stevie's hand. 'I will do it.'

A smile curved Dolph's lips, his grey eyes warming, and Leah's pulse responded with a pleasurable skip. That almost made up for the fear coursing through her entire body. Almost.

'I promise not to let you fall, Miss Thame.'

## Chapter Twelve

Half a dozen villagers were already on the pond by the time they reached the village. The carriage was sent back to Dolphin Court, with instructions to return in three hours to collect them, and the moment had arrived. Philippa glided towards them across the ice, graceful as a swan, and the solid weight of dread that had settled inside Leah stirred, churning her insides, making her feel sick. To cover her nerves, and while the two men greeted Philippa, Leah crouched down to strap on first Stevie's and then Nicky's skates, fixed their mufflers more securely around their necks so there were no loose ends flapping, and made sure their gloves and caps were on.

She stood up, once she was sure her nerves were under control, and greeted Philippa. The men, she noticed, were busy donning their own skates. With any luck they would forget about her, and she could watch them safely from the bank. There were a few wooden chairs set around the edge, presumably for spectators, and they looked far more enticing to Leah than the wide, glittering expanse of ice before her.

'You make ice skating look remarkably easy, Philippa,' she said.

Philippa laughed gaily, her eyes sparkling. 'It is, Leah. It is so...*liberating*, to travel at such speed as a result of one's own skill and momentum.'

Before Leah could respond, a shriek split the air. Stevie! Leah had been vaguely aware of Nicky tugging his older brother towards the ice as she spoke to Philippa, and now she desperately searched the skaters on the ice, looking for Stevie, expecting to see him in a huddled heap. But no. There he was, at the far side of the pond already, and actually skating. He had a little wobble now and then but, in the main, he looked in control, and even at this distance Leah could see the huge grin on his face. The shriek had come from Nicky, just a few feet from the edge of the ice and still on this side of the pond. His legs resembled those of a newborn foal trying to stand for the first time and his arms cartwheeled as he fought to keep his balance.

'We'll help him,' Hinckley said.

He grabbed Philippa's hand and they hurried to the edge of the ice. Within seconds, they had Nicky securely between them, steadying him. Hinckley called back, 'You help Miss Thame, Dolph. We'll stay with Nicky until he finds his balance,' and off they set across the ice, each holding one of Nicky's hands.

Leah sought Stevie again and, if anything, he looked even more adept as he glided in front of Nicky, showing off. Leah couldn't help but laugh.

'To think Stevie was petrified of today, and now look at him.' She glanced at Dolph, who was watching both his sons with clear pride. 'He was afraid of making a fool of himself. Worried Nicky would outshine him, as he so often does in physical challenges.'

'It's a joy to see him so confident.' Dolph turned to

Leah. His eyes searched hers. 'It is your turn. Unless you are too nervous to even try?'

Leah tilted her chin. Stevie might no longer need her on the ice, but how could she possibly refuse to try when he had been so brave? She would not allow herself to appear a coward in front of the boys.

'No. As I said, I will try. But I shall not promise to persevere if I fall over.'

He nodded, his lips pursing with a suppressed smile. 'I knew you would rise to the challenge but, rest assured, I shall ensure you remain on your feet. If you sit there—' he indicated a nearby chair '—I shall help you with your skates.'

Her heart in her mouth, Leah sat down and Dolphinstone crouched before her, the brim of his beaver hat concealing his face. Unobserved, she watched him, her stomach fluttering with more than just nerves about the skating ordeal to come as he stripped off his gloves and lifted her booted foot, his grip warm and firm around her ankle, even through the leather of her half-boots. He pushed the hem of her gown up from her foot, to give him access, and tingles chased each other across Leah's back. Although there were people all around, it was as though the two of them existed apart from them, contained in their own separate bubble. She swallowed, clasping her gloved hands together as he fitted the skate to her foot and buckled the straps to secure it in place. He placed her foot back on the ground, and then he tipped his face up, catching her watching him.

Time appeared to stand still as their gazes fused. Now she knew why they had both avoided being alone together since that kiss. This attraction was definitely not one-sided; Dolph felt it as keenly as she. Her heart lurched and her entire body heated. Then he bent his head once more, and she released the breath that had seized her lungs, uncertain of what that moment might have meant to him, although she knew very well what it meant to her.

*Fool! Have you learned nothing?*

Twice she had lowered her defences to allow a man close. Twice she had been tricked into believing a man's feelings for her were genuine. And the fact still remained Dolph was an earl, and she—although soon to be wealthy, and thus elevated in Society—was still his governess, and baseborn, to boot. If he was ever to remarry—and he had been clear in his snub to Hinckley when the subject had arisen—he would look much higher than Leah, for the sake of his children.

'Now for the other one.' Dolph's voice was firm and emotionless as he strapped on her other skate. But, when he looked up at her again to say, 'Now, Miss Thame. It is time to put you through your paces,' the heat banked in his eyes was clear, even to a novice about men and their desires such as Leah, and her pulse leapt anew.

Dolph stood in one fluid motion. He pulled on his gloves before extending both hands. Leah took them, relishing the feeling as his fingers closed around hers, and his strength as he tugged her to her feet. Her ankles knuckled over immediately; balancing on the skates proved even trickier than she'd anticipated.

'Whoa! Steady! You're not even on the ice yet.'

Dolph released her hands to steady her under the elbows as she straightened her ankles, concentrating on the strangeness of balancing on the thin blade. The effect was to bring their bodies close together, chest to breast, and Leah resisted the urge to lean into him. With an effort, she stepped back, forcing him to relinquish his grip on her elbows. This time, *she* took *his* hands. This was *her* nightmare. She would be in control.

'That's the way.'

His murmured approval was the spur she needed to face the next step. She lifted her chin.

'I am ready.'

There weren't so very many people on the ice, and no one was watching. Nobody—surely—would notice or care if she fell. Besides, Dolph had promised he would not allow her to fall. She would put her trust in him.

They stepped onto the ice, and Leah found her worst fears were nothing compared to the actuality of losing— it seemed—all control over her legs and her feet, which seemed to be trying to slide in every direction at once. Dolph swapped her left hand from his right to his left, and wrapped his right arm around her waist, giving her added support.

'Relax,' he said. 'Allow your foot to slide forward and move with it…keep your body above it. That's it. Right foot first, stay in time with me. I have you. I won't let you fall.' His voice lowered to a deep, throaty murmur. '*Trust* me.'

Leah shivered. *I do.* But she held back the words and directed her attention to her feet instead. She'd trusted other men. Peter. Usk. They'd lied to her. Doubts rose to peck at her.

'Try not to look down at your feet,' he said. 'Look straight ahead. *Feel* your body and its balance as you look where you're going.'

'I cannot. I'm scared if I look up, I will fall.'

'I am here. You can trust me.'

But her eyes remained stubbornly fixed on the ice as her legs continued to misbehave and her feet shot away at impossible angles until a jubilant shout jerked her gaze up to Stevie as he sped past, grinning hugely. Her stomach dived as she saw they were right in the middle of the pond. The bank…safety…looked an impossible distance away.

'Miss Thame! Papa! Look at me!'

Stevie skated a circle in front of them and then skidded to a halt. He wobbled a little, and Dolph's arm firmed around Leah's waist as he brought them to a halt by Stevie. He released Leah's hand to reach out and grip Stevie's shoulder.

'Steady, son.'

'I'm all right, Papa. I *love* skating.'

'And you are exceptionally good at it, Stevie,' said Leah. 'Unlike me, I'm afraid.'

'But Papa will make you like it, Miss Thame, won't he?'

'I will certainly try my best, Stevie. Why don't you go and help your brother?'

Nicky was still in between Hinckley and Philippa but he did look as though he was improving.

'Yes, Papa.' Stevie skated away, full of self-importance.

'Now. Let us try again.' Dolph took Leah's hand again and softened the arm wrapped around her waist. 'Ready?'

She had no time to reply, for he was already moving, and all she could think of was that distance to the edge and to safety. Her feet slid this way and that, and the more she frantically fought to stay upright, the less control she seemed to have.

'Whoa!'

She was vaguely aware, and somewhat irritated, that Dolph was laughing as he pivoted—all masculine elegance and control—to face her. Before she realised his intention, he bent his knees and in the next instant he swung her up into his arms, cradling her against his chest. Her arms snaked around his neck in a purely reflexive gesture as he glided towards the edge of the pond, and her heart, already racing, pounded still further as she delighted in the sensation of being picked up as though she were a child and cradled against his solid chest.

He halted but, rather than setting her down immediately, there was a pause. Leah sneaked a look at his face. His grey eyes stared into the distance. His expression was inscrutable as his arms tightened and he hugged her closer, his breathing ragged. She wondered what he was thinking—she did not even pretend to believe he was thinking about her.

'My lord?'

She felt his body jerk, as though his mind had been far away. His cheeks flushed slightly, and the thought sneaked into her brain that a memory had struck him… Maybe he and Lady Dolphinstone had skated here together, in the past.

'Now you will accuse *me* of being a wool-gatherer, Miss Thame.' He lowered her carefully to the ground. 'We shall try that again but, this time, please try not to hold your breath while you stare at your feet. Your mind needs to stay quiet. Allow your instinct and your natural balance to control your body.'

'Would you not rather go and skate with Lord Hinckley and Miss Strong?' Leah nodded towards where the pair were skating together, Stevie having taken charge of Nicky, who was now finding his balance. 'I am persuaded you will enjoy yourself more than attempting to teach me. I fear I am a lost cause.'

'Firstly, you are not a lost cause, Miss Thame. And secondly…'

The silence stretched. Leah glanced up at Dolph, to find him staring down at her, his brow bunched in a puzzled frown.

'Secondly?'

'Secondly…' He hauled in an audible breath. 'No. I would not enjoy skating with them more than I am enjoying teaching you.'

Heat flushed up from her neck to wash her face, and that accursed glimmer of hope deep inside her—the one she had been at such pains to banish—glowed a touch brighter. 'I…thank you.' She gulped, before saying, unsteadily, 'Teaching others is rewarding, is it not? That is why I like teaching children—seeing them learn and become more confident.'

His chuckle sounded a little strained. 'Rewarding,' he said. 'Yes.'

He reached across to take her left hand in his left, and again put his arm around her back. Even through her thick cloak she was aware his fingers tightened into her waist for a fleeting moment before relaxing once again. 'Here we go, Miss Thame. Try to look ahead and keep your weight above your front foot.'

She tried. She really did. For half a circuit of the pond she even began to enjoy the sensation of gliding smoothly across the ice, and she definitely enjoyed the sensation of her hand in Dolph's and of his arm around her. But, all too soon, she lost control of her front leg, which shot sideways instead of forwards, and the doubts and fears piled onto her, and instead of her right arm elegantly extending to assist her balance, she reached across to grab frantically at Dolph's forearm, involuntarily spinning to face him and getting in his way. He swerved and lost his balance. Time seemed to slow, his fall taking an excruciatingly long time, and Leah felt herself begin to overbalance too. Somehow, though, he grabbed her and twisted, cushioning her fall. Rather than a hard landing on the ice, she found herself for the second time that morning held tightly to his chest.

'Oh! Oh, my!' Leah just lay there, not hurt but shocked into immobility, her bonnet knocked awry.

'Are you hurt?'

His words seemed as though they were spoken right by her ear. She twisted her head to look at him, but her bonnet brim covered her eyes.

'I'm fine,' she breathed. 'But what about *you*? You broke my fall.'

She felt, rather than heard, the chuckle rumble deep in his chest. 'I did tell you to trust me, did I not? I couldn't quite stop you falling, but I could stop you getting hurt.' He pushed her bonnet back to its rightful position. His face was remarkably close, and his familiar scent filled her as his eyes searched hers. 'I would hate for you to get hurt.'

His voice was low and intimate, there was heat in his gaze, and the hard ridge pressing against her belly confirmed that, physically at least, he desired her. Her heart hammered in her chest as her breasts ached. She became aware of a strange yearning deep inside her and a tiny pleasurable pulse of…something…that beat within the feminine folds between her thighs. She swallowed and waited for a second pulse, but it did not come. Was this how a woman felt desire? She had heard others speak of it, in whispers, but never had she imagined experiencing it herself. She had never felt anything physical for either Peter or for Lord Usk—any attraction on her part had been solely in her mind. She swallowed, knowing that Dolph, too, felt it. But she also knew that male physical desire did not necessarily mean emotional attachment.

A loud swishing, scraping sound broke the spell between them, and two hands thrust unceremoniously under her arms to swing her up and away from her employer's recumbent form.

'Up you get, Miss Thame. You don't want to squash poor Dolph, do you?'

And Leah was plonked unceremoniously onto the ice although, luckily, Philippa was there to help steady her as Hinckley laughingly extended one hand to Dolph and hauled him to his feet.

# *Chapter Thirteen*

Dolph busied himself brushing imaginary slivers of ice from his coat and breeches, as George exclaimed, 'Whoops! I do believe old Dolph here was winded there for a moment, Miss Thame! But how lucky for you he managed to save you from a painful landing.'

Dolph's immediate relief George had noticed nothing untoward was quickly dispelled by his friend's wink—a wink that informed Dolph that George had not only noticed but was thoroughly entertained by the entire interlude. Nevertheless, Dolph gave his friend credit for intervening at exactly the right moment to save Dolph from committing the social gaffe of kissing his sons' governess in full public view.

Whatever had he been thinking? How had he so forgotten himself, and their surroundings, to so nearly be overcome by temptation? He cast a sidelong look at Leah in an attempt to gauge how much she had noticed. Her downcast eyes and the blush tinting her high cheekbones suggested she was fully cognisant of the frisson of awareness that had sizzled between them.

'Indeed it was.' If he kept his tone matter-of-fact, as though he'd noticed nothing, hopefully both George and

Leah would soon wonder if they'd been mistaken. 'Think how awkward it would be if Miss Thame broke a bone— who would look after the boys?'

'Perhaps—' and the governess's brisk tone suggested that she, too, was ready to deny that spark between them had ever occurred '—it is unwise for me to try again. As you say, my lord, it would not do for me to fall and break something, and quite apart from the effect on the boys' care and education, *I* have no wish to suffer such an injury.'

'That is entirely understandable, Miss Thame,' said George, soothingly, 'and I am quite sure Dolph has no desire to see you suffer either. But you cannot give up now. You were beginning to enjoy yourself…and do not deny it, for both Philippa and I remarked upon it. Allow me to offer my assistance. With me on one side and Dolph on the other, you cannot possibly fall.'

Dolph clenched his jaw, seeing no alternative but to go along with George's suggestion—damn him and his interference. 'Splendid idea, George. Come, Miss Thame. We will make a skater of you yet.'

And they did. Within half an hour, Leah was skating independently, albeit with both Dolph and George within touching distance in case they needed to catch her quickly. She soon grew overwarm and she discarded her cloak, leaving Dolph to admire her willowy figure, and how the shade of blue she wore complemented her colouring even as he puzzled over his reaction to her. He had met any number of beauties in Europe, but he'd had no interest in them whatsoever and had carefully avoided any hint of entanglement.

Had that been too soon after Rebecca's death? Was this merely a signal that that side of his life was not over, as he'd repeatedly told himself? Had his body simply decided it had been deprived long enough? After all, such urges were natural for a man of his age—surely he would respond in the same way to any attractive female. They were not triggered by Leah specifically.

'I need to rest.' Leah sounded breathless, her cheeks flushed, her eyes bright as she glanced at Dolph, then quickly looked straight ahead again. 'I am afraid to stop…afraid I will fall if I try to slow.'

Almost before he realised what he was doing, Dolph skated close to her and passed his arm once again around her slender waist, even though he could quite easily have simply taken her hand. He excused his action by telling himself she would feel more secure this way, and he steered her towards the edge of the ice. George followed them.

Miss Strong had already left the ice and was sitting on a chair to remove her skates.

'It is starting to rain,' she called as they approached. 'Mrs Hubbard—' she indicated an elderly woman who had hobbled across to the pond, leaning on her stick, and settled onto one of the chairs to watch the fun '—tells me the pond will be half thawed by tomorrow, because the wind has veered to a south-westerly. It is fortunate we took advantage of the ice when we did.'

'Indeed it is.' Dolph peered up at the sky and the grey clouds that had gathered in the short time they had been skating. A fine, cold drizzle hit his face, cooling and welcome. 'It is a good time to stop—that sky looks like it means business. The temperature does not feel much warmer to me, though.'

'Not yet, perhaps, but if Mrs Hubbard forecasts a change in the weather, you can be confident it will happen.' Miss Strong smiled at him, raising her brows. 'I hope you will still join us at the vicarage for a bowl of soup?'

'Delighted to; thank you for the invitation.'

George went to assist Miss Strong while Dolph helped Leah to the chair where he had earlier placed her discarded cloak. His arm was still around her waist and he relished the feeling of her leaning into his support.

'Here.' He shook out her cloak, then swung it around her shoulders and fastened it at the neck, gazing down at her bowed head, her face shielded by her bonnet's brim. A few auburn tendrils had worked free and he admired the contrast of her red hair against the rich blue of her bonnet. She sat, and he knelt before her, his heart hammering faster now than when they were skating. 'Allow me to unbuckle your skates.' His fingers trembled, causing him to fumble the straps, and his mouth felt horribly dry as he scrambled around for something innocuous to say.

*What the devil is wrong with me? I'm behaving like a green lad.*

Was it the awkwardness of not knowing how to behave with a woman he admired but who was out of bounds? This was not like a mild flirtation with a lady at a ball or a house party. Leah was employed by him. She lived in his house. He was responsible for her. His principles forbade him to flirt with her—let alone anything stronger— unless his intentions were honourable. And they could not possibly be honourable. He would never marry again.

He finished removing her skates and, with a profound sense of relief, he stood up before bending to remove his own. Only then did he look at her. Her attention was on the boys, who were still out on the ice. The visibility had lessened in even those few minutes since they had stopped skating. Dolph watched his sons with pride—

Nicky had clearly got the hang of his skates, but he was nowhere near as confident as Stevie, who was watching over him as they circled the pond. As they neared the side where the adults now stood, Dolph hailed them, telling them it was time to stop.

'You should wear vivid colours more often,' he heard himself say to Leah, his eyes still on the boys. 'They suit you.'

By his side, he heard Leah's gasp, quickly stifled. And little wonder—her appearance was far too personal a subject.

'What I mean is —' he scrambled to save the situation '—there is no need to confine yourself to dull-coloured gowns if you have other garments in your possession. *I* should not object, and I doubt the boys would even notice.'

'That would be...inappropriate, I fear, my lord. I should not like to provoke criticism from others within the household or from any in the neighbourhood.'

'Of course. I understand.'

'Besides, my usual gowns are more practical for caring for the boys, especially when we are confined to the house and play hide-and-seek. Those secret passages are horridly dusty.'

Dolph was saved from having to say more by the arrival of Stevie and Nicky.

'Let me help you with your skates, boys,' Leah said, crouching down. 'Miss Strong has invited us back to the vicarage for hot soup and sandwiches. It will help us warm up again—Mrs Hubbard might declare the temperature is on the rise, but I cannot say it feels any warmer to me now we have stopped skating.'

The party of five tramped across the village green towards the vicarage as the drizzle turned heavy. The vicarage was warm and cheery, and the Reverend and Mrs Strong were most welcoming. The time passed quickly and, before they realised it, a knock at the door heralded the carriage's arrival.

Back at Dolphin Court, Leah shepherded the boys upstairs, still avoiding Dolph's gaze, much as she had both at the vicarage and on the journey home, concentrating on his sons instead. Dolph watched them go, wondering how to deal with the flare of attraction between them.

'Miss Thame, Dolph?'

He started at George's quiet question. 'What about her?'

'You seem…taken with her. Philippa commented on it as well. It's the first time I've seen a spark of interest in another female since you lost your wife.'

Guilt poked at Dolph's conscience and he vowed to take more care to keep their relationship professional, most especially when there were others around. He knew *he* would reap no repercussions should gossip begin to circulate about him and Leah, but her reputation would surely suffer.

'I confess Miss Thame is growing on me,' George continued. 'I have never known a woman I initially dismissed as plain to suddenly appear alluring. When she is animated, she is quite arresting. Most odd.'

Nothing would induce Dolph to admit as much. Her eyes haunted him. Her smile kindled his blood. He'd thought he'd been seized by a peculiar fancy for a woman not his usual type simply because he had not been intimate with a woman for so long. Now…ought he to wonder if there was more to it?

But George's words did prompt Dolph to retort: 'George. You are *not* to flirt with my governess.'

George laughed and held up his hands in surrender.

'Nothing could be further from my thoughts, Dolph. I should hate to upset your domestic arrangements. Just sayin', in case you hadn't noticed. I know what a monk you've become since you lost Rebecca.'

'Well, you and Miss Strong are both mistaken if you imagine my interest in Miss Thame is of a personal nature, George. I admire her ability with the boys. She is good for them, and I appreciate her work. Nothing more.' Dolph led the way to the drawing room. 'You know how it is with governesses—they are more than servants and yet not really part of the family. It is a fine line to walk.'

'Indeed it is. Especially when said governess is from good bloodlines.'

'George! You make her sound like a racehorse. And marriage to *anyone*, as I have repeatedly told you, is not on my agenda.'

'Oh, you know what I mean. Philippa told me about Miss Thame's family—her father was a vicar; a younger son. And *his* mother was a Weston—Baverstock's family, you know.'

The Earl of Baverstock's country estate was also in Somerset. But Leah's breeding made no difference. Dolph remained firm in his resolve to never marry again—never to risk driving another woman to suicide. Besides, she was still his governess—he had no wish to invite scandal onto his family name.

'A bit like Philippa…' George continued, his expression turning dreamy. 'Her parents are from excellent families too. Her father told me he is the grandson of Grosdale, and her mother was a Davenport. All good stock. Very respectable.'

His thoughts dragged away from his own difficulties, Dolph stared at his friend and wondered anew at his intentions towards Miss Strong, particularly after having spent time in their company and seeing for himself the ease with which George made himself at home at the vicarage. If he didn't know George so well, he might well believe he was truly in love this time. But he did know his friend and he had seen all this before. He knew the ease with which his mercurial adoration could shift from one lady to the next.

He changed the subject. 'Talking of racehorses, that reminds me... Frinton knows of a farmer over towards Hewton whose children have outgrown their ponies. If Mrs Hubbard is right, and the thaw has begun, I shall take Steven and Nicholas to view them one afternoon this week. I'll see what the weather is like in the morning, and send one of the grooms over with a note if the ground has softened sufficiently. Would you care to accompany us? You can help entertain the boys on the journey.'

'Delighted, old chap. Will Miss Thame come with us too?'

'Of course not. Buying horseflesh is a matter for us men. We can look after the boys between us.'

*And that will leave Leah free to visit Miss Strong and hopefully confide in her about whatever is causing those sleepless nights.*

'Now.' He slapped George on the back. 'Shall we indulge in a glass of brandy?'

'Yes, let's.' George, easily distracted, grinned. 'I need something to chase the chill out of my bones.'

Leah brought all three children down to say goodnight later, as had become her routine. Dolph always looked forward to this quiet time, and he enjoyed the chance to cuddle the sleepy Matilda, for, during the day, she was too lively to submit to being held for more than a few minutes before wriggling free. As Leah walked through the door, carrying Matilda, he drank in the sight, his heart twitching with sadness that Rebecca was not here to see her children grow, and that Matilda would never know her mother. Her arms were wound around Leah's neck, and she sleepily fingered a loose tendril of hair. Dolph went to them and held out his arms. For one heart-stopping second, Matilda clung to Leah before allowing the governess to pass her to Dolph, but he noticed, as he sat down, that his daughter's eyes followed Leah as she ushered the boys towards Dolph.

'Well, boys.' He pitched his voice low so as not to rouse Matilda too much. Leah had told him that, often, Matilda was asleep by the time they reached the nursery again. 'How did you enjoy the ice skating today?'

Steven puffed out his chest. 'I loved doing it, Papa. I can spin circles.'

'You were particularly good, Stevie. And you, Nicky... you soon got the hang of it too. Well done.'

Nicky's eyes brightened at Dolph's words. 'I liked it too, Papa. I'll soon be better than Stevie, won't I? And I'm already better than Miss Thame.'

Leah smiled, and their eyes met. His heart jolted as a bolt of energy surged through him. He swallowed hard as she wrenched her gaze from his, blushing.

'Well, I am not sure about that, Nicky,' he said, willing his voice to remain even. 'Stevie seems to have a talent for skating, so, although you might be as good, you may never overtake him, but that is all right, for you have other talents, do you not?'

'I can climb higher than him.'

Dolph had watched from the window one day, his heart in his mouth as his sons both climbed the same old elm he had used to climb as a boy. Nicky had scrambled up, as agile as a monkey, while Stevie had been far more cautious and clearly did not enjoy the experience.

'That is true. And I have good news. The thaw appears to have set in, so, either tomorrow or the next day, we shall go to view those ponies Frinton told us about. What do you think of that?'

'Hurrah!'

Both boys shouted simultaneously, and Nicky jumped up and down, waving his arms, while Stevie grabbed Leah's hand, shaking it while grinning up at her. Their sister stiffened in Dolph's arms. Her face screwed up and, as she let out a wail, Leah sent him a fulminating glare, and Dolph sent her an apologetic look in reply, knowing she disliked the boys getting too excited at this time.

'Quiet, boys.' Dolph tightened his arms around Matilda, cuddling her into his chest. 'Hush, Tilly,' he whispered, and feathered his lips across her soft forehead.

Leah had grabbed hold of Nicky to restrain him and put her other arm around Stevie.

'That will give you both something to look forward to,' she said calmly. 'Now, it is time for bed, children.'

She walked towards Dolph, who stood up and handed Tilly to her. Their hands touched in the exchange, sending sparks sizzling through his veins. How did she have this effect on him? Her eyes remained downcast, but he was almost certain she experienced that same ripple of excitement. He bid the children goodnight and watched as they all left the drawing room, his stomach stirring uneasily as he wondered where this inexplicable attraction between him and Leah might end.

During dinner that evening, Leah appeared subdued, but George was as talkative as ever and appeared not to notice her mood. Dolph buried all his uncertainty beneath a light veneer of conversation, and the meal passed quickly.

'I shall go and practise on the pianoforte, if you gentlemen will excuse me,' Leah said when they finished eating.

The two men stood as she left the room, and they settled down to a glass of port. To Dolph's relief, George did not return to his earlier teasing about Leah and, instead, the conversation veered onto their experiences of estate management and tenant farmers, with the distant piano music providing a pleasant background. Before long, they joined Leah in the drawing room, where Wolf sprawled in front of the fire. She glanced up as they entered, a smile in her eyes, her pleasure in the music plain to see. A feeling of calm settled over Dolph as he sat down, leaning back and closing his eyes to listen. But when the piece ended, George's voice interrupted his reverie.

'My apologies to you both.' Dolph's eyes opened. George had remained standing. 'I am very tired and ready for my bed.' He nodded to Dolph and bowed to Leah. 'Beautiful piece, Miss Thame. Was that Mozart?'

'It was.'

'Good old Wolfgang, eh?'

At the sound of his name, the dog opened one eye and gently thumped his tail.

'Goodnight, then, Dolph; Miss Thame. I shall see you in the morning.'

As they both bid George goodnight, Dolph silenced the inner warning voice demanding he follow suit. With a full belly and after a couple of glasses of both wine and port, he felt relaxed and mellow but not yet ready to sleep. He watched from under heavy lids as Leah rose to her feet.

'Do not retire just yet,' he said. 'Come. Sit down a moment so we may talk.'

A frown twitched between her brows, but she did as he asked.

## Chapter Fourteen

Leah knew she ought to follow Hinckley out of the drawing room, despite Dolph's request she remain, especially now she was aware of the risk of their being alone together. Until that moment on the ice, she had persuaded herself that—no matter her own blossoming feelings—Dolph would make certain there was no repeat of their kiss from three nights ago. But his desire for her had been obvious and her own physical response to lying full length on him had been…troubling. A prudent woman would leave, but she was clearly *im*prudent because, heaven help her, she *wanted* to kiss him again.

She chose the sofa opposite the chair upon which Dolph sat. She smoothed the skirt of her gown as she sat and then folded her hands in her lap.

'I wish to speak to you about our plans for tomorrow,' he said. 'It would appear Mrs Hubbard was correct— I spoke to Frinton after the boys went to bed, and the ground has already begun to thaw. As long as it does not freeze again tonight, I shall send a note to Hewton in the morning to tell them to expect us in the afternoon. And, Leah…please take the opportunity to call upon Miss Strong tomorrow, as we discussed before.'

'Thank you.' She was grateful for his discretion, and that she did not have to deny, yet again, that she was troubled. 'And I also intend to set my mind at rest by warning Philippa not to take Lord Hinckley too seriously, even though I know she is far from naïve and he is not the wicked sort who would ravish an innocent and desert her.'

*Unlike my real father.*

That thought made her feel physically sick, and she diverted her gaze to stare into the dancing orange, yellow and blue of the flames rather than risk Dolph reading her sudden distress.

*Although Tregowan did, at least, arrange matches for his three victims.*

Why, though, did Mama, and the mothers of both Aurelia and Beatrice, succumb to Lord Tregowan? They would all three have known he was a married man, and yet… The nausea rose to choke her. The only conclusion she could draw was that either her mother had lacked morals, or her natural father had, somehow, forced her mother to…

She clenched her jaw and swallowed desperately.

Was this yearning for Dolph somehow in her blood? Did she take after her mother? No, she could not believe that of her mama—perhaps it was Lord Tregowan's bad blood? After all, he had ruined three young girls' lives… She thrust down any further conjecture, afraid of where it might lead. She had enough to worry about in the here and now, for the time had come when she must ask Philippa to step in and look after the boys until Dolph found a replacement governess. After tomorrow, she would have no more excuse to cling on to her life at Dolphin Court. Her heart felt as though it were being ripped to shreds, but that only confirmed this was the right thing to do. She had lingered here too long.

'Is that what happened to you?'

Leah started at that quiet question, rattled that she had retreated into her own thoughts so completely in his presence.

'You were lost in thought again,' he said. 'As though your words triggered a memory.' He leaned towards her, his grey gaze intense. 'The other night…the night we kissed… At the time, it seemed as though maybe it had resurrected an unhappy memory. Forgive me for asking, but did someone in the past…a man…take advantage of you? Let you down? Desert you?'

Her heart leapt into her throat that he had guessed so much, but she bristled at the idea he might view her as a victim.

'Not in that way,' she said. 'Please do not allow that one kiss to give you the wrong impression of me—I am not a loose woman.'

He reared back, his eyes hurt. 'I did not intend to imply it. My apologies. There are multiple ways in which one person can let down another.' A muscle bunched in his jaw, and he rubbed his hand over it, as if to soothe the tension. 'So many ways.'

Those last three words, spoken so softly, and his suddenly bleak expression prompted Leah's curiosity, but how could she phrase the question she now burned to ask? It seemed too personal for a governess to ask her employer. But…she would soon leave Dolphin Court, and that knowledge encouraged her to speak more boldly than she might otherwise.

'You have been let down in the past?'

His laugh was cynical. 'No. It is I who have been guilty of failing those I love. Those whose welfare should have been my only concern.'

'The children?'

'Not only the children.' He surged to his feet then, his cheeks flushing. 'I beg your pardon. I should not be talking to you about such things.'

'And yet...' Leah paused.

He stared at her for long, silent seconds. Then he raised one eyebrow.

'And yet...?'

'Please sit down again.' Leah indicated his chair. 'I find it somewhat intimidating with you looming over me like that.'

He did so, his brows beetled together as he stared into the flames. The firelight warmed his ruggedly handsome face but also highlighted the signs of strain around his eyes, and the harsh lines bracketing his mouth, and she realised how effectively he normally hid the strain he was clearly under. The only hint until tonight had been his involuntary glance at the cliffs, that first day at Dolphin Bay, and that moment today, on the ice, when the memories seemed to lure him into the past.

'I have no wish to pry, nor to anger you, but as you once advised me to confide in a friend if I was troubled, I feel emboldened to offer that advice back to you. Could you not talk about your feelings to Lord Hinckley?'

He barked a laugh. 'You know little about men, Miss Thame. That is clear. Men,' he added, 'do not discuss their feelings.'

It was Leah's turn to raise an eyebrow, despite the accuracy of his first remark. She focussed on the second. 'Because they have far more important matters demanding their attention?'

'Oh, indeed.' His eyes glinted with amusement...and a hint of admiration.

Her stomach swooped as she took in his rugged good looks—his square jaw, broad shoulders and chest, and strong thighs. That pull of attraction grew ever stronger. How could she not be enticed? He was so big; so masculine; so very, very male.

'You speak as though you feel guilt over the past but, surely, burying feelings…not bringing them into the open…surely that can lead to consequences that might otherwise be avoided?'

Papa—the father who had raised her—had speculated that suppressing worries and feelings could result in mental disorders, an observation born out of years of tending to his parishioners. Dolph's skin had now leached of colour. His grey eyes were stricken, and Leah's heart went out to him.

'I am a good listener. And you may trust my discretion.'

He shook his head. 'I cannot burden you…anyone… with this.'

'Why do you presume it will be a burden? Truly, I should like to help, if I can, by listening. *Truly*,' she emphasised, as he clearly wavered.

He rubbed his hand across his jaw and then propped his elbows on his knees and stared into the fire. How she longed to take him in her arms and comfort him, but she could only offer words.

'Guilt,' she said, 'is a destructive emotion. Do not allow it to fester inside you and taint the rest of your life. And that of your children.'

He stared at her. 'You think it will affect them?'

'It is bound to. It will bring you low, and *that* will upset the children. They are more sensitive to such moods than you might realise. Some children more than others, of course. I am speaking of Stevie, in particular. He is your heir. You do not wish him to suffer because he cannot understand his father's unhappiness, do you? A sensitive child such as he might interpret your unhappiness as a sign of discontent with *him*. He will lose confidence.'

She'd pushed him as far as she could. She could tell it, by the firming of his jaw and the sudden shuttering of his expression. He would not confide in her—hardly surprising, when she was nothing more than his governess. She'd been in danger of forgetting the difference in their status; she'd been close to thinking of him only as a friend in need of help and understanding.

'My children will not suffer. From now on, *they* are my only priority. I am perfectly able to control my mood when I am with them, I assure you.'

There was nothing to be gained by pursuing the topic. She must be content she'd said her piece and that Dolph might reflect upon her words. She burned to know what else he had referred to—who else he had let down—but she doubted she would ever know for sure. She suspected, however, he meant his late wife. Rebecca.

'I doubt not your ability, nor your good intentions towards the children, for you have already made great progress. All children have a need to feel secure and to feel loved, and already both boys are more confident in your company. Tomorrow will surely only help to build upon that foundation.'

He smiled at her then. 'That is my hope. And I plan to take them out riding every afternoon, when the weather allows...always supposing their strict governess will permit such outings.'

Leah laughed to hide the shaft of pain she felt on hearing those words. She would not be here to approve or disapprove, and that knowledge cut deep. She rose to her feet.

'I shall bid you goodnight, sir. It is late.'

He stood too, bringing them face to face. So close she

could make out the black flecks that dotted his irises and the silver threads scattered through his dark brown hair. She should step back, but her muscles would not obey her. His musky male scent surrounded her, wreathing through her senses. Her pulse hammered, and all she could hear was the sound of her own blood pounding through her veins. Saliva flooded her mouth, and she swallowed. She wanted to kiss him. Wanted to taste him again, before she left. Without volition, her hand rose to rest on his chest, the silk of his waistcoat cool and smooth to her touch.

His eyes darkened. 'You are a remarkable woman, Miss Thame.' His voice deepened. 'Leah.'

Leah's stomach swooped. She could not tear her gaze from his.

'Your hair...' He threaded one finger into her hair at her temple and lifted it away, working a tendril loose to slide through his fingers. 'It reminds me of the colours of autumn...all the colours interwoven and changing according to the light.' He repeated the action, freeing more of her hair, allowing it to fall to her shoulder and over her breast. 'Stunning,' he murmured, closing his hand around it, lifting it and then allowing it to slide through his grip. Before she knew it, the pins that had secured it were on the floor and her hair was loose, spilling over her shoulders.

Leah's pulse quickened as her breasts grew tender and her limbs heavy. She stared up at him, captured by the intensity of his eyes, more black than grey behind the heavy lids. She licked lips that had suddenly dried, and his gaze released hers as it moved down to her mouth. His hand cupped her chin and he lowered his face to hers, but the moment before their lips met, he whispered, 'May I kiss you, Leah?'

Her heart tumbled in her chest. She would be gone by

the end of the week. She may never see him again…and, God help her, her lips craved his. This need had been building since the moment she had seen him again…his stark masculinity attracting her like no other man ever had. It was nothing more than a kiss… As long as she remembered that and did not allow herself to indulge in foolish daydreams, there would be no harm. And where was the harm if she wanted to taste him before she left? They were both adults. He was trustworthy; she felt it deep in her bones. *He* would not kiss and tell, unlike Viscount Usk.

She nodded. For whatever reason, he found her attractive—red hair, freckles and all—and he wanted to kiss her, and it was a pure thrill for a woman like her to know she aroused desire in such a man.

His mouth touched hers, warm and smooth and tasting of brandy. His arm swept around her waist, supporting her, and she needed no urging to step closer, relishing his solid strength as she moulded her soft curves to his hard, muscular body. Her eyes closed as his fingers curved around the back of her head, threading through her hair, his lips moving over hers. Her lips parted to the nudge of his tongue, and a low groan rumbled through him as he deepened the kiss.

It was a dreamy kiss, a kiss to melt into, slow and sensuous as tongues caressed and lips moved. Despite her best intentions, a myriad of hopes spun through her, overcoming her caution. What if Dolph did have feelings for her, beyond the physical? What if he *could* grow to love her?

Eyes closed, Leah gave herself up to the sensations tumbling through her. Her fingers hooked into his shoulders as the strength in her legs dissolved and pure need flooded her body, thrumming through her with every beat of her heart. A groan vibrated in her throat, and she pressed closer in an attempt to soothe the ache in her breasts. Every nerve in her body seemed to be linked to the sweet spot between her legs, and her hips moved, tilting of their own volition. She met each thrust of his tongue with one of her own, opening to him, responding to a rhythm that came as instinctively to her as breathing.

His hands dropped to her bottom. His fingers spread and gripped, lifting her against him. She moaned to feel his thick, hard length press against her belly, and without volition, she moved, rubbing her body against him, her nipples aching. He tore his mouth from hers, trailing hot, open-mouthed kisses along her jaw. Her head tipped back, and he feasted on the sensitive skin of her neck, nibbling, licking, kissing. Then his hand was on her breast, squeezing, moulding, and the yearning sensation between her thighs exploded, craving more. And more.

But just as her conscience began to reassert itself, with the reminder this was wrong, she must stop this now, Dolph abruptly released her, steadying her with his hands at her waist. Both were breathing hard as they locked eyes.

'I am sorry. I should not have done that.'

'You asked. I said yes.'

'That is true.' Dolph swept one hand over his head, then half turned from her. 'But I had to stop it going any further. It would be unfair when I can make you neither a reputable nor even an irreputable offer.'

*He means as his mistress.* Horror flooded Leah. Why would that even enter his head? She would *never* accept such a position, even without the children to consider.

'I pay your wages. You are a respectable female living under my roof and I am responsible for your welfare and your reputation.' He paced the room a moment before halting in front of her, his grey eyes rueful. 'I cannot deny I am attracted to you, Leah—you would not believe me if I tried—but the children are my main concern. They need you far more than I do. I will not risk their happiness.'

How she longed to tell him then she was leaving—that the boys would lose her anyway—but she did not, for the conviction grew that it would make no difference. Dolph had been clear he would never remarry—his love for Rebecca must have been true and strong—and even though, in her fantasies, she had been guilty of imagining a future here as Dolph's wife and as the children's stepmother, she knew in her heart that could not be. Even if Dolph did not still love Rebecca, the fact remained he was an earl and she, Leah, was a baseborn nobody. Besides…would she truly choose to marry a man whose sole purpose was for her to be a replacement mother for his children? Even if she loved that man?

'I understand,' she said.

'I'm sorry. I think we must agree to redouble our efforts to avoid being alone together in future.'

'I agree.' What more could she say?

Tomorrow…as soon as she had spoken to Philippa… she would tell him then. And she would leave immediately. There was no point in further delay; it would just get more and more painful. And though she reminded herself she had a whole new life to look forward to in London, the thought of her future resulted in the taste of ashes in her mouth, and the pain of sorrow in her heart.

## Chapter Fifteen

Steven and Nicholas could barely contain their excitement the following morning when their father decreed the ground had softened enough to allow them to go and look at the ponies that afternoon. Leah was exhausted by noon, especially after her restless night. She wondered if Dolph had any idea how demanding they would be on the drive over to Hewton, and how he and Hinckley would cope with two small boys in such a highly excitable state. But Dolph managed the problem by the simple expedient of allowing the boys to sit up on the box seat next to Travers, the coachman, while Frinton—the Dolphin Court head man who was going with them to help judge the suitability of the ponies for the boys—climbed into the carriage with Dolph and Hinckley. Leah watched the carriage drive away and then climbed into the buggy that had been brought around for her to drive over to the vicarage.

Philippa was expecting her, as Leah had sent a note that morning, asking if she might call upon her, and had received a delighted reply in the affirmative.

'This is delightful,' Philippa said, as she and Leah settled in front of the fire in the parlour with a pot of tea and a plate holding a delicious-smelling, freshly baked apple cake.

Philippa poured a cup of tea for Leah. 'Would you care for a slice of cake?'

'Yes, please.'

Philippa cut a slice and handed a plate to Leah with an impish smile. 'Look at us…social visits and taking afternoon tea like two ladies.' She cut one for herself and bit into it, chewing with a beatific smile on her face. 'You never know,' she continued after finishing her mouthful, 'one day, maybe we *will* both be ladies.'

Leah balanced her plate on her knee as she sipped her tea, ruthlessly crushing the little kernel of hope that had sprung into existence at some point during the long, sleepless night. She was afraid of that hope, for what good would it do? Hope born out of the realisation that Dolph liked her. Desired her. And she must marry someone in the next twelve months. Under *eleven* months by now.

But Dolph was still an earl, still grieving his wife's tragic suicide, still battling his own guilt, and she had heard herself his vehement vow to never marry again. Allowing her hopes to stray in his direction was futile. Besides, she still had her dream of love within her marriage, and she was sure marriage with a man she loved but who could not offer her love in return would be a recipe for heartache.

She longed to unburden herself to Philippa but, now she was here, she didn't know where to start. So she began with the easy—for her—bit.

'May I speak to you about Lord Hinckley, Philippa?'

Philippa's smile disappeared. 'Uh-oh. This sounds serious. He has asked me to call him George, you know.'

'I don't doubt it.' Lord Usk had begged her to call him Harold, too. It meant nothing, but silly females gave too much credence to such matters. 'But…do take care, my dear. Hinckley is an earl, living a very different life from yours. I cannot help but be concerned—'

'That I have fallen under the spell of his silken words and extravagant compliments?' Philippa shook her head and laughed. 'Leah, you goose. Do you really imagine I am such a country miss I do not understand His Lordship is amusing himself with a flirtation while he rusticates in the country? Believe me… I am in no danger of expecting anything more from George than the chance to spend time with an amusing gentleman who, I admit, makes me laugh. I enjoy his company—and I believe he enjoys mine—but I will not lose my heart to a man who will be gone from here in a few weeks with never a backward look.'

Leah stared at her friend, then shook her head, smiling ruefully.

'I have underestimated you, have I not?' Philippa's customary good sense appeared firmly in place where Hinckley was concerned. 'I am relieved you are blessed with such clear sight. Please forgive my interference.'

Philippa reached across and squeezed Leah's hand. 'I appreciate you were concerned enough to warn me. You truly are a good friend.'

Leah then found herself the subject of a searching look.

'And, as *your* friend,' Philippa continued, 'I would be remiss if I did not mention you are looking fagged to death, Leah. What is it?' She moved to sit next to Leah and took her hand. 'Tell me,' she urged in a soft voice. 'Are you…are you ill?'

'No. It is nothing like that. But I do have something to tell you.'

She told Philippa about Lady Tregowan's will, and that she must leave Dolphin Court soon.

'There are conditions to our inheritance. We must all move to London by Easter at the latest, and we must live together there for the duration of the Season, after which we may choose to live either at Falconfield Hall or remain in London. And we must each marry within a year, but we must not marry the current Lord Tregowan.'

'Would he not be your half-brother, though?'

'No. The Tregowans had no children. The current Earl is the son of a distant cousin who fell out with the former Earl over some matter or other.'

'But…' Philippa's brow wrinkled. 'So…you have two sisters you knew nothing about?'

'Half-sisters. Yes, but please do not tell anyone—that secret is not mine alone to reveal.'

'You know you may rely on my discretion. But…why are you still here working for a pittance as a governess now you are wealthy? It makes no sense to me. What has Lord Dolphinstone to say about your good fortune?'

'Ah.' Leah fiddled with her skirts, pleating and re-pleating the fabric.

'Leah! You have not told him, have you? Why ever not? You must give him time to appoint another govern-ess. You cannot leave him in the lurch.'

Leah bit her lip. 'I know. You are right. But…you were there when I arrived home that day, Philippa. You saw how angry he was. I was afraid he would send me away immediately if I told him the truth, and how could I leave the children at the very moment their father returned? I just wanted to help the boys adjust to their papa being home before I unsettled them further with the news I must leave.' Leah forced her next words through a throat clogged with unshed tears. 'Philippa… I dread saying goodbye to the boys.' She closed her eyes and groped for her friend's hand. *I cannot pretend to myself my heart is not breaking twice over now.* 'And to their father,' she added in a strangulated whisper.

'Oh, Leah.' Philippa hugged her. 'I suspected... I noticed, yesterday...but I did not like to say anything. But His Lordship appears very taken with you, and George said it's the first time he's shown an interest in anyone since his wife died. Is there no chance? After all, your circumstances have changed. You will no longer be a governess but a lady of means. And if you must marry anyway...'

Her voice trailed away. But Leah could not allow herself to believe, not after what had happened in the past and despite that tiny seed of hope still lodged deep inside her heart—the hope that, faced with the fact of her leaving, Dolph might realise he could not let her go. But pride would never allow her to admit as much, not to anyone.

'No,' she said. 'His Lordship is adamant he will never remarry. And although that inheritance will make me more acceptable, the circumstances of my birth will count against me. Except, of course, with gentlemen with pockets to let who will, of course, overlook such unsavoury details.'

Philippa squeezed her hand. 'We are a fine pair, are we not?'

Leah dragged in an unsteady breath and opened her eyes. The time had come. If she stayed, she would only fall more hopelessly under Dolph's spell. She must try to look forward instead, to the new life that awaited her with Aurelia and Beatrice.

'Philippa?'

Philippa tipped her head to one side, her eyes big with sympathy. 'Leah?'

'Might I impose upon our friendship? Would you agree to step in and care for the boys until His Lordship appoints another governess?' There. She had said it. The die was cast. 'I will tell him at the earliest possible opportunity,' she rushed on, 'and then I shall tell the children, and…and… Oh, Philippa!' She gulped back her emotions as they threatened to erupt. 'I could not bear to linger once they all know. It will be too painful.'

'Hush.' Philippa squeezed Leah's hand. 'Of course I will. Just send me word when you know the day.'

Leah forced a smile and squeezed her friend's hand in return. 'Thank you. I shall miss you, my dearest friend.'

Philippa's smile was sorrowful. 'I shall miss you too, and I wish you all the luck in the world when you go to London.'

Leah forced herself to smile back, but her heart was heavier than she had ever known it. She would have a hard task to hide her anguish from Dolph and the boys until she left, but she was determined to try.


'No! For the last time, you cannot ride the ponies home.'

'But… Papa…*pleeeease*.' Nicky gazed up at Dolph with huge, beseeching eyes that grew more teary by the second. 'We will be careful, won't we, Stevie?'

Stevie scuffed his boot on the ground. 'I do not want to. I want to go in the carriage with Papa.'

*Thank God one of my sons is biddable. How does Leah cope with this?*

The thought of the governess stirred a conflicting mix of emotions, the same mix that had kept him awake long into the night—desire, first and uppermost; admiration and gratitude for how she had cared for his children; shame that he had taken advantage of her. Again. And dismay that the first woman to stir his blood since Rebecca's death happened to be a woman in his employ and therefore under his protection.

*I must not lose control again. I cannot risk driving her away... The boys would be distraught if they lost Leah. She's like a mother to them.*

He directed a stern look at his youngest son. 'You heard your brother, Nicholas. Get in the carriage.'

Nicky's lower lip thrust forward. Dolph cast a pleading look at George, who grimaced and shrugged before climbing into the carriage. Stevie followed him, leaving Dolph facing his recalcitrant younger son. Rescue came in the form of Frinton.

'Now, then, Master Nicky. You do as your father tells you, and less of your nonsense. That there pony ain't fit enough to be rid one mile, let alone four—they'll both find it hard enough tied behind the carriage. Their little legs'll have to work twice as fast to keep up. Now. Less of your stubbornness. You'll have plenty of time to ride once they're back at the Court, all safe and sound.'

Dolph watched, amazed, as Nicky flushed, hung his head and trailed over to the carriage to clamber up the steps. He turned to Frinton.

'Thank you.'

'You was much the same when you was that age, milord. Far too full of what you wanted and no stopping to think of the wisdom or rights of your demands. *And* you was as easy to steer. You might be experienced with bargaining with politicians and the like, but I'll tell you this for free. You never bargain with young'uns. Never. Or sure as certain you'll be making a rod for your own back.'

Having delivered his homily, Frinton climbed up to

the box seat, leaving Dolph to join George and the boys in the carriage.

'I feel sick,' said Nicky.

'The carriage,' said Dolph, 'has not even begun to move. You cannot possibly feel sick.'

Nicky crossed his arms, lower lip once again protruding. 'I don't like being inside. I want to drive with Travers and Frinton.'

'Well, you can't.' Dolph tried very hard to control his exasperation. 'We will be home before you know it. Close your eyes and try to sleep.'

George, he noted, would be of no help, for he had already tipped his hat over his eyes and stretched his legs across the carriage, giving a good impression of a man taking a nap. The slight smirk on his mouth suggested, though, that he was listening to, and enjoying, this test of Dolph's fathering skills.

Nicky wriggled in his seat, kicking his legs, which reached nowhere near the floor. His lip protruded further. 'Not tired. Get sick if I close my eyes.'

'Look, Nicky. Look at the river. There's a heron. Can you see it?'

Stevie cast an anxious glance at Dolph, whose heart clenched. He prayed that, by riding out together daily, Stevie would relax a little more in his company. He still seemed so formal—very different from the boy he saw interacting with Leah. As for Nicky... Dolph heaved a silent sigh. Before today, he'd found Nicky the easier of his sons to understand, but he couldn't fathom why his younger son was hell-bent on testing his patience today. He should be happy at getting a pony of his own but, if anything, his behaviour had worsened as the afternoon wore on. Dolph now regretted not bringing Leah with them although, after the night before, he was also relieved not to face an hour's journey in an enclosed carriage with her.

The memory of that kiss set his blood pounding and his lips tingling. If only she weren't his governess. If only she were a lady of his world...then he might... But no. He could not risk it. Rebecca had been so unhappy with him she had taken her own life, and he had failed to see any warning signs. How could he risk putting any other woman through the same? Especially one he was beginning to care about.

At least Stevie's distraction appeared to have worked, for both boys now knelt on the seats, peering out of the window at the river snaking through the meadow alongside the road. Dolph sighed and closed his eyes, trying without success to quieten the thoughts racing around inside his head as a headache threatened to take hold. He felt more out of his depth than ever. He had not even realised children could be so different. In the past, children had, in his head, been lumped together into one homogenous mass. But his sons were little people—individuals—and he was determined to get to know their characters. He'd missed so much of their earlier years, distracted by politics, business and the estate. He'd allowed anything and everything, it seemed, to take precedence over family. He'd barely even noticed his children, other than as a natural step in his life. He'd gone to school and university, taken over the title and estate when his father died; married; had children. He'd followed the natural order of life for a man in his position, but he now felt ashamed of his neglect of his entire family. If he'd paid more attention...if he'd spent more time with them... Rebecca might still be alive.

He'd been a bad husband. Not cruel. Not even mean. But careless and dismissive. Rebecca had deserved better. And instead of staying to comfort his children after their mother died, he'd left them in the care of a stranger, more concerned with dealing with his own grief by distracting himself with the negotiations in Vienna. It was fortunate Leah had proved such a good woman. The children clearly loved her.

At least he'd got that bit right, although it was only by luck, not judgement.

Well, it might be too late to make amends to Rebecca, but his relationship with his children was getting better. And now they would have their own ponies, meaning he could spend more time with them outside the schoolroom. Which meant he need see even less of Leah. It was for the best. He must not risk his behaviour becoming a reason for her to resign.

He would not allow his children to suffer another loss in their lives.

'Papa?'

He opened his eyes. 'Yes, Nicky?'

'I don't feel well.'

Dolph studied his son. It was true. His face did have a greenish pallor... Dolph rapped on the carriage ceiling with his cane and it rocked to a halt.

'Papaaaa...'

'Hell and damnation!' Dolph sprang to the door, flung it wide, jumped down—straight into a patch of mud at the side of the road, into which his booted feet sank up to the ankles. 'Grrr!' He tugged his feet out of the cloying mud.

'Dolph!' George's shout was urgent.

He spun around, took in Nicky's face with one look, grabbed him unceremoniously under the arms and swung him out of the vehicle.

'Bleurghhhh...'

All down the front of Dolph's greatcoat. The sour

stench of vomit reached his nostrils and curdled his own stomach, but at least Nicky had not soiled his own clothing. About to yell at Nicky—in pure reflex—Dolph managed to bite his tongue in time.

Tears streamed down his son's face as he sobbed, and Dolph couldn't even hug him to reassure him, or they would both be covered in sick. Then Frinton was there. He took Nicky and put him down on the road.

'Best take that coat off, milord, or you'll all be puking with the stink. There's a rug up top. Hi, Travers. Throw down the spare rug, will you?'

The coachman did as bid. Dolph stripped off his greatcoat, handing it to Frinton, who grabbed a stick from the verge and scraped off the worst of the vomit before folding the coat carefully, with the stain on the outside.

'No sense in spreading it over more of the coat than necessary,' he said cheerfully. 'Mrs Frampton'll soon have that sponged clean.'

Dolph crouched down next to Nicky and put his hands on the trembling shoulders. The next minute, Nicky pressed his warm little body into Dolph's chest, and his arms wrapped around his father's neck.

'Want Miss Thame,' he sobbed.

'Shhh. Yes. I know.' Dolph stood up, still holding Nicky in his arms. 'You shall have her soon. But we must get home first, Nicky. It won't take long, and the next road will be less bumpy than this one.' Dolph looked up at Frinton. 'Have you any water?'

A canteen of water was produced, and Nicky was persuaded to rinse out his mouth before sipping a little.

'Master Nicky can ride up front with me and Travers,' said Frinton. 'How about it, Master Nicky?'

Nicky's head shook vehemently. 'Wanna stay with Papa.'

Dolph's heart lurched, and joy spread through him like warm honey. 'Then you shall,' he said.

He climbed into the carriage and, as he settled in his seat with Nicky on his lap, he noticed George watching him with an indefinable look on his face.

'Never thought to see you so...fatherly,' he said. 'You're a lucky man, with three such fine children.'

'I am,' said Dolph. And was surprised to find he meant it. *Maybe,* he thought, as he cuddled Nicky, lying slumped against his chest, *I can become a good father after all.*

'Papa?'

'Yes, Stevie?'

'What's hell and damnation?'

Dolph caught George's eye and saw the wretch trying hard not to laugh. Maybe he still had some work to do to become a good father.

'It's a special grown-up phrase. It's not for children to use, so you must not say it. Do you hear me, Stevie? Miss Thame will *not* be happy if she hears you repeat it.'

Nicky stirred, lifting his head so his hair tickled Dolph's chin.

'Hell and damnation,' he murmured under his breath.

'Nicholas...' Dolph put as much warning as he could muster into his son's name.

'Sorry, Papa.'

Nicky relaxed again, and Dolph breathed a sigh of relief. Not long now till they reached home. He was exhausted. His gaze settled on his older son, sitting quietly and obediently as he watched the passing scenery. Stevie's lips moved, and Dolph would swear he mouthed, *Hell and damnation.*

He felt the press of failure once again. What sort of a father used such bad language in front of his young sons?

## Chapter Sixteen

Dolph could see Leah waiting at the window when the carriage pulled up outside the house, and relief flooded him. By the time the steps were down, she was outside, her shawl wrapped tightly around her.

Her amazing eyes widened when Dolph emerged from the carriage with Nicky still in his arms and the carriage rug around his shoulders. There had been no further unscheduled stops—for which Dolph was profoundly grateful—and Nicky had, in fact, fallen asleep. He now roused, his eyes drowsy as he looked around. Then he tensed, and wriggled, as he saw Leah.

'Miss Thame! I puked over Papa!' He wriggled harder, and Dolph gave up trying to hold him, putting him down on the ground.

'Oh, no. Poor Papa.'

Her eyes danced with amusement, the low-lying winter sun catching them and making them sparkle like the sea on a bright day. Dolph's pulse kicked, and his heart jolted in his chest. Desperate to disguise his reaction and determined to stick to his vow to allow no repeat of last night's intimacy, Dolph raised one eyebrow in the aristocratic manner he had learned would repress all but the most insensitive individual. Leah bit her lip, but the sparkle of amusement remained in her gaze and Dolph realised how good it felt to be teased, and how nice it was to see Leah in such a light-hearted mood. He recalled her mission today and he hoped her visit to Miss Strong would mean no more sleepless nights.

'I came out to find out if your trip had been a success,' Leah went on. She nodded towards the two ponies tethered to the rear of the carriage. 'I can see it was.'

'Come on, Miss Thame.' Stevie grabbed the governess's hand and pulled her towards the ponies. 'The bay one is mine. He is bigger than Nicky's 'cause I am the biggest.'

'He is very handsome, Stevie. What is his name?'

'He is actually a she,' said Dolph as he joined them. 'And she is called Dolly.' He caught Steven's grimace at the name. Dolph sympathised—it was not a name for a budding knight's charger. 'But she will not mind if you change it to a more appropriate name, I am sure, Stevie.'

'I want to change my pony's name too.' Nicky pushed his way between his brother and Miss Thame and pointed at his pony, a grey. 'She is called Prudence. It's a silly name.'

'Well, I agree,' said Leah. 'No self-respecting young man would want to ride a pony called Prudence.'

'What would you like to call them, boys?' Dolph asked. 'You can choose.'

'Ummmmmm.' The two boys looked at one another, clearly bereft of ideas.

'There is no hurry,' Leah said. 'It is cold out here, and you do not want your ponies to catch a chill now they have stopped moving. Why not let Frinton get them all warm in their stalls with some nice hay to eat, and we can go indoors to think of suitable names?'

She glanced back at the house, and for a split second, Dolph swore her smile slipped to reveal an expression of misery, but when she looked back at them, she was again all smiles.

'Wolf is waiting inside, full of excitement now you're all home—I had to leave him inside in case he frightened the ponies.'

Dolph couldn't remember her being this talkative. Ever. Either confiding in Miss Strong had lifted an intolerable burden from Leah's shoulders, or she was hiding something.

'When I arrived home,' she carried on, 'poor Wolf was full of sulks and wouldn't talk to me because we all went out without him. He's forgotten his bad mood now, however, and is bounding around full of excitement, as I said. A bit like the boys before you set off.'

Dolph grimaced, pushing to the back of his mind his uneasiness at the thought of more secrets in his household. 'Don't remind me.'

'Come along, boys. Inside the house now, please.'

Miss Thame shepherded Stevie and Nicky towards the front. Dolph watched them go until a nudge from George grabbed his attention.

'Quite the touching family scene, old fellow. If someone was to offer me odds, I'd confidently wager you will end up in the luscious Miss Thame's arms before very long. I trust you appreciated my timely withdrawal last night so you could spend a little time alone together?'

'George.' Dolph forced his words through gritted teeth. 'If you wish to be throttled, you are going the right way about it. So, if you care anything for your health, you will not say another word on that particular subject. It is all in your imagination. Miss Thame is a valued member of my *staff*. She is a respectable woman and has done nothing to deserve you speaking of her with such disrespect.'

George grinned. 'Of course she is, Dolph. I offer you my unreserved apology.'

Dolph stalked ahead of his friend into the house, not trusting himself to say another word.

Leah took the three children down to the drawing room to say goodnight to Dolph that night, only to find George was present—a blatant departure from the norm and, she soon realised, a deliberate ploy on Dolph's part. He'd clearly meant what he said the previous evening: he would risk nothing that might result in the boys losing their beloved governess. There was no opportunity to request a private interview and, if she was honest, she was grateful to put off the moment she dreaded until later.

George dominated the conversation all through dinner that evening, as usual. When the time came for Leah to withdraw, both gentlemen rose as she did.

'Will you play for us later, Miss Thame?' George asked.

Leah caught the expression of dismay that flashed across Dolph's features and—even though she knew he had forsworn marriage and that, even had he not, he would not marry his own governess, no matter how attracted he might be to her—it still felt as though a dagger had pierced her heart.

*Stupid, stupid woman. Will I never learn?*

It seemed no amount of brutal home truths was enough to fully destroy her foolish daydreams or her pathetic hope he might experience some kind of epiphany and realise he loved her, and not his dead wife, after all.

'My apologies, sir, but I have the beginnings of the

headache and I intend to retire now. I bid you goodnight, gentlemen.'

'I hope you will feel better after a good night's sleep,' Hinckley said.

Dolph inclined his head, with a brief 'Goodnight, Miss Thame,' before sitting again and gesturing at Palmer to pour the port.

As she climbed the stairs, Leah knew she must find the opportunity tomorrow to speak privately to Dolph, to tell him she was resigning her post. She would then tell the boys, and she would leave just as soon as she could.

The worry about how she would tell Steven and Nicholas kept her awake long into the night, but she refused to fret over what she would say to Dolph. He had made his position clear, and she would not waste her time wallowing in self-pity. She had an exciting change ahead of her and she would be a fool not to take advantage of the opportunity fate had thrust in her path.

If she told herself enough times, she might begin to believe it.

The next day—the first day of March—dawned with dark clouds massing on the horizon, and by mid-afternoon, the rain was sheeting down. It was clear to Leah that Dolph was taking even more stringent steps than ever to avoid being alone with her. He visited the schoolroom as normal in the afternoon, taking care to concentrate wholly on the boys and their work. Leah was unsurprised, but it still hurt every time he avoided meeting her eyes and every time she recognised the small manoeuvres with which he ensured they could not exchange so much as a private word. She was still determined to speak to him today about her resignation, however, even if it meant writing to him to demand an appointment. She was relieved when, after his usual half-hour, Dolph stood up—his signal it was time for him to go.

'I must attend to estate matters,' he said, 'but before I leave, I wondered if you boys had thought about names for your ponies yet? It is raining today, but if tomorrow is dry, I thought we might ride out, with me and Lord Hinckley leading you. Would you enjoy that?'

'Yes, please, Papa,' said Stevie, while Nicky beamed.

'Excellent,' said Dolph. 'So, have you chosen names?'

Leah held her tongue. She had discussed suitable names with the boys and suggested maybe the names of birds might be appropriate. Nicky, up to then, had been determined to call his grey mare Wellington, with Stevie favouring Apollo for his bay.

'I have chosen mine,' said Stevie. 'I shall call her Falcon.' He beamed at Leah, and she nodded approvingly.

'That is a good name, Stevie,' she said, 'for some falcons are indeed females, are they not, Lord Dolphinstone?'

He shot her a hard look upon her use of his title. She mentally shrugged. Why should she care? She was leaving. Soon.

'They are, and I agree. It is a good name for your pony, Stevie. Have you decided on a name, Nicky?'

'Swift.' Nicky bounced off his stool. 'Swifts are faster than an arrow, aren't they, Papa?'

'Indeed, Nicky. And falcons are extremely fast as well. I shall have to hope my horse can keep up with two such speedy ponies.' He nodded to Leah. 'Thank you, Miss Thame. I shall attend lessons at the same time tomorrow, following which I shall take the boys out on their ponies if it is not raining.'

'Hurrah!' Stevie, too, jumped to his feet.

'Now settle down again, boys. Miss Thame has not yet

dismissed you, and if I hear you have not paid attention after I leave, I may have to rethink our ride.'

Both boys subsided and, after the door closed behind Dolph, they bent their heads obediently to their school-work until three o'clock, when Leah decided they had been patient for long enough.

'That's it, boys. Lessons are over. Would you like to play with your soldiers?'

She did not really expect them to agree—with no opportunity for a walk today, they would be itching to be more active.

'May we play hide-and-seek? Pleeeease, Miss Thame.'

Nicky stared up at Leah with a beseeching look she could not resist.

'Stevie? What about you?'

'Hide-and-seek, miss.'

Leah could not refuse. How many more days would she have to play with them? She must make the most of the time they had left together. Their little faces blurred as the reality of saying goodbye to them hit her again, and she turned away to straighten the items on her already tidy desk.

'Of course we can play hide-and-seek,' she said. 'Shall you boys go and hide first? But, I warn you, do not venture near your father's study, for he is busy and will not wish to be disturbed.'

Dolph put down the letter he was reading as George wandered into his study with Wolf at his heels. He stifled a sigh.

He had so much to do—correspondence to catch up on and various reports on the state of his tenanted farm-steads—but, somehow, he had achieved virtually nothing since leaving the schoolroom. His thoughts kept wandering away from business matters and onto Leah. Her calm acceptance of his attempts to avoid any private talk had needled him, even though he knew it was the only solution. His body, however, paid no heed to his logic. It was a dilemma. One he was uncertain how to resolve, other than to seek out a lonely widow and reach a mutual arrangement, sordid as that sounded.

Dolph knew his friend would only interrupt him for a good reason and so, rather than resenting the intrusion, he welcomed it, telling himself George could be the very distraction he needed to keep his thoughts from Leah.

'What can I do for you, George?'

'Is that claret in that decanter, Dolph? I've just returned from the village and I'm awash with tea. Need something to bolster my spirits and you might find yourself in need of fortification as well, when you hear what I've got to tell you.'

His curiosity piqued, Dolph poured two glasses of the rich red wine and crossed to the pair of green leather wingback chairs flanking the hearth. Wolf sat by his chair, leaning against his lower leg.

'That sounds ominous.' Dolph frowned. 'Is this about Miss Strong?' Had George compromised her? That would create a tangle of worms, for certain.

'Yes. No. Well, it only concerns her in that she let something slip she was not meant to tell me.'

Dolph raised his brows and fondled Wolf's ears as he waited for George to continue.

'It would appear, old chap, that you are about to lose the services of Miss Thame.'

## Chapter Seventeen

'Lose…? No.' Every muscle in Dolph's body clenched. 'You must be mistaken.'

Leah would never leave the boys. Would she? He thought they'd resolved that kiss… Was that not why they had agreed to avoid being alone together in future? Why they'd agreed to avoid temptation?

'She has not seemed unhappy in her role here.'

'There's no mistake, Dolph.' George sipped his claret. 'Philippa mentioned Miss Thame's visit yesterday, and how much she would miss her. Of course, having said that much, she was obliged to explain further, but she was also surprised I was not aware—Miss Thame told her she would speak to you at the earliest possible opportunity.'

*And I have purposely avoided giving her any chance to do so.*

Wolf nudged his hand reproachfully, and Dolph absent-mindedly resumed stroking his silky head and ears.

'Evidently,' George continued, 'Miss Thame has come into an inheritance, and she has asked Philippa to step in to teach the boys until you are able to appoint another governess.' He cocked his head. 'She did not inform you of her plans, then, Dolph?'

'No.' He felt sick. He must think of a way to stop her leaving. Wolf stood up and laid his head on Dolph's knee, watching him with worried eyes.

'And you knew nothing of this inheritance?'

'No.'

The boys... What would this do to them? They adored Leah. Losing her would break their hearts. He knocked back the remains of his claret and placed the empty glass on a side table, his hand trembling as he realised the full impact on the boys of losing Leah.

*And what about you? How will you feel if she goes?*

Dolph ignored that inner voice. His feelings were not the point. Only the boys mattered. He had nothing to offer any woman. Not after Rebecca.

His fist clenched on his lap, and Wolf licked it with his warm tongue.

'It will be a shock for you, no doubt.' George scratched his head and frowned. 'I thought the two of you were growing close.'

Dolph shrugged. 'Not in the way you're suggesting.' He worked to keep his voice level and light. He was not proud of the way he lusted after Leah. 'We share the common objective of the well-being of my sons. Nothing more.'

'Ah. I see. The *boys*, then, will miss her terribly.'

'They will.'

Unable to remain still, Dolph surged to his feet and paced the room, sweeping his fingers over his hair, almost tripping over Wolf, who was shadowing him.

'Get out of the way, Wolf!' Dolph pointed to the fireplace and was immediately seized by guilt as the dog slunk over and lay down on the hearth rug. 'This is dreadful, George. I have to do something to stop her leaving. I *cannot* allow the children to lose another mother figure—they will be inconsolable. I—I'll do anything to keep her here. Did Miss Strong tell you any more about Miss Thame's plans?'

'I only know she has inherited a house in London together with sufficient funds to provide her with an independent income.'

'An income?' He sank down onto his chair again, that sudden surge of energy depleted and his gut churning. The laugh he forced sounded hollow even to his ears. 'So, there is little point in offering her a pay rise.'

'Is this still about the children?'

The understanding and the sympathy in George's eyes squeezed his gut even harder.

'Of course it is. Don't be ridiculous. But I must do something to persuade her to stay. I will do whatever it takes, but...tell me, George. What *can* I do? What can I offer her to make her stay?'

'You could marry her.'

A startled laugh burst from Dolph. 'Marriage? You are not serious? You know full well I shall never marry again.'

'I know you said you would not, but it would make sense, Dolph. Think about it... The children will have a stepmother they already adore, and you cannot deny you are attracted to her, so bedding her will be no hardship.'

No hardship? It would be a pleasure. Bedding Leah had been on his mind since he had first kissed her. But marriage? The thought had never once entered his head. They had only known one another a matter of weeks. Besides, how could he risk another woman's happiness? What if it happened all over again—the gradual growing apart and the slow sinking of her spirit, until... He jerked his thoughts from following that thought through to its conclusion. How could he risk it? He could not face that burden of responsibility.

He sank down onto his knees beside Wolf and petted him, to make amends for snapping at him earlier. His thoughts continued to whirl.

Although…was marriage such a ridiculous notion? What if he made it clear it was a business arrangement, as so many marriages were? Could that help to steer any expectations away from romantic nonsense and onto the purely practical aspects of a union? If she had no expectations of him, then he could not let her down.

He liked Leah. Found her attractive. Many marriages were built on less.

*That's not the point. You do not deserve happiness after what you put Rebecca through. The children, though…*

But there was Leah herself to consider, too. She had confessed her wish to marry for love—he could never offer her that. He was incapable of love. He could never make her happy. Could he?

'And consider her inheritance,' George continued, while Dolph's head was still full of conjecture. 'A property in London is not to be sneezed at. It makes all kind of sense. You must see that. It is the perfect solution for both you and the children.'

Burning with humiliation, Leah crept quietly back along the secret passage that stretched from the library to Dolph's study. She'd been so sure she would find the boys here, having been unable to locate them in any of their usual hiding places. She'd been convinced they had disobeyed her and had, after all, hidden in the passage that led to Dolph's study. She'd been wrong. She hadn't found the boys crouched down, giggling, as she'd expected. Instead, she had heard Lord Hinckley telling Dolph of her plans. And Dolph's response.

Why, oh, why had Philippa told Hinckley about her inheritance? Although, to be fair, she had not told him the whole, thank goodness. She could not face the humiliation of Dolph knowing his sons were being taught by a woman whose father had discarded her mother like a worn-out nag once she became a liability to him.

She must go at once to Dolph and resign. She would leave in the morning. Her pride would not allow her to stay a moment longer after hearing that conversation in which Dolph and Hinckley had discussed her as though she were no more than a horse to be traded. Hot fury evaporated any tears before they could even form... How *dared* they? She was a person. With feelings. Not just a convenience to make his life easier by substituting the children's mother.

Although...was not that idea all Hinckley's? *Dolph* had said nothing to suggest marriage was a business transaction. Despite the hurt, a shoot of hope unfurled. What if, now the notion had been put in his head, Dolph realised he loved her too much to let her go? What then?

*Don't be an utter fool. Has experience taught you nothing?*

She emerged from behind the secret panel into the library and stood irresolute, doubts ricocheting inside her head. She must find the boys first. And then she would go to Dolph. As she spun on her heel and headed for the door, she was brought up short by a muffled giggle. She tilted her head.

'What is that I hear?' She rotated slowly, her eyes searching every nook. 'Is it a mouse, I wonder?'

Another giggle, and a movement of one of the floor-length curtains. Despite her longing to curl up into a ball and wallow in her pain, Leah ran across to the window and tickled the solid little body concealed within its drape.

'I've got you!'

With a shriek and a burst of laughter, Nicky erupted from behind the curtain. Leah immediately investigated the other curtains in the room and, before long, Stevie too was winkled out.

'Bravo, Miss Thame.'

Leah stiffened at that amused masculine drawl. By the time she faced Dolph, her expression had sobered. He'd kissed her. Twice. And then regretted it. True, she had been a willing participant, but only because she'd stupidly hoped he might develop feelings for her. The triumph of hope over experience! Well, no more. She would not wait for him to broach the subject. She'd had enough of not being in control of her own life. Now was the time to begin. She captured Dolph's gaze and held it.

'My lord. I am glad you are here, as I must speak with you as a matter of urgency. Stevie, Nicky, would you please go up to Cassie in the nursery? I shall be up very shortly.'

Dolph's grey eyes narrowed as he frowned. The air between them appeared to crackle with suppressed energy, and Leah's heart thumped against her ribs as nerves curdled her stomach.

'But what about our game, miss? It is your turn to hide.'

Their gazes remained fused as Dolph said, 'Do as Miss Thame tells you, boys. And take Wolf with you.'

Audibly grumbling, Stevie and Nicky left the room, accompanied by the huge dog, who had come in with Dolph. Leah's nostrils flared as she inhaled, steeling herself, but before she could speak, Dolph held up his hand, palm forward, silencing her.

'Before you say anything, I have something I should like to say. Or ask, rather.'

Leah raised a brow but nodded, her breath growing short.

'This might seem as though it comes out of the blue, but I wish to request your hand in marriage.'

Pain sliced through Leah. No words of love. No hint of any feeling for her. Just a bald proposal. A *business-like* proposal, made only after prompting by George. She searched his expression, noting the tic of the muscle in his jaw and the compression of his lips. Despite her idiotic hopes, he looked nothing like a man who had discovered he was in love.

'Why?'

*'Why?'*

His expression was almost comical as his brows shot skywards, but Leah had never felt less like laughing.

'Yes. I have heard you swear never to marry again. So, I should like to understand why you are proposing to me. And why now?'

'Does it matter why now? The fact is, I have no wish to risk losing you, and I fear our recent…um…encounters… my behaviour…might prompt you to leave. The children love you and I'll do anything to protect them against further loss and heartache.'

'Anything?' She could feel tears prickling behind her eyes. 'Including marrying their governess?'

'Yes! No…that is not what I meant. I will do my utmost to make you happy, of course, and not to let you down. Think of the advantages—you will be a countess; I am wealthy; you love the children and they love you. They *need* you.'

She crossed to the window, staring out, desperately trying to quash the hurt that spiked through her. There had been nothing personal in that proposal. He could have been proposing to any woman.

*What did you expect, you stupid fool? When will you ever learn?*

She had seen marriages where the men viewed their wives as just another possession, someone to do their bidding and to produce heirs. And Dolph would not even need her for that, as he had Steven and Nicholas. She swallowed. If she did not already love Dolph, then maybe such a marriage would work. But he had spoken no words of love, and a marriage where one partner loved and the other did not…*could* not… No. She could not bear such a life.

'Leah?'

With a start, she realised she had not answered him. Slowly, she turned back to the room. She had always been honest with him, ever since his return, and he had seemed to value it. She would not be coy about her reason for refusal, especially as she'd already confessed her silly dream of a love match, so it wasn't even a matter of salvaging some pride. She faced him, her back straight, hands clasped before her.

'As I understand it, you are offering me an arrangement akin to a business transaction. For a practical reason, to keep me here as a convenient replacement mother for your children. My answer is no. You already know that is not what I want from a marriage and, as I can now afford to support myself without working, I should prefer to remain single rather than be trapped in a loveless union with a man still in love with his late wife.'

A flash of something like shock crossed his face before his expression blanked.

'I… I am fond of you. You know I am.'

*Are you? Or has any interest in me been driven by lust? No doubt my real father was fond of Lady Tregowan. That did not stop him seducing and ruining three young ladies.*

'I am sorry. That is not enough for me. My answer is no.'

There was indecision in his face. Silently, she willed him on. *Please. Find out you cannot bear to lose me. Persuade me we can be happy together.* His indecision did not last. His brow lowered.

'You can afford to support yourself, you say?'

'I can. I have come into some money. I no longer need earn my living as a governess.'

That was all he needed to know. She would not tell him about the marriage stipulation—that was still a humiliation, in her opinion. All she could hope for now would be marriage to a decent man with whom she could be content, without any of the heartache of unrequited love. Neither would she tell him about her sisters or their link to the Tregowans—thank goodness Philippa had kept that titbit from Hinckley. Of course, if Dolph was aware she was the illegitimate daughter of Lord Tregowan, he might very well withdraw his offer anyway. So, no. She would tell him none of it. It was *her* business.

'And you have known this how long?' he growled. He began to pace the room. 'No. Let me guess. You have known about it ever since your trip to Bristol. Ever since I came home. And yet you have left it until now to tell me, and you are prepared to leave me in the lurch by giving me no notice whatsoever?' He halted before her, towering over her. 'I thought better of you, Miss Thame.'

Leah stiffened and raised her chin. '*That*, my lord, is grossly unjust. I remained here to help the children settle after you reappeared without warning in their lives. But you no longer need me. Besides…' she narrowed her eyes at him '… *I* did not say I was leaving immediately— I have not even proffered my resignation, even though that is my intention.'

His jaw squared. 'I inferred as much from your previous comment.'

Clipped and dismissive. No hint of the man who had sounded so desperate to stop her leaving when he spoke to George. She moistened her lips and her hand rose of its own volition to touch Mama's ring, concealed beneath her bodice, giving her courage.

Her chin lifted higher, pride driving her on. 'Then I congratulate you on your perspicacity, sir…at least in *certain* matters. You are correct, and I therefore now tender my resignation, effective immediately. Miss Strong has agreed to teach the boys until you are able to appoint a new governess.'

A single flicker of the eyelid was his only reaction. 'Might I ask why the haste?'

She searched his expression but saw no hint of dismay at the news her departure was imminent.

'You and I both know it is for the best after what happened between us the other evening.'

'Then marry me.' He gathered her hands in his. 'We would not have to deny ourselves. Think of the advantages.'

Yet another blow to her heart and yet another good reason why she was doing the right thing. Better to leave now than risk falling any deeper in love with him. And if she were to marry, better to find a man she liked and could respect. She might not experience the highs of love, but at least she'd be spared the lows.

Her voice chilled. 'I have already told you I have no

wish to be married simply for the sake of your children. Allow me to add neither do I harbour any ambition to be wed simply to provide a convenient bedfellow for my husband. I deserve better.'

His expression shuttered. He dropped her hands and turned away. Dismissing her. 'I see. Well, I cannot deny my disappointment you fail to appreciate the benefits of my proposal. You have made your wishes crystal clear and it would be wrong of me to persist in any attempt to change your mind.'

His indifference was proof enough to Leah she had done the right thing, and it confirmed the glimpses of fire and longing she had seen in him were merely the frustration of a widower with no outlet for his physical needs. And that, to her, was probably a worse reason for marrying a man than to be a surrogate mother for his children.

There was nothing more to say.

'I will tell the boys now.' Her throat ached at the thought. How could she explain it to them? She resolutely consoled herself with thoughts of her new family. 'I shall leave tomorrow, if I may beg the use of the carriage as far as Bristol.'

'How will you get to London?'

He didn't seem to notice she hadn't told him her ultimate destination. That had come from George. But she had not the heart to challenge him on that fact. It was all too much.

'I shall purchase a ticket on the London stagecoach, of course.'

'No.' He faced her, his features harsh. 'You will not travel alone in a public conveyance. The carriage will take you all the way. I shall instruct Travers. And you will take a maid with you. You are a respectable woman, and your reputation must be protected.'

The relief was huge—she had quailed at the thought of how she would cope with such a lengthy journey, all alone. She had never in her life travelled so far from the West Country.

'Thank you. I am grateful. I will, of course, reimburse all costs.'

'You will not.' His face softened. 'Allow me to do this for you, Leah. Please.'

She forced her smile. 'Thank you. I accept.' She walked to the door, but paused before opening it. She looked back at him, her heart breaking but, still, that foolish hope flickering deep inside, fanned anew by his urge to protect her on that journey. She could not resist a final challenge. If she never saw him again, what would one more slice of humiliation matter?

'If you should decide you want me for the *right* reasons, my lord, you know where I will be.'

## Chapter Eighteen

Leah stepped down from Dolph's carriage and peered up at the town house that would be her home for the next few months. Despite the anguish of leaving Dolphin Court—and the heart-wrenching memories of the tear-stained faces of Stevie and Nicky, and their sobbing pleas for her not to leave—she had worked hard not to dwell on what she was leaving behind during the carriage ride to London, instead setting her thoughts firmly on the future.

*Her* future. Her half-sisters. The new life that awaited her.

That was the only way to banish the memory of Dolph and his kisses, that awful proposal, and his utter lack of emotion as he bid her goodbye. She was grateful to him for the comfort of her journey, however, so she would not become bitter that a man she had fallen in love with did not feel the same way towards her. That thoughtfulness—to send her to London in his own carriage, with the maid, Sally, to lend her respectability—confirmed her basic instinct that Dolph was a good man. Sally's presence had also stopped Leah brooding, helping her control her misery, and now they had arrived, she couldn't deny the thrill of excitement that raced through her at what was to come.

The coachmen unloaded Leah's trunk as the front door opened to reveal a nondescript man with mousy hair and a prominent nose, dressed in a black tailcoat. His sharp gaze took them all in, and then he bowed to Leah.

'Miss Thame? We have been expecting you.' Before leaving Dolphin Court, Leah had written to Aurelia to tell her she was on her way. 'I am Vardy, your butler.'

Two footmen hurried out past him to collect Leah's trunk and carry it inside.

'I am pleased to meet you, Vardy.'

'Will your people require accommodation?' He eyed the carriage. 'I'm afraid we cannot stable the horses—there's only the two stalls in the mews.'

'Don't you worry about us, miss,' Travers said. 'His Lordship said we was to put up at his town house for the night. It's closed up, but there's a caretaker there and we'll make do for one night, never fear.'

'Thank you.' Leah looked from one to the other, all faces grown familiar to her, and tears prickled behind her eyes. 'I am grateful for all your help on the journey.'

She fumbled in her reticule and withdrew some coins to give to the three. 'In appreciation. Thank you again. And goodbye.'

A parting less painful than that with the boys. Or, even worse, with Dolph—although the memory of his shuttered expression fired her determination to forget all about him as soon as she could. Her heart might have been torn into pieces, but he showed no remorse at losing her. Decent man or not, that proposal really had been all about her staying for the sake of the children. She welcomed the hot flare of anger inside—anger she would need to help her put the past behind her without too many backward glances.

The carriage rattled away, and she followed Vardy along the entrance hall and up the stairs.

'Mrs Butterby and Miss Croome are in the drawing room.' He opened a door off the landing. 'Miss Thame has arrived, ma'am.'

He stood aside, and Leah—her insides a tangle of nerves—walked into a pleasant room with high windows and decorated in shades of gold and green. Her nerves soon disappeared as Aurelia crossed the room with her hands outstretched. She looked altogether different from the gaunt, dull-haired woman Leah had met in the solicitor's office just under five weeks ago. Now her fair hair shone, her hollow cheeks had filled, her skin glowed and her high-necked morning dress with blue bodice and blue and white striped skirt accentuated her blue eyes. She looked every inch the Society lady and Leah felt dowdy in comparison.

'Leah! I am so pleased you are come at last. Come and meet Mrs Butterby, our chaperone. I warn you, she takes her role *very* seriously,' she added in a whisper, rolling her eyes.

Leah peered over her half-sister's shoulder at the elegant grey-haired lady standing by the sofa. The name Butterby had conjured up a plump, motherly figure vastly different from this slender, unsmiling female.

She switched her gaze back to her sister, contentment spreading through her. 'I am happy to meet you again, Aurelia. Thank you for the welcome.'

Daringly, she kissed Aurelia's cheek, breathing in an exotic, spicy scent that conjured up images of faraway lands, colour and sunshine.

'And, Mrs Butterby.' She crossed the drawing room

to the lady and, not knowing quite what would be expected, bobbed a curtsy. 'Thank you for taking on the role of our chaperone.'

The lady's smile was unexpectedly sweet, relieving the severity of her face as her eyes crinkled at the corners. Leah immediately felt more at ease.

'I am happy to meet you, Miss Thame. And Aurelia is correct—' a censorious look was levelled at Aurelia, who elevated one perfectly arched eyebrow in response '—I do take my role seriously. It is my ambition to see you all successfully wed by the end of the Season and, to that end, you will both do well to remember I have cultivated the hearing of a bat, the eyes of a hawk and a nose for trouble—essential attributes for a chaperone with three wealthy young ladies' reputations to protect.'

Leah caught a second eye-roll from Aurelia and bit back a smile. Battle lines, it seemed, had already been drawn between them. She could hardly blame Aurelia for being put out when she, like Leah, had been earning her own way in life—she would understandably chafe at such restrictions. For her own part, Leah did not much care. She had no desire to go out there and flirt with various men. Mentally, she wafted away the black cloud that descended whenever her thoughts drifted in Dolph's direction. Soon, she hoped, she would feel genuine enthusiasm for the Season ahead instead of the fake excitement she must project to the world to disguise her inner heartache.

'And, speaking of reputations, I ought to forewarn you, Miss Thame—Lady Tregowan's will, and the identity of the beneficiaries, has been the gossip *du jour* from the moment of Aurelia's arrival. I counsel you to keep the details of your paternity a secret, however. An air of mystery will do none of you any harm and the truth that you are half-sisters might well blight your chances with some of the most eligible gentlemen.'

Leah disliked the idea of hiding her relationship to her half-sisters but, seeing Aurelia's quick shake of the head, she said nothing. For the moment.

'Have either of you heard from Beatrice?' she said instead. 'Do you know when she is likely to arrive in London?'

'No.' Mrs Butterby frowned. 'I hope she will arrive soon—we have all manner of appointments with mantua-makers, milliners and dancing masters, and the later she arrives, the more of a rush it will be to prepare her for when the Season proper begins. As it is, she will miss out on the earlier entertainments. There are already a few families in Town, and I expect invitations to start to arrive as soon as word spreads about three heiresses on the hunt for a husband.'

*On the hunt for a husband...* What a dreadful phrase. What a dreadful prospect.

'Shall I ring for refreshments? I dare say you are fatigued after your long journey, Miss Thame.'

'Oh, please. Call me Leah. Every time I hear Miss Thame, I am transported straight back to the schoolroom, and I intend to leave all memory of my time as a governess in the past.'

Surreptitiously, she crossed her fingers, praying that if she told herself that enough times, it would be true.

'Leah. Thank you. Although I shall stick to the formalities in public.'

'Of course. Might I freshen up first? I feel decidedly grubby.'

'I asked the kitchen to heat water ready for you. Come. I shall show you up to your bedchamber.' Aurelia headed for the door. 'Your maid will have unpacked your trunk by now, I dare say.'

'My *maid*?'

'Yes indeed.' Mrs Butterby's eyes twinkled. 'If you are to take the *ton* by storm, you will, first and foremost, need to look the part. Unless you wish to spend hours coaxing your own hair into the latest fashionable style?'

'Of course.'

Life would be easier if she agreed to everything until she worked out which aspects of this new life suited her and which did not. It would take time to become used to the fact she was a wealthy woman and, as such, in control of her own life. Until she married, that was. *If* she married. She had already decided she would not wed just any man for the sake of it because, if that was to be her fate, why would she not have accepted Dolph?

*Except you already love him. And he still loves Rebecca. That is why.*

Nevertheless, she would try to find a husband to suit her—a man she could respect and with whom she could be comfortable. Life might not reach the peaks of excitement with such a spouse, but she would at least be protected from the despair that would result from her loving too much and him too little.

She joined Aurelia and followed her upstairs to the second floor.

'My bedchamber and one other overlook the street, so we put you in that one,' Aurelia said. 'Beatrice's room and Prudence's are at the back.'

The name Prudence conjured up a picture of Nicky and his pony, now renamed Swift. It felt as though a knife stabbed her through the heart, but Leah forced a laugh. 'Prudence?'

Aurelia's blue eyes narrowed. 'What's wrong?'

Leah shook her head. 'Nothing. I—I used to know someone called Prudence, that's all.'

'And is *Prudence* the reason you crossed your fingers when you claimed you wished to leave all memories of your time as a governess in the past?'

*I shall have to take care around Aurelia. She is altogether too perceptive.*

'I don't know what you mean.' Leah swallowed. 'Is Prudence Mrs Butterby's name?'

'Clever diversionary tactic there, Leah. And yes, although she has not suggested I use it, so I don't call her that to her face.' An impish grin lit Aurelia's face. 'One has to take one's pleasure where one may.' She winked. 'Here we are.' She opened a door. 'My bedchamber is next to yours.'

Leah stepped inside a room decorated with a trailing light pink and green floral-design wallpaper. Two tall windows were dressed with rose-coloured curtains that matched the drapes around the bed and the eiderdown. Matching walnut furniture, including a wardrobe, chest of drawers, washstand and dressing table, was placed around the walls, and a gently steaming jug and a basin stood on the washstand, ready for Leah to wash. Her trunk was already empty, and a dark-haired woman of around five-and-forty was placing Leah's clothing in the drawers. She turned as they entered and curtsied.

'Good afternoon, miss. I am Faith, your lady's maid.'

Her gaze travelled over Leah from head to foot and back again, making Leah squirm as she imagined the thoughts running through Faith's head. No doubt she would regret not having a rewarding subject like Aurelia to dress. She drew herself up to her full height.

'I am pleased to meet you, Faith.' Leah turned to Aurelia. 'Thank you. If you will excuse me, I should like to

wash and to change my gown. I'll join you in the drawing room shortly.'

Aurelia smiled. 'I am glad you've arrived, Leah. I'm
looking forward to getting to know you.'

Faith helped Leah to remove her carriage gown.
'Which gown shall I lay out, miss?'

'The green muslin, please.' Leah washed her hands
and face, and then, enjoying the warm water on her skin,
she stroked the washcloth over her bare arms and legs.

'Have you only just started here, Faith, or did you work
for Lady Tregowan before?'

'Mrs Butterby appointed me a fortnight ago, miss.
Me and Maria, who will be Miss Fothergill's maid when
she arrives. Bet started earlier—she is working for Miss
Croome.' Faith had found Leah's muslin and laid it on the
bed. 'This colour must suit you very well, miss, if you
don't mind me saying? It will bring out your eyes—such
a lovely colour, they are. And it'll be a stunning contrast
with your hair.'

She handed Leah a towel. Leah dried her face, then
patted her limbs dry before handing it back, Faith's words
running through her head the entire time.

'Red hair is unfashionable,' she ventured.

Faith cocked her head to one side. 'In my book, to
be different is a good thing. All those young misses…
they are like peas in a pod! You… Look at you, miss. I
count myself lucky to have you rather than Miss Croome.
Golden hair? Pah! You are tall. Slim. Elegant. Your hair
is stunning, and your eyes are amazing. We will work
to make the most of you, and you will end up the toast
of the Season. You see if I am not right.'

*I don't want to be the toast of the Season. I want
Dolph!*

Would pain slash at her every time he entered her

thoughts? Would she ever forget him? She turned to the dressing table. 'Well, I count myself lucky to have you too, Faith. You have bolstered my confidence no end. Thank you.'

'Ah, bless you, miss. I love my job…' Faith moved behind Leah and began to unpin and then brush out her hair. Leah closed her eyes, enjoying the luxury of someone else teasing out the tangles. 'I used to work for Lady Yeovil,' Faith continued, 'until she passed away. She was also, as they say, not in the common way, but in her heyday the gentlemen buzzed around her like bees around blossom.'

The remainder of the afternoon was spent being lectured by Mrs Butterby on all aspects of tonnish life. Aurelia—having, as she said, heard it all before—soon excused herself, claiming she wanted to read her book in peace. Mrs Butterby watched her go.

'Really! She will be the death of me, that girl.'

'Why do you say that?'

'I know she is your half-sister, Leah, but she is determined not to accept my advice. Headstrong, that is what she is. I fear for her reputation—let alone her virtue—when she is let loose in Society.'

'Do not forget Aurelia has been looking after her own life—and virtue—since her mother died. I am sure she hears what you are saying, even if she appears unwilling to take your advice. I'm certain your fears are unfounded.'

'I hope you are right. I am keen to see all three of you happily settled, that is all. Do not misunderstand me, Leah. I like Aurelia. She has a quick mind and she is a beautiful woman. But she is stubborn; she has a sharp tongue at times; and she is, I find, guarded. Mayhap she will confide more in you, as you are nearer the same age. You might prove a calming influence on her.'

Leah intended to love Aurelia as her sister, whether or not she proved stubborn, sharp-tongued and secretive. She hoped they would also become friends.

The conversation then veered onto the coming Season. Later, when they were dining, Leah broached the subject of their unexpected inheritance.

'Will you tell us about Lady Tregowan, Mrs Butterby? Apologies if you have heard all this before, Aurelia, but I long to understand why she left her entire estate to three strangers. And why those particular conditions were included.'

'I have no objection,' said Aurelia.

'Very well,' said Mrs Butterby. 'Now, let me see… I lived with Lady Tregowan—Sarah—for many years. She took me on as her companion after Beatrice's mother left. Sarah was a semi-invalid following a bout of illness soon after she wed Lord Tregowan, hence her need for a companion. She didn't know the real reason for Beatrice's mother's departure until much later, when His Lordship confessed all to her.'

Mrs Butterby shook her head, her expression one of contempt. '*He* experienced an epiphany when he himself fell ill. He wanted to clear his conscience before meeting his maker, and so he did just that, with no regard for the pain it would cause Sarah. He did not say it directly, but the implication was it was *her* fault he had strayed because she was unable to give him children. And nothing I said could shake her of the belief she was responsible for the ruin of your mothers' lives.'

*Always the woman's fault!* Sympathy for Lady Tregowan and both anger and shame for her father filled

Leah. 'And so she thought to make amends by leaving us money?'

'Yes. Eventually. It was Aurelia's circumstances that prompted her to act.'

'Not that Her Ladyship ever set eyes on me that I know of,' Aurelia said. 'All I knew of her was as a lady who came to our milliner's shop in Bath once. I was not there, but I remember Mama telling me and hoping she would become a regular client. But she never came back.'

'She rarely went out and therefore had little need for new hats,' said Mrs Butterby. 'But that was not when she altered her will. After His Lordship died—eight years ago, now—Sarah discovered the circumstances of all of you and, as none of you appeared wanting, it never occurred to her to intervene. But then she grew sicker. We leased a house in Bath for the winter months in order that she could take the waters regularly and, while there, we learned of Aurelia's mother's death, which had left Aurelia in difficult circumstances.'

Aurelia hunched a shoulder but offered no clarification. Leah hoped to find out more as they became closer.

'You say she altered her will,' Leah said. 'But who were the original beneficiaries?'

'The current Lord Tregowan. He inherited the title and the entailed estates when your father died, but Falconfield and this house were unentailed and your father left them to his widow.'

'The current Lord Tregowan?' Leah frowned. 'But... she must have experienced a sudden change of heart, for is it not Tregowan we are forbidden to marry?'

'It is.' Mrs Butterby sighed, laid down her knife and fork, and leaned back in her chair. 'It all happened very quickly. One thing on top of the other. Do not misunderstand me—what I am about to say does not mean I disapprove of you inheriting Sarah's estate, but the decision to change her will was made rather hastily.

'After learning Aurelia was in dire straits, she sent a man to find out how both you and Beatrice were faring, Leah. He reported back that the man who had raised Beatrice had died, leaving her nothing, and she now relied on the charity of her brother, and that you, Leah, were earning your living as a governess, and had been dismissed from a previous job after kissing the son of your employers.'

Leah's face heated. 'That was not the whole story,' she protested.

'It never is,' said Mrs Butterby, not unkindly. 'Sarah fretted so, fearing that any one of you—or all of you— would follow in your mothers' footsteps. She became obsessed with how she could stop that happening.

'Then she learned Lord Tregowan was in financial difficulties, and it was rumoured he had substantial gambling debts. You must understand, Sarah loved Falconfield Hall. She grew up there. She brought it to the marriage as part of her dowry, and she spent almost her entire married life living there. She hated Tregowan, which is in Cornwall, and very remote. It was Tregowan where Sarah fell ill and, rightly or wrongly, she always blamed the place, flatly refusing to live there afterwards.

'It was the only thing they ever argued about. His Lordship wanted to sell Falconfield to raise funds to invest in Tregowan, but Sarah stood firm and he, in the end, gave in to her. She was adept at using her poor health to get her own way, and I do believe he felt guilty that she contracted her illness at Tregowan.

'Sarah convinced herself the current Lord Tregowan would sell Falconfield to pay off his gambling debts and to invest in Tregowan, and she couldn't bear the idea after she had fought so hard against it. She hoped one of you would fall in love with Falconfield and would make it your marital home.'

'Is that the reason why we must give first refusal to the others should one of us—or our husbands—decide to sell our share?' asked Leah.

'Yes. She had a new will drawn up straight away. She would not even wait to consult the solicitors who had acted for Lord Tregowan but used a firm in Bath. She signed it and gave it to me to have delivered to Henshaw and Dent in Bristol, but I delayed, fearing she might change her mind again. Two days later, she died, quite unexpectedly even though she had been ill. Her heart, the physician said.' She paused, to swallow some wine.

'And the other conditions?' Leah asked. 'Why were they included?'

'It was her way of ensuring you did not fall from grace, as your mothers did.'

'Fall from grace?' Aurelia's eyes narrowed. 'How dare she? Her husband had a role in every one of those seductions. *He* knew what he was doing whereas my mother, at least, was young, unworldly and innocent. She was seventeen years old when I was born. Seventeen!'

Mrs Butterby held up her hands in a gesture of calm. 'I am aware of it, my dear. Please believe me. But Sarah… As I said, she was somewhat obsessed. She was housebound. Bedridden for much of the time. She had little else to occupy her thoughts.'

'That explains the stipulation we must marry,' Leah said, 'but why the insistence on our spending the Season in London?'

'It was to give you all the best chance of finding a good husband.'

'Good?' Aurelia's laugh was bitter. 'Aristocrats who

care for nothing other than their own pleasures; who freely spend money they do not have, and care not how many debts they leave in their wake; aristocrats with their inherent belief in their own superiority over the rest of us. I do not consider men like that to be "good".'

Leah gripped her hands together under the cover of the table. Dolph was not like that—superior, and obsessed with money and status. Was he?

*No. He cannot be, or he would not have offered for me, a lowly governess.*

Even though his offer was for the wrong reasons.

'They are not all tarnished with arrogance and greed,' said Mrs Butterby quietly, 'just as not all poor people are dirty, lazy and feckless. There are good and bad individuals in every walk of life. Look at Lady Tregowan— would she have even considered your fate if she had been as you described?'

Aurelia lowered her gaze to her empty plate. Leah wondered even more what Aurelia's experiences had been. It was clear there was a great deal of anger locked inside her, and she hoped the challenge of getting to know and understand her prickly half-sister would help to distract her from the fact her heart had been torn into pieces.

## Chapter Nineteen

Tomorrow would be one week since Leah left Dolphin Court but, to Dolph, it felt like a year. Miss Strong had stepped in to teach the boys, and her father had turned up trumps when he'd suggested his cousin, Miss Pike, for the role of governess. Dolph had interviewed her, liked her, and she was due to arrive tomorrow to take up her post.

Today was therefore Miss Strong's last day in charge of the boys, and Dolph found himself walking with her to the stables after lessons had ended for the day—she to be driven home by a groom and Dolph to ride out with Stevie and Nicky on their new ponies. The boys had raced ahead to the stables and were already lost to sight—their daily ride with Dolph and Frinton had become the highlight of their days, but they still missed Leah and talked about her incessantly, oblivious to their father's heartache and how every time her name was mentioned another fragment was ripped from his soul.

'Well, Miss Strong—how are the boys coming along with their lessons?'

Dolph had ceased to visit the schoolroom daily, with the excuse his presence at lessons would make Miss Strong uncomfortable. But the truth was that the schoolroom reminded him too much of Leah at a time he strove with every fibre of his being to forget her.

'They keep asking when Leah is coming home, my lord.'

His stomach clenched. 'I have explained to them Miss Thame had to leave and they know Miss Pike is due to arrive tomorrow. They will soon settle down.'

Out of the corner of his eye he saw Miss Strong frown. 'I hope you are right. I am sure the boys will like Cousin Miriam, but that won't stop them missing Leah.'

They reached the stables where the buggy was waiting, and Dolph handed Miss Strong up next to the groom. 'I thank you for all your help, Miss Strong. I very much appreciate you standing in at such short notice.'

She studied him for a long moment, the minuscule lift of her eyebrows enough for him to understand she probably agreed with George he had been a fool to let Leah go, let alone aid her by sending her to London in his carriage.

*What else could I have done? I proposed. She refused me. I could hardly force her to the altar!*

'Good afternoon, my lord.'

The groom slapped the reins on the pony's broad back, and the buggy set off on the short drive back to the village, leaving Dolph to continue his silent argument with himself. He had only proposed for the boys' sake—his children were his priority now. And although he would have been happy had Leah accepted his offer, he still thought she was better off without him.

*I don't deserve to be happy, not after what happened to Rebecca.*

'Milord?'

Frinton was in front of him, holding both his own and Dolph's horses, with Steven and Nicholas already mounted on Falcon and Swift. Dolph shook his head clear of arguments, regrets, and memories of both Rebecca and Leah, and quickly mounted up.

Upon their return, as they walked back to the house from the stables, Nicky ran on ahead, but Stevie stayed back to walk beside Dolph.

'Papa? I should like to ask you a question.'

'Go ahead. I shall do my best to answer it.'

'It is about Miss Thame.'

Dolph's heart sank. Was everyone in a conspiracy to ensure he could not forget her? 'What about her, Stevie?'

'Well… I do not understand.' Stevie's forehead wrinkled in thought. 'Mama died and left us, so I know you cannot bring her home again. But Miss Thame did not die. So why did she leave us? Does she not love us any longer?'

'Of course she still loves you, Stevie, but sometimes life changes and grown-ups must do things they would rather not do.'

'Can't you bring her home, Papa? She will listen to you. I tried to tell her not to leave, but she still went.'

'You will have a new governess tomorrow, Stevie. And you will soon love Miss Pike just as much as you did Miss Thame.'

*I won't, though.*

That thought stabbed Dolph, bringing him to an abrupt halt. He could not catch his breath… Where had that come from? He missed Leah, yes. He'd been attracted to her, physically. He'd enjoyed her company. But…*love*?

'Papa?'

With an effort, Dolph took in Steven's upturned face, his expression anxious.

'Why have you stopped? You look funny. What's wrong?'

'Nothing, son. Nothing is wrong. Come. Cassie is waiting for us.'

Dolph pointed at the front door, where Cassie—Tilly in her arms—was standing with Nicky. Wolf was there too, his tail waving. For one brief second Dolph's mind played a trick on him, and it was Leah who stood there, holding Tilly. Then Wolf barked and bounded to meet them, and the vision cleared.

*Love, though. Could it be? Truly?*

Dolph placed his hand on Stevie's shoulder and urged him on, even as his spirits soared, energised by that revelation. Was it love he felt for Leah? How had he not realised? Then, as quickly as joy and hope erupted through him, it subsided. What difference did it make? She'd gone. He fended Wolf away automatically as the great dog bounced around him and Steven, and as they reached the front door, Dolph concentrated on his children. *They* were what was important.

*But they love Leah, too. If I can persuade her to come home...*

*No! You don't deserve it. Not after what you did...*

He shook his head to clear it again. Tilly was reaching out to him, her chubby cheeks beaming, and his heart flipped in his chest as he took her in his arms.

'Papa!' She squirmed and bent over his arm, her own arms straining towards Wolf. 'Papa. Woof!'

Dolph crouched down and Tilly giggled as Wolf licked her cheek. Several minutes later, having carried Tilly up to the nursery with Cassie and the children, Dolph—Wolf padding behind him—descended the stairs again. He paused at the foot and gazed around as if seeing the house for the first time. It was still his home, but now it felt as though some of the heart and soul of the place had gone with Leah.

'Dolph! There you are. Why are you standing there like a mooncalf? Come in here. I need to talk to you.'

Glad of the interruption to his melancholy thoughts, Dolph followed George into the drawing room.

'What is it, George?' Dolph took up his customary stance by the fireplace as George sat on the sofa. Wolf stretched out before the fire with a contented sigh.

'The new woman arrives tomorrow, doesn't she?'

'Indeed she does.'

'So you have no excuse not to go to London and persuade Miss Thame to come home.'

Dolph's heart lurched. *Home?* He blanked his expression and stared at his friend. 'What nonsense is this, George? As you just pointed out, the new governess arrives tomorrow.'

'All the more incentive for you to persuade Miss Thame to return as your wife.'

'My *wife*?'

Emotion churned in the pit of Dolph's belly. George watched him patiently, and it occurred to Dolph his friend had changed over the past weeks. He was more thoughtful. Less erratic. More settled, somehow.

'If you recall, I did propose to her—at your suggestion—and she refused me.'

'You must have made a pig's ear of it, old fellow, for it was crystal clear she held a *tendre* for you and you for her. Did you declare your feelings for her?'

'Declare…? No! I was not…am not…in love with her.' His denial came automatically, but his doubts were already mushrooming. 'If you are so eager for a wedding, George, why do you not follow your own advice and propose to Miss Strong?'

George grinned, cocking his head to one side. 'Attack

is the best form of defence,' he murmured, before adding, 'Why did you let her go, Dolph?'

'I did not let her go. She went. There is a subtle difference.'

'You could have stopped her.'

'I tried!' Dolph pushed away from the mantel and took a hasty turn around the room, energy pumping through him as he fought the urge to unburden himself of all the contradictory thoughts that tangled his brain. No matter how George appeared to have altered, Dolph needed to work this out for himself.

'Try again. Go to London.'

'And repeat the mistake I made after Rebecca died? I abandoned the children immediately after I appointed Miss Thame. I will not do so again. The children will soon forget her.'

'Out of sight is out of mind?' George stood and brushed his hands down his breeches. Then he sighed and fixed Dolph with a knowing look. 'Any fool can see it's not only the children who are devastated by Miss Thame's departure.'

Dolph stiffened. 'I do not know what you mean.'

'I cannot make up my mind whether you lie to me or to yourself. It is time you stopped blaming yourself for Rebecca's death, my friend. Accidents happen. It was nobody's fault.'

*It was! It was my fault.*

'Will you spend the rest of your life denying yourself happiness? Do you really imagine Rebecca would want you to keep punishing yourself?'

Dolph shook his head in denial. 'You are talking nonsense. It is the children who are important... It is they to whom I must make amends, for abandoning them in their hour of need.'

'And yet it is the children who are suffering now. Why continue with this pretence? I swear I do not understand you, Dolph.' George gripped him by the shoulders. 'Face up to the truth, man. Even I can see the heart has gone out of you since Miss Thame left. There is no shame in it. If you love her, go after her and tell her before it is too late.' He released Dolph and stepped back. 'There. I have said my piece. I can do no more. I shall go and change for dinner.'

He paused after opening the door and looked back.

'You're a stubborn fool, Dolph. Do not lose this chance for you and the children—*and* Miss Thame—to find happiness.'

He left the room, leaving Dolph staring after him, dumbstruck. George… *George*…had recognised the depth of his feelings for Leah while he, Dolph, had remained blind. He slumped on the sofa. But George did not know the truth about Rebecca. No one knew but Dolph. If only he could understand why she'd taken her own life, maybe he could change. Wolf, who had lain quietly till now, scrambled to his feet. He laid his head on Dolph's knee, and Dolph fondled his ears and smoothed his domed head.

'I miss her, Wolf.' He cradled the dog's head between his hands and spoke to those trusting brown eyes. 'Why is life so complicated? I wish Herr Lueger were here. I wish there were someone I could unburden myself to.' He smiled then, at Wolf. 'Other than a dog, of course.'

Loneliness rose up to swamp him, and he could feel tears scald his eyes. The elderly Austrian's long-ago words sounded in his head.

*'You bury your feelings. You shut them away. You believe you have dealt with them, never to bother you again, but I tell you that is not so, my friend. You simply delay*

*the time you must face what happened and the guilt you carry. I was not there. I cannot tell you this is the truth or that is the truth. Only you can know that, and only you can decide to forgive yourself for your part.'*

Wolf pressed forward and licked Dolph's chin.

'Only I can know, and only I can decide.' Still those internal arguments raged in his head. 'How can I risk history repeating itself, Wolf? What if I married Leah and then drove her to suicide? Isn't it better for the children—and me—to lose her this way than to risk that?'

He leaned forward to bury his face in Wolf's thick fur, drawing comfort from him but no nearer a solution. After several minutes, he rose to his feet and made his weary way up the stairs to change his clothes for dinner.

In London, the days passed in a whirlwind of shopping, dressmakers, dancing lessons and promenading or driving in Hyde Park in the late afternoon. Leah and Aurelia were introduced to the members of polite society who were already in Town, and invitations to suppers, card parties and soirées began to arrive.

Leah's confidence had grown in the week since she'd arrived—wearing the right gown for the right occasion, and wearing colours and styles that suited her, whether or not those colours and styles were the height of fashion, boosted her self-esteem. Faith had proved herself invaluable, especially with her skill in styling Leah's hair, pinning it up in a soft chignon and allowing gently waving tendrils of hair—'*Not* ringlets, miss. They are not for you!'—to frame and soften her face.

It was all new and exciting, and Leah worked hard to convince herself she was happy. But she could not quite control the skip of her heart whenever she spied a dark-haired gentleman of a certain height, nor the plunge of her spirits when that same gentleman turned to reveal the face of a stranger.

She missed Dolph; missed him with a visceral ache that only deepened as the days passed. She had thought... *hoped*...that pain would lessen. She had thought her memories of him would start to fade—that the novelty of being in London and of meeting so many new people and of participating in so many new experiences would slowly push all thought of Dolph to the back of her mind. She was wrong.

The constant effort of hiding her erratic changes in mood exhausted her, but she told herself it was worth it to escape sharp eyes of her half-sister, who was the one bright spot in her life. The two had grown closer, encouraging and advising one another on their shopping trips, and giggling together—in private, for Mrs Butterby was always on hand to nip any hint of public unladylike behaviour in the bud—at some of the more outrageous fashions and customs of the *beau monde*.

But Leah soon learned her acting skills were not enough to fool Aurelia. She'd known her sister was observant but, as the days passed and Aurelia said nothing, she believed she had succeeded in fooling her as well as Mrs Butterby.

'I *told* you Prudence would find some arrogant lord to introduce us to,' grumbled Aurelia one evening as she and Leah entered the drawing room and waited for the tea tray to be delivered. They had just arrived home from the theatre, and Mrs Butterby, pleading fatigue, had gone straight to bed. 'She watches us like a hawk. There is never any chance to meet any suitors other than those *she* deems suitable. The theatre was the perfect place to meet a wider variety of men, not just overprivileged aristocrats, half of whose pockets are to let in any case.'

Aurelia did not hide her contempt for the aristocracy from Leah, but she was single-minded in her pursuit of a wealthy husband—understandable when she had been all but penniless before inheriting her share of Lady Tregowan's fortune.

'She has our best interests at heart, Aurelia, and she does understand this world better than you or I.'

'Hmmph.' Aurelia moved to sit next to Leah on the sofa and took Leah's hand. 'I am pleased we are alone, for I should like to talk to you without fear she might overhear us.'

She sounded serious, with no hint of her usual slightly mocking tone. Leah waited, hoping Aurelia would finally trust Leah enough to open up about her past. Mrs Butterby's suggestion that Aurelia was not a woman who easily shared confidences had proved correct, and Leah had been careful to curb her curiosity, wary of antagonising her secretive sister.

'I know we are still unfamiliar with one another, Leah, but we *are* sisters, and I want you to know I am here for you, if you wish to talk about whatever it is that haunts you.'

Leah straightened, instinctively preparing to deny it.

'No!' Aurelia raised her hand, palm forward. 'Do not pretend with me. You are unhappy. I see you when you think no one is watching you, so I say it again—if you wish to talk, I am here for you.' She flashed a smile. 'I can be discreet, you know.'

*Dolph.* Leah longed to pour out her despair. But she could not. It was too raw. Too recent. And Aurelia was too…unknown.

She changed the clasp of their hands, so she was holding Aurelia's.

'And I am also here for you, Aurelia, should *you* wish

to confide in *me*. I have noticed how you change the subject whenever your father is mentioned.'

'Ah.' The corner of Aurelia's mouth quirked up. 'The difference there, my dear sister, is I have no wish to share. The past is the past. May it remain there.'

'Very well. I thank you for your offer, and I shall bear it in mind should *I* wish to share.'

Aurelia laughed. 'Touché. And yet...' with her free hand she reached to brush a lock of hair back from Leah's forehead '... *I* am not haunted by my past. I do not retreat into *my* past and long for...something...from there to appear in my present.'

Leah flinched at the gentle understanding on her sister's face. She looked away. 'I cannot. Not yet.' Tears prickled her eyes and her throat constricted. She swallowed hard.

'Then I shall pry no further, my dear. Maybe, in time, we shall both welcome a confidante. Now, in the meantime...' Leah's hand was released. She swallowed again, making sure her emotions were under control, as Aurelia continued, '...*what* are we to do about Beatrice? Do you think we should write to her, despite what she said about her brother? I am worried we have heard nothing from her.'

'As am I. But as to what to do... I am not sure.' They had already discussed Beatrice's apparent fear of her brother. 'She was adamant we should not write to her, and I should hate to cause trouble for her.'

Aurelia sighed. 'I hate having to just sit here and *wait*, but maybe it is too soon to panic—it is still over four weeks to Eastertide. Oh! How I wish she would hurry up and join us. I cannot wait until we can openly acknowledge our connection.' She eyed Leah. 'You do still agree with me we should openly admit we are half-sisters?'

'Yes. Although not, of course, if Beatrice should object.'

They had agreed any acknowledgement must wait until Beatrice joined them and had her say, as any adverse reaction to the news would affect all three of them.

'I have a feeling Beatrice will be as eager as us to show the world we are proud to be sisters,' said Aurelia. 'Even in the face of Prudence's predictions of scandal and disaster.'

Leah laughed. 'She did not use quite such incendiary words, Aurelia. She fears the truth will put off many genuine gentlemen and leave us with hardened fortune hunters from whom to choose.'

'Well, if a little thing like that is enough to put off a gentleman, I do not think he would make a particularly good husband, do you? And it would mean a lifetime of lies to your spouse. Think of that. What if he discovered the truth after marriage?'

Janet, the maid, brought in the tea tray then, and Aurelia sprang up to pour them both a cup while Leah pondered her sister's words. How would Dolph have reacted had Leah told him the truth about her inheritance and her paternity? She absent-mindedly took the cup and saucer handed to her and sipped the hot tea, her head full of Dolph. Would he have changed his mind and withdrawn his proposal?

'There you go again.'

Leah jumped at Aurelia's softly spoken comment, feeling her cheeks heat.

'Where *do* you go inside your head, Leah? It does not make you happy.'

Leah shook her head, fearing if she spoke, the whole might flood out.

'I know I said I wouldn't pry, but…is it Lord Dol-

phinstone? Did you fall in love with him? Do not think I
haven't noticed you dropping his name into the conversation at odd moments—*Dolph says this; Dolph did that.*'

Hot embarrassment flooded Leah. *Do I do that?*

Aurelia sat next to Leah and put her arm around her.
'It is all right, Leah. I know you don't wish to talk about
it, but I will say the man is a fool to let such a diamond
slip through his fingers, and a fool such as that is not
worth a moment more of your regret.'

Leah felt Aurelia stroking her nape, and she realised
she had bowed her head.

'You will tell me one day, when you know I may be
trusted,' Aurelia whispered.

Leah firmed her jaw, then raised her head, forcing
her eyes open.

'Going back to Beatrice,' she said, 'do you think we
should go to her brother's house and bring her to London ourselves?'

'I don't know.' Aurelia nibbled one finger, her brow
puckering in thought. Then she directed a mischievous
grin at Leah. 'This may surprise you, but I think we
should discuss it with Prudence. If she agrees, we could
all go down to Somerset together.'

Leah laughed. 'I am *astonished* you might suggest
we talk to Prudence about *anything*, let alone Beatrice.'

The confinement of this life continued to chafe Aurelia, and her frustration was all too often targeted at
Mrs Butterby.

Aurelia huffed a laugh. 'I know our situation is not
her fault, but I cannot help being irritated by her determination to see us "marry well", as if good breeding is
the only essential measure of a suitable match. I tell you,
Leah, I should far prefer a man who has earned his position and wealth than one who merely inherited them,

but who is nonetheless convinced of his own superiority, and who will no doubt secretly despise me for the circumstances of my birth. There was no stipulation in Lady Tregowan's will as to what position in Society any husband must occupy, but Prudence is determined we marry into its upper ranks. Well, I do not know about you, but I can do without a spouse who will look down upon me throughout our marriage because of my birth.'

'Is that how your father treated your mother? And you?'

Leah was aware she had been fortunate. Papa and Mama had fallen in love, and their marriage had been happy. Her childhood had been happy.

Aurelia stiffened, her cheeks colouring. 'Did I say that?'

'There is no need to be defensive, Aurelia. *I* do not judge you. How could I?'

'Hmmph. I suppose not.' Her eyes remained downcast.

It was Leah's turn to comfort Aurelia. She put her arms around her and pulled her into a hug.

'We will each tell the other, one day.' She pressed a kiss to Aurelia's cheek. 'On the day we both fully believe the other may be trusted.'

## Chapter Twenty

Dolph stared helplessly at Steven's tear-drenched face. 'I must go, Stevie.' He rounded his desk, dropped to his knees, put his arms around his eldest son and pulled him in for a hug. Wolf, who had been snoring by the fire, lumbered to his feet and padded across to join in. 'But I won't leave until the beginning of next week, and I promise I will only be gone a matter of a week or so.'

He had finally accepted the truth. He loved Leah… had for a while, but he'd blinded himself to his feelings, dismissing them as lust, or friendship, or anything rather than admit the truth. And his reluctance to admit the truth was because he did not believe he deserved to be happy, as George had said. And now he had lost Leah, and he missed her more with every passing day. There was little point in regretting he had not spoken of love when he proposed—he had not been ready to confess his feelings to himself, let alone to her. But he was ready now, and the need to see her again and to be honest with her, to declare his love, was near overwhelming. He'd had to force himself to remain in Somerset—all the time frantic Leah would meet someone new—until the new governess had moved in and the boys settled into their new routine. Fortunately, Miss Pike had proved herself a gem almost immediately but, still, Dolph worried he'd left it too late or that she would refuse him again.

He took heart from her words: *If you should decide you want me for the right reasons, my lord, you know where I will be,* but he also faced the hard truth that, should she refuse him again—if he had hopelessly messed everything up by not being honest with her, let alone with himself—then his only option would be to return to Dolphin Court and to learn to live with his own failure. However much he loved Leah, he would not abandon his children again by spending weeks on end in London while he proved his love for her.

'But, Papa…'

A figure darkened the door of Dolph's study. 'Stevie! *There* you are. I am so sorry, my lord, but he slipped away when I was busy with Nicky.'

'It is quite all right, Miss Pike.' Dolph stood up, keeping one hand on Stevie's shoulder. 'Stevie and I have a few matters to discuss. I shall return him to the schoolroom when we are done.'

Miss Pike had only been with them six days, but the boys had taken to her immediately, helped by her one-eyed pet parrot, Horatio, who could say *Fiddlesticks* and *Stow it*, fascinating the boys, and who frequently terrorised poor Wolf, with its swooping, airborne attacks.

'Very well, my lord. I shall return to Nicky, or he will be up to some manner of mischief, I'll be bound.'

She flashed a smile and hurried away.

'Come, Stevie.' Dolph led his son to the chair by the hearth, sat down and lifted him onto his lap. 'Listen. It will not be like last time. You have my word as a gentleman I shall return as soon as I humanly can.'

Steven sat still for a few minutes, pouting. Then he

scrambled from Dolph's knee and stood to attention in front of him. 'Is it business, Papa?'

Love for his small solemn boy flooded Dolph. 'It is business of sorts, Stevie, yes.'

'In London?'

Dolph frowned. He had the feeling of walking into a verbal trap set by a seven-year-old. 'Ye-es.'

'I am your heir, Papa. I need to help with business. I shall come with you.'

'Stevie. That is imposs…' Dolph paused. It wasn't impossible. 'Do you know something, Stevie?' he said slowly. 'That is an excellent idea. We will all go to London. The whole family. And we won't wait until next week. We shall go tomorrow.'

'Hurrah! We're going to London.' Stevie capered around the room, Wolf prancing at his heels, his tail waving. 'Can we go and see Miss Thame, Papa?'

He should have foreseen it. His heart sank. How would they cope with seeing her again when they were only just getting used to her absence? Stevie halted in front of Dolph and patted his hand.

'Do not worry, Papa. We love Miss Thame, but we know she had to leave us. We won't get upset again, I promise.'

Dolph grabbed Stevie and hugged him close, not only to hide the tears in his eyes but also his grin of pure delight. How had he ever worried Steven was too sensitive and needed toughening up?

He told George he was going away after dinner that evening, after the servants had withdrawn and while they lingered over their port and cigars.

'I am pleased you are easier about leaving the children now,' said George. 'The boys have certainly taken to Miss Pike and her parrot—I never saw such looks of delight as on their faces when she descended from the post-chaise carrying its cage.'

'I am not leaving them. They are coming with me.'

George stared. 'You're a brave man, Dolph. Don't you remember the horror of that journey back from Hewton with their ponies?'

'Oh, I remember all right. That is why I hoped to prevail upon you to return to London too. I can keep you company in your carriage while the children, Miss Pike and Cassie occupy the other.'

'Ah.' George fell silent, staring at his glass while he twiddled it between his thumb and forefinger. 'The thing is, old fellow… I am not quite ready to go yet.'

Dolph waited, watching a succession of expressions flow across George's face. Eventually he looked up.

'You may take my carriage—it'll be more comfortable than all cramming into yours or hiring a post-chaise. Winters can return here for me. There's no rush…as long as you have no objection to my staying here?'

'Not at all.' Still Dolph waited, until the words burst from George in a torrent.

'You see…the thing is… I didn't expect… I never expected…' He snatched up his glass and gulped the remaining port in one swallow. 'I don't want to leave her, Dolph. I *cannot* leave her.'

'So…what do you intend to do about it, my friend?'

'I shall ask her to marry me.' George poured another measure into his glass and shook his head in disbelief. 'It very much looks as though we are both on the brink of entering the parson's mousetrap, Dolph.'

'In my case, there will be bridges to mend first. I can only hope I shall succeed.' He raised his glass. 'To you and Philippa, George. I hope you will be very happy together.'

'Thank you, my friend.' George's glass chinked against Dolph's. 'And, in my turn, a toast to wish you luck on your mission to repair those bridges in London.'

Two weeks to the day after Leah's arrival in London, Mrs Butterby suggested they take advantage of a dry afternoon by taking a drive in the Park in Lady Tregowan's barouche.

Barely had they arrived in Hyde Park when Aurelia said, 'May Leah and I walk for a spell, Mrs Butterby? The crowds are sparse enough that you won't lose sight of us.' Only then did she look at Leah and add, 'If you should like to walk with me, that is, Leah?'

'I shall be happy to.'

'Of course you may.' Mrs Butterby peered all around and then tutted. "Tis most vexing. Lord Sampford assured me he would ride in the Park this afternoon. Veryan too.' She sighed. 'Oh, well. 'Tis early yet... I dare say they will be here later.'

Leah smiled at their chaperone's disgruntled tone even as she wondered how long it would be before one of their approved admirers, such as Sampford or Veryan, joined them. Not long, she suspected—their possession of a tidy fortune each had guaranteed the persistent attention of several gentlemen of the *ton*. Mrs Butterby was kept on her toes warning the undesirables away, but both Sampford and Veryan had earned her approval as being suitable marriage prospects even though neither Leah nor Aurelia could stand either gentleman, whose conversation appeared to consist entirely of tittle-tattle.

Without warning, Dolph's image materialised in her mind's eye. *His* conversation had never been dull or trite.

She sucked in a deep breath, willing her emotions down, determined to reveal no sign of distress as she swallowed past the aching lump in her throat. When would it get easier, this sense of loss? She missed him. She missed the children. She missed her home. This—she cast a sweeping glance around the Park as she and Aurelia strolled, taking in the members of Polite Society who had already returned to Town and who, like them, were promenading in order to see and be seen—*this* was not what she wanted.

'Leah…' Aurelia halted and faced Leah, a tiny crease stitched between her fair brows. 'I wanted to talk to you alone… Oh! Not about your precious Dolph,' she added quickly. 'I promised, did I not? No. It is Beatrice. We can delay no longer… We *must* go down to Somerset to rescue her. I have an uneasy feeling, right here—' she pressed her hand to her midriff '—and it will not go away.'

'Rescue her? Do you imagine her brother has her locked away?'

'I would put nothing past him,' Aurelia said darkly. 'She was scared of him. I know she was.'

'Yes. I know it too. I am sorry. I have been preoccupied—it's almost a week since we agreed to talk to Prudence, isn't it? I quite forgot, I'm afraid.' Guilt curled through her. 'I have been selfish.'

Aurelia tucked her arm through Leah's, and they began to stroll once more. 'As you said, you have been preoccupied. We still have time.'

'Then we shall talk to Prudence today.' Leah's heart sank at the sight of two gentlemen on horseback. 'Uh-oh. Here are Veryan and Sampford. Prepare yourself for another sparkling display of wit and intelligence.'

Aurelia giggled. 'You wicked woman! You know you

ought to be grateful for their condescension in even noticing us.'

'Oh, I assure you, I am fully aware of the honour they do us,' Leah murmured.

They curtsied as Their Lordships halted their horses and bowed.

'Good afternoon, Miss Croome; Miss Thame. What a splendid afternoon for a stroll.'

Leah smiled dutifully. 'Splendid indeed, my lord.'

'You have escaped the clutches of the good Mrs Butterby today, I see.'

Veryan's patronising tone set Leah's teeth on edge.

'Not entirely,' Aurelia responded. 'She is being driven in the barouche. Miss Thame and I wished to enjoy a quiet stroll together.' She tilted her chin. 'So, if you will excuse us, we shall be on our way.'

'Now, now, Miss Croome. I know you do not mean it, for I am familiar with your teasing ways. Indeed, I have a fancy to take a stroll myself,' said Sampford. 'What say you, Veryan? Shall we take a turn about the Park with the ladies?'

Aurelia cast a speaking look at Leah as Their Lordships dismounted and handed their reins to the groom riding in their wake. Leah knew her sister was quite capable of sending this pair of peacocks packing, if Leah did but give her the nod. But even though she resented the interruption to their conversation, she was aware the Season had a long way to go yet, and there was little point in insulting prominent members of the *ton* just for the sake of it.

Their Lordships proffered an arm to each of the sisters. Leah sent a resigned smile to Aurelia before laying her hand upon Veryan's forearm. This might spell the end of their conversation about Beatrice, but she would not allow herself to become distracted from the subject again. How awful if they did nothing and Beatrice was in trouble.

As the four of them strolled, Leah directed her gaze straight ahead.

'Oh!' The exclamation escaped her before she could stop it.

'Are you well, Miss Thame?' Veryan laid his hand over hers and squeezed it solicitously. 'Shall I summon your chaperone?'

'No. Indeed, I am well, my lord.' Leah could not tear her attention from the figure approaching them. His head was tilted down, and the brim of his hat was low so she could not fully distinguish his features, but the set of those shoulders...the power of those breeches-clad thighs striding along... She swallowed, her pulse fluttering. *Could it be?*

Veryan followed her gaze. 'Well,' he tittered, looking past Leah to Lord Sampford, 'Dolphinstone's vow to shun Society did not last long, did it? I wonder what could possibly have prompted him to come up to Town so soon after losing his governess?'

Leah cringed inside. She knew what he implied—she'd made no secret she'd worked as a governess, most recently for Dolph, and she'd heard the snide comments as to why he had let an heiress such as her slip through his fingers. But she would not gratify Veryan by rising to his sly dig.

Not so Aurelia. 'What is it you imply, sir?' Her eyes snapped fire.

Veryan smiled mockingly. 'Nothing that need concern you, my dear.'

'Then you should not have mentioned it,' said Aurelia. 'It was impolite.'

Leah caught Veryan's barely disguised smirk, and anger at his superiority roiled her insides. No wonder Aurelia resented these arrogant aristocrats. And then her fury was further fuelled by anger at Dolph for breaking his word by leaving the children again.

Dolph nodded at Sampford and Veryan but clearly had no intention of stopping. Then his gaze met Leah's, and shock flashed across his expression before he successfully blanked it. He halted, raised his hat and bowed, his jaw muscles bunched, brows low over frowning eyes.

'Well met, Miss Thame.'

Leah curtsied, determinedly blanking her own expression. 'My lord.'

'You are in good health?'

'I am. Thank you.' She longed to demand why he had left the children, but refrained, knowing any hint of discord between them would only encourage further gossip. 'Will you allow me to introduce Miss Aurelia Croome?'

'Indeed. I am pleased to meet you, Miss Croome.' Dolph's smile did not reach his eyes.

Aurelia curtsied, her smile equally cool. 'I am fascinated to meet you, my lord, after hearing so much about Miss Thame's life at Dolphin Court.'

Dolph's eyes narrowed and he shot a questioning glance at Leah. Who lifted her chin. Dolph's jaw firmed again.

'If you will excuse me, I have a meeting I must attend.' He studied Leah, and she felt her colour rise. 'I shall call on you if I may?'

Leah dropped a curtsy. 'Of course, my lord.'

She did not turn to watch as he walked away although every fibre of her being screamed at her to do so…to run after him…to know why he was here. Instead, she battened down her emotions and set herself to the interminable exchange of small talk that passed for entertainment in Polite Society.

## Chapter Twenty-One

'Are you all right?' Aurelia whispered to Leah twenty minutes later, after Sampford and Veryan delivered them back to Mrs Butterby. They were already seated side by side on the backward-facing seat, opposite their chaperone, who was distracted as she ascertained Their Lordships' attendance at Lady Todmorden's rout that evening. 'You have been so quiet, and you look even paler than usual.'

Leah merely nodded. The effort of concealing her shock from their escorts had left her with a mouth too dry and brain far too jumbled to trust herself to say anything. Aurelia squeezed her hand and Leah desperately tried to calm her breathing as she pushed aside her conjectures—and, to her dismay, her *hopes*—as to why Dolph was here, in London.

'Thank goodness *that* ordeal is over,' Aurelia declared as the barouche pulled away. 'Do you think they have any notion how exceedingly *tedious* their conversation is?'

'Aurelia! Please!' Mrs Butterby indicated Hall, who was driving the barouche. 'You do not wish for such opinions to become common knowledge.'

'Do I not?' Aurelia rolled her eyes at Leah, who forced

a smile, grateful to her sister for diverting Mrs Butterby's attention away from her.

'You really are hopelessly outspoken—it will win you no friends in Society. Please, Leah, will *you* tell her?'

Leah hated their chaperone's tendency to try to get Leah to side with her against Aurelia. She shook her head. 'It is not my place to tell Aurelia how to behave.'

Aurelia squeezed her hand again, and Mrs Butterby spent the rest of the journey delivering a homily to Aurelia on ladylike behaviour. When they arrived home Leah and Aurelia headed straight for the drawing room, and Mrs Butterby said she would join them shortly.

'Really!' Aurelia flung herself onto the sofa. 'She is infuriating. Have you noticed how she constantly tries to set you against me? I can only view her strategy as one of divide and conquer—she no doubt believes we will be easier to manage as individuals than as friends who support one another.' She directed her bright blue gaze at Leah. 'We are friends, are we not, Leah? I know I am sometimes a touch…shall we say, confrontational—' a smile flashed across her face '—but I would do anything for you. You do know that?'

Touched, Leah sat next to Aurelia and hugged her. 'Yes, I do know it, and yes, we are friends.'

'And, as your friend… I know I said I would not pry, but… Leah… Lord Dolphinstone.'

Leah's heart somersaulted in her chest, and her pulse picked up again. Just at the mention of his name.

'You did not tell me he was so handsome.'

When Leah did not reply, Aurelia sighed. 'Well, it is hard to contain my curiosity, but I *did* say I would not pry, and friends should stick to their word. And sisters, even more so.'

Leah's arm was still around Aurelia, and she hugged

her again. 'I am so happy we are sisters,' she said. Then she frowned. 'And I would be far happier to admit that outright. Which brings us back to what we should do about Beatrice.'

'Yes, I shall accept your change of subject,' Aurelia said, nudging Leah gently. 'So, speaking of Beatrice...' She chewed her lip. 'How would we feel if we did nothing, and she simply did not turn up?'

Leah shoved all thought of Dolph from her mind. Beatrice was important too.

'We would regret it. Deeply.'

Mrs Butterby entered the room as Leah spoke. 'Regret what, pray?'

'We are worried about Beatrice,' Leah said. 'We would like to go to her brother's house and bring her back to London before Easter.'

Mrs Butterby sat in a chair and fussed about, smoothing her skirts. 'She has over three weeks yet.'

'But what if she misses the deadline?' said Aurelia. 'You did not see her when she spoke about her brother. She is scared of him. He is a brute.'

'She told you so, did she, Aurelia?'

'She didn't have to tell me. I can feel it here!'

Aurelia clapped a hand to her chest, covering her heart, and Leah puzzled again at the contradictions in this sister of hers. Defensive about her own past, and about her future too, scathing of many people she met, but fiercely protective of Beatrice, whom she barely knew, and of Leah too.

'It does you credit you are concerned about Beatrice, and I promise we will not allow her to miss her chance. If we have heard nothing by early next week, then we shall all three go down to Somerset and fetch her. Although...' she looked from Leah to Aurelia and back again '...you do realise that if Beatrice fails to arrive in time, you two will benefit from it?'

Leah gasped, horrified it would even occur to Mrs Butterby that she might think such a thing. Before she could speak, however, Aurelia leapt in.

'As if *that* would make any difference! She is our flesh and blood, and that is worth more than any amount of money. Is that not right, Leah?'

'It is.'

Aurelia had again surprised Leah, but had also delighted her because, when Leah looked inside her own heart, she knew exactly how fortunate she was—finding Aurelia and Beatrice meant more to her than any amount of wealth.

Dolph's head spun as he strode away from Leah and her companions.

*Sampford and Veryan! What the devil is she doing with that pair of scoundrels? And* what *is she doing promenading in the Park anyway? Dressed in the height of fashion, too...*

His thoughts stuttered to a halt. George had told him she'd inherited a house and some money. He'd *assumed* it had been a modest amount—sufficient to enable her not to work for her living.

With a silent oath, he turned for home. He'd arrived an hour ago, tired and stiff after close to five days of travel, making slow progress for the children's sake, although they had travelled better than Dolph expected, especially once they reached the well-maintained road to London. As soon as they had arrived at his town house, Dolph had taken advantage of the dry weather to walk in the Park in order to blow the cobwebs away.

Never had he imagined Leah would be one of the

first people he saw. His plan had been to call upon her the next day, after a refreshing night's sleep, and to tell her the truth about Rebecca's death, and to confess his own culpability, and to throw himself upon her mercy and beg her to take a chance on him and to be his wife.

Now he realised he'd never even thought to ask Travers for Leah's address, and he also realised, with a wash of shame, that he'd never *really* believed she would refuse him again, even after he confessed the truth about Rebecca's suicide. He had *assumed*—and there was that word again—she would forgive him because what he could offer her was superior to what she already had.

For the first time, doubts assailed him. She was clearly in better circumstances than he'd imagined. What if she was enjoying her life here in London? *What if she said no?*

As soon as he arrived home, he walked straight through into the mews and asked for Travers. When his coachman emerged from the stables Dolph drew him aside.

'It occurs to me I should pay my respects to Miss Thame while I am in Town, and I shall therefore need her address.'

He gritted his teeth at the amused gleam in Travers's eyes.

'South Street, milord. Tregowan House.'

*Tregowan House? What the devil...?*

Dolph fought to hide his bewilderment.

'Thank you, Travers. I shan't need the carriage in that case.' South Street was only around the corner from his own house in South Audley Street.

The first thing Dolph saw when he walked into his house was Nicky with Miss Pike's parrot on his shoulder.

'Wolf. Wolf. Say Wolf, Horatio. Wolf.'

'What are you up to, Nicky? Where is Miss Pike?'

Nicky looked at him guiltily. 'She is upstairs, Papa.'

'And where does she think you are?'

'Putting Horatio's cage in her chamber.'

'And is Horatio meant to be *inside* his cage?'

Nicky pouted. 'He has been inside his cage for *days*, Papa. He needed to fly.' He gazed up at Dolph, all innocence. 'He *needed* to blow the cobwebs away.'

Dolph bit back his grin at having his own words recited back to him. 'Go now and do as Miss Pike bid you,' he said, sternly. 'And then ask her how else you may help her.'

'Yes, Papa.' Nicky headed for the staircase.

Horatio suddenly stirred and stretched out his wings. 'Wolf!' he screeched. 'Wolf!'

The click of claws on the tiled floor sounded as Wolf emerged from the parlour and trotted along the hall, ears pricked.

'Wolf! Wolf!' Horatio took flight and dived at Wolf—aiming at his rump, too wise to venture too close to the dog's teeth. Wolf twisted, snapping ineffectually at empty air.

Dolph rubbed his hand around the back of his neck. He needed peace and quiet to think through what he'd learned about Leah. But first...

'Wolf. In.' He pointed at the parlour door. The dog obeyed, and Dolph shut the door. 'Come along, Nicky. Let us go and find Miss Pike. I doubt she will be happy you have taught her parrot to call Wolf—it'll cause chaos.'

Nicky beamed. 'It will, won't it, Papa? Are we going to see Miss Thame while we are here? Stevie said she lives in London now.'

'I do not know, Nicky.' And he really didn't know. Not now. He didn't know what to think. 'We shall see.'

\* \* \*

In the end, with so many unanswered questions whiz-zing around his head, Dolph abandoned his plans of a quiet evening in, followed by an early night, and ven-tured out after dinner. A visit to his club elicited the in-formation from the doorman that the foremost event that evening was Lady Todmorden's rout. Dolph knew Lady Todmorden's spouse, Sir Horace, from his governmental work, and so he strolled from St James's to their house in Bruton Street, confident of a welcome despite his lack of an invitation. Here he hoped to find acquaintances who could fill in the gaps in his knowledge as to why Leah appeared to have been bequeathed Tregowan House.

The Todmordens' house was ablaze with light and the road hectic with carriages lining up to deposit their oc-cupants at the door. A cacophony of laughter and con-versation drifted through the open windows.

'Dolph! Good to see you again.' Sir Horace Todmor-den's magnificent side whiskers quivered in his enthu-siasm. 'It must be—what—close on a year and a half since we last met? You fellows did a grand job over in Europe, by the way. Thank God Napoleon got his come-uppance at last, eh?'

Lady Todmorden placed a hand on her husband's arm and smiled at Dolph. 'Welcome, Lord Dolphinstone. We were so sorry to hear of your loss last year, were we not, Horace?'

'What? Oh, yes. Quite. Condolences, my dear fel-low. I quite forgot in all the kerfuffle over that bounder Bonaparte. Yes…welcome indeed.' He waved his arm in an expansive gesture. 'Do go ahead and mingle. I'm sure you'll find some familiar faces in there.'

Dolph smiled and then headed for the room indicated by Sir Horace. He paused in the open doorway and accepted a glass of champagne from a passing footman as he scanned the occupants for one of those familiar faces.

The first person he saw was Leah, holding court. Really, there was no other way to describe the scene before him. Leah, surrounded by half a dozen gentlemen—Veryan included—who were clinging to her every word and vying with one another to earn a smile, or a glance from those brilliant eyes. The sparkle was obvious, even from clear across the room, as the men flirted with her and she...*she* appeared to relish the attention.

*Fortune hunters. Every one of 'em. They're only after her money. They don't know the real Leah as I do.*

Jealousy spiralled up through Dolph at a dizzying speed. His free hand fisted at his side as he forced himself to sip nonchalantly at the champagne and watched, his gaze unwavering.

Her appearance was nothing short of regal as she stood straight and proud. She was inches taller than most other ladies present, but she did not slouch. And her hair gleamed like a beacon... It was braided up behind—bright, glossy, threaded with pearls—to reveal her elegant neck and ivory shoulders. Gentle curls softened her temples. Her gown—the colour of emeralds—clung to every inch of her willowy frame, draping the long, elegant line of her thighs, and the off-the-shoulder wide neckline exposed an expanse of bare skin unmarred by any decoration save for a green ribbon threaded through her mother's wedding ring. Strangely, that ring reassured him that this gleaming, polished lady of quality was still the same Leah he knew and loved.

'Dolph! Back in Town so soon?'

Dolph turned to see his old friend Sir Charles Pidgeon, who claimed a horror of the countryside and lived in London the year round with his wife and family.

'Pidge. Good to see you again.'

'I thought you were determined not to set foot in the place again, and yet here you are, not three months later. Is Hinckley back as well?'

'No, he's stayed down in Somerset for the time being.'

'And you? Why have you graced us with your presence again, so soon? Ah…'

Dolph stiffened as his old friend grinned knowingly.

'Could it, perchance, have something to do with the exceedingly popular Miss Thame? She was your governess, as I understand it.'

Dolph frowned. 'That is common knowledge?'

'She has made no secret of the fact. Neither has Miss Croome hidden that she was in dire straits before Lady Tregowan bequeathed them her fortune.'

'Miss Croome was also a beneficiary? In the same will? Lady Tregowan's will?'

Pidge's brows shot up. 'You did not know?'

'I only knew Miss Thame had inherited a house in London and an amount of money that meant she no longer had to work for a living.'

'Ah. Then allow me to fill you in, my dear chap, although there are still gaps in what we know, and rumours galore to fill those gaps, as you might imagine. One of those rumours is that there is another beneficiary, so no one is quite sure whether your Miss Thame has inherited one half or one third of Lady Tregowan's entire estate. Still, either way, she is a very wealthy lady.'

'*All* of it?' Dolph's brows shot up. 'Including Falconfield Hall? What about the current Earl? He would surely have expected to inherit something?'

'Ah, poor Tregowan. No one's seen hide nor hair of him—rumour has it he's licking his wounds back home in Cornwall. It's to be hoped the blow doesn't drive him to despair... Rumour is his finances are shot.'

Dolph felt a swell of sympathy for poor Tregowan. He didn't know him well, but he hoped his situation wasn't as serious as Pidge implied. And Leah...she had inherited a small fortune, and yet she had remained at Dolphin Court, working, when she could have been a lady of leisure. And that, he knew, was out of the goodness of her heart and from her desire to help the children become accustomed once again to their own father.

'The speculation, as you can imagine, is rife,' Pidge went on. 'Two young women appear from nowhere and take up residence in Tregowan House under the chaperonage of the late Lady Tregowan's companion? Society hasn't had this much excitement this early in the Season for many years. The tattlemongers are busily whispering behind their hands, questioning the link with Lady Tregowan, while the sticklers are already peering down their noses at the ladies in question. I doubt they will be honoured with vouchers for Almack's when it opens, but both *are* of respectable enough breeding on the face of it, and money does have a way of blinding those in debt to such negative connotations, does it not?'

Hence Leah being in company with Veryan and Sampford that afternoon. No wonder she had refused his offer when she had such wealth and excitement awaiting her in London.

'Thank you for bringing me up to date, Pidge.'

Pidge slapped Dolph's back. 'You're welcome, my friend. And if your appearance here has anything to do with Miss Thame, I honestly wish you luck, for she seems a decent woman and she will do far better with you than with any of those chancers cosying up to her. And, if you ask me—which you wouldn't, but I shall tell you anyway—the lady might give a good impression of lapping up all that attention but, in my opinion, her heart is not in it.'

With a final smile, Pidge wandered off while Dolph remained in place, searching the room with his eyes, seeking Leah. Someone was in the way, and Dolph shifted until he could see her. As she came into view—still surrounded by admirers—he battled a primeval urge to drag her away from them, to warn them away from her, to warn *her* they cared only for her money.

Her head turned, as if she felt the force of his gaze, and their eyes locked. He felt the blow as though it were physical. The air shot from his lungs and he strove to refill them, his legs suddenly weak. He could not move but remained as if frozen in place as he watched Leah's reaction. And, of course, there was no artifice. Not for her the coy lowering of her lashes. Not for her the turn of the shoulder to punish him. Not for her the revenge of flirting even more outrageously with her admirers simply in order to prove she had no need of him.

No. She excused herself from her coterie and she crossed the floor to him. Her smile, though, was hesitant. She was unsure, but she would not use that as an excuse to cut him. She had always been forthright and uncomplicated with him, and London had not—yet—changed her. She stopped in front of him and looked up, directly into his eyes.

## Chapter Twenty-Two

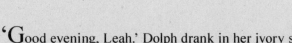

'Good evening, Leah.' Dolph drank in her ivory skin dotted with those fascinating freckles, and her stunning turquoise eyes. Oh, how he had missed her.

'My lord.' A frown of disapproval creased her brow. 'I was unaware of your intention to come to London. You have left the children? After all your promises to put them first?'

'I had some unfinished business to attend to, but I have brought them with me.'

Her frown cleared at his words. Dolph sent his gaze around the room and saw several pairs of resentful eyes watching them. He crooked his arm. 'Would you care to stroll? I have news for you.'

Leah placed her hand on his forearm and Dolph reined in his urge to cover her hand with his. Her scent wreathed through his senses, in part familiar, and yet her own scent was overlaid with an unfamiliar, evocative floral perfume.

'Did Lord Hinckley accompany you to London?'

'No. He found he could not tear himself away from Somerset.'

'Ahhhhh.' Her lips curved as she sighed with satisfaction. 'He could not leave Philippa?'

'He offered for Miss Strong on the morning we left, and she accepted him.'

'I am delighted. Philippa deserves to be happy.'

They strolled on, through an open door at one end of the room and into another, equally crowded but with one distinct advantage, as far as Dolph was concerned. It did not contain Leah's flock of admirers but instead consisted of an older group of guests, mainly gentlemen recognisable to Dolph as ex-military.

Dolph glanced sideways as Leah spoke. Her mouth might smile but her eyes were sad. Without volition, his hand now covered hers, and he gently squeezed. If George was right about Leah's feelings for Dolph, then he had hurt her. Badly. He'd been a blind idiot not to see what had been in front of his nose.

'We *all* deserve to be happy,' he murmured.

Her head bowed, and he noticed her eyes screw shut for an instant, as though she were in pain. 'Tell me. The children are well?'

'They are.'

'Your business must be exceedingly important for you to come rushing up to London like this.'

'Oh, it is. It is, without doubt, the most important business of my entire life.'

'I see.'

He knew she would question him no further. He needed to explain himself—to throw himself upon her mercy—but this was neither the time nor the place for such an intimate and emotional discussion. She would know everything soon enough, and he would find out if her feelings for him were strong enough to withstand the truth about Rebecca. Frustration bubbled through him.

He longed to find a quiet spot, to take her in his arms and to kiss away her doubts. But only a scoundrel would do that before telling her the full truth and giving her the chance to reject him.

Wouldn't he?

Almost without conscious thought, he scanned the library and spied a single door set into the far wall. It was closed, meaning what lay beyond was not open to guests. Dolph changed the direction of their stroll to ensure they passed close by it even as a voice inside clamoured he was being unfair.

'Who is caring for the boys? Have you found a new governess for them?'

'I have. Miss Pike. She is a cousin of the Reverend Strong. And she has a one-eyed parrot. Horatio.'

'A *parrot*?' Her lips quirked, and the memory of their taste, their texture, their eagerness, exploded through him. She soon sobered. 'Then the boys will have forgotten all about me already, I fear.'

'No. *None* of us have forgotten you. Nicky asked only today if they may visit you.'

Leah's fingers tightened on his arm, and Dolph sent her a sideways look, just in time to see the glint of a tear on her lower lashes, and to catch the hitch in her breath.

'I am sorry. I did not mean to distress you.'

'And I did not intend to allow my emotions to overcome me.' Leah touched the corner of her eye with one gloved finger. 'Foolish woman! I do apologise.'

Dolph reached for his pocket handkerchief and moved to shield her from view, although, judging by the general hubbub, the other guests were too engrossed in their own conversation to take much notice of the two of them. He pushed his handkerchief into Leah's hand. She snatched it from him and quickly thrust it out of sight in her reticule.

'Not in front of everyone, please,' she hissed. 'There are already people who look to find fault with every little thing about us—about me and Aurelia, I mean—without handing them more ammunition with a display of *vulgar emotion*, as Mrs Butterby would say.'

Dolph stared down at her. Her eyes still brimmed with tears and, as he watched, one drop spilled over her lashes and slowly tracked down her cheek. She bent her head and another tear plopped to the floor. With a muttered exclamation, he cupped her elbow and steered her to that door, opened it and nudged her through. A glance behind showed nobody taking any notice, so he followed her, shutting the door behind them. The room was dark, but another door, slightly ajar, allowed enough light to reveal they were in a small parlour. Dolph strode to the second door and peered out to see it opened into the back of the entrance hall. He used a tinderbox upon the mantelshelf to light a candle.

'Why do you imagine people are looking to find fault in you?'

A quiet, bitter-sounding laugh escaped her. 'We have seen the looks. Heard the comments. It would appear the purity of our *breeding* is in question. As if we were a couple of racehorses.'

Dolph bit back a laugh at her disgruntled tone. 'You should ignore them. It is pure jealousy and spite, for the most part. They are envious of your good fortune.' His voice deepened as he stepped closer to her. 'And of your beauty.'

She stared up at him. 'Beauty? Now I know you are flannelling me. And I thank you for it, but there is no need to try and make me feel better with false compliments.'

'The compliment was not false. You stand out as a

diamond among all the other females here, despite your lack of jewels.' He stroked one finger down the silk ribbon and paused as he reached the ring. 'You still wear your mama's ring, I see.'

Her hand rose to her chest, and her fingers brushed his as she touched the ring. 'It is more precious to me than any jewels. It keeps her memory close.'

His heart ached at the sadness in her voice. She had lost both parents. She had no family. She had been forced to earn her living at what was often a thankless task, and he—the one person who should have protected her against more hardship—had effectively driven her away from where she was happy. Nothing could excuse his behaviour. He hadn't recognised his love for Leah just as he hadn't recognised Rebecca's despair. He truly was a failure, and he was ashamed.

Dolph placed two fingers beneath Leah's chin, tilting her face to his. 'Leah... I—'

The door behind them opened, and they jumped apart as Miss Croome stalked into the room, glaring at Dolph.

'Leah! Mrs Butterby is hunting high and low for you. You had better come with me before she creates an uproar over your disappearance. It is fortunate I was watching you and saw Lord Dolphinstone spirit you away.'

'Spirit me away? Aurelia... I am in no danger from His Lordship, I assure you.'

'Your *reputation* is in danger.' Miss Croome's blue eyes, flashing like sapphires, scrutinised Dolph from head to toe and back again. 'Why have you come to London?'

Leah gasped. 'Aurelia! Please—'

Dolph touched Leah's arm. 'It is all right, Leah. Miss Croome is entitled to wonder why we are here alone, and to question my motives. I am in London on *personal* business, Miss Croome.'

His gaze sought Leah's as he spoke. A blush stole up her neck to her cheeks, and her fingers sought her mother's ring. Her throat moved as she swallowed.

Her eyes clung to his as she said, 'Aurelia, will you kindly go to Mrs Butterby and reassure her I am found and perfectly safe?'

That suspicious blue gaze transferred to Leah. 'Come with me.'

'I will be right behind you. I promise.'

Miss Croome drew herself up to her full height, meaning the top of her head barely reached Dolph's shoulder. Her eyes narrowed. 'If Leah does not appear in *three minutes*, I shall return, so be warned.'

She stalked from the room.

'I see I have no need to fear for your safety when you have your own personal bodyguard,' Dolph said, with a laugh. 'She is rather protective, is she not? It makes me wonder what you have told her about me.'

'I have told her nothing. She is aware you were my employer, and that is all. I only met Aurelia for the first time at that meeting in Bristol. I do not know her well enough to share confidences...not that there are any confidences to tell, of course. And,' she added, 'you are no longer responsible for me, so there is no need for you to fear for my safety or to concern yourself about anything to do with me.'

'Touché.' Dolph cupped Leah's shoulders. 'Leah... listen... I am aware we do not have much time. That personal business...' He watched her closely. 'It involves you.'

'Oh.' Her smile wavered. 'I appear to be lost for words.

Can you enlighten me with more details of this personal business?'

'I cannot. At least, not fully. There are things I must tell you that will take more time than we have available now. May I call upon you tomorrow?'

'Yes. I shall look forward to it.' Her expression belied her words and the tremor in her voice signalled her doubts.

*He* had caused this. And, all at once, he understood Pidge had been right. Her performance as a queen among her entourage had been precisely that. A performance. And his treatment of her had added to her doubts about her own allure.

Dolph's hands firmed on her shoulders and he drew her slowly towards him.

'I have missed you more than you could ever know, my sweet Leah.' He lowered his face as hers tilted towards him. His mouth brushed hers and then settled. Her response was, as ever, heartbreakingly honest—her lips softening beneath his in a slow, sensual kiss that set his pulse racing. Too soon, she pulled away, her hands flat upon his chest.

'I must go.' Her deep turquoise gaze searched his. 'You should know—my reasons for refusing your offer have not changed.'

Forever honest. He gently brushed back a stray lock of her hair at her temple.

'But my reasons for making that offer *have* changed, dear Leah. However...' he placed his forefinger against her lips as her mouth opened to speak '...there is something I must tell you first. Something you need to understand, before we speak of the future. So we will talk tomorrow.'

He put his arms around her and pulled her close, just

holding her. His eyes closed and he breathed in her floral scent. What would tomorrow bring? Would she understand why he had hesitated to admit—or even recognise—his feelings for her? Would she willingly face the risk of being his wife? And yet, even as those thoughts crossed his mind, he began to realise the benign neglect that had dogged his marriage to Rebecca need not be repeated. His future was in his hands. Unlike then—and whether it was because he was now older and more mature, or whether it was because it was Leah rather than Rebecca, and he loved her with his whole heart—he no longer viewed his decision to give up his government business as a sacrifice. He felt as though he would be content to stay at Dolphin Court with Leah for the remainder of his days. He loved her. Never in his life had he felt that emotion so deeply, so naturally, so *passionately*.

With reluctance, he released her.

'Come. Let us go before Miss Croome returns to savage me once again.'

He took her hand and led her to the door into the entrance hall. A swift peek revealed only servants—a footman on duty by the front door and two maids waiting to assist guests with their coats upon arrival and departure. Dolph urged Leah through the door and followed her out into the hall and then into the room in which he had first seen her. It was still packed with guests.

Miss Croome pounced the minute they entered. 'I was about to come looking for you again,' she hissed. 'Mrs Butterby has the headache now, no doubt from all the worry you've caused.'

'Nonsense!' said Leah. 'There is no need to be overly dramatic, Aurelia.'

Miss Croome's blue eyes raked Dolph once again. 'If there was nothing clandestine in your little *tête-à-*

*tête*, why did *His Lordship* not introduce himself to your chaperone?'

'*Aurelia*. Please...'

Miss Croome's expression softened, and she took Leah's hand. 'I am sorry. I am worried for you, and that has sharpened my tongue, perhaps.' She bit her lip and looked up at Dolph. 'I apologise, my lord.'

'You were rightly concerned for your friend,' he said. 'And now, Miss Croome, perhaps you will be kind enough to conduct us to your Mrs Butterby, for you are quite right, and I should have made myself known to her at the outset.'

Leah's smile warmed his heart. They followed Miss Croome through the throng to a slender, grey-haired lady, whose drawn features did indeed give the impression she was in pain.

'Mrs Butterby,' said Leah. 'May I introduce Lord Dolphinstone? My lord, this is Mrs Butterby, who is kindly standing as chaperone for myself and Miss Croome for the duration of our time in London.'

Mrs Butterby curtsied. 'I am pleased to meet you, my lord. I do hope you will call upon us while you are in Town.'

Dolph bowed. 'Thank you, ma'am. I have already asked Miss Thame if I might call upon her tomorrow.'

Mrs Butterby's eyes widened. 'I shall look forward to your visit, my lord.'

Leah took the older woman by the arm. 'Are you quite well, dear ma'am? Aurelia said you are suffering the headache.'

'Oh. Well. Yes, indeed, but it is only very slight.'

'It does not look to me to be only slight. It is unbearably hot and stuffy in here, not to mention the noise. Shall we go home?'

'Well, if you and Aurelia have no objection, I must confess it would be a relief.'

'I have no objection,' said Miss Croome.

'Nor I,' said Leah.

Mrs Butterby scanned the room distractedly. 'In that case, I shall find Lady Todmorden and say our goodbyes while you girls bespeak our carriage and our cloaks. Lord Dolphinstone, I am sorry we must leave, but I shall look forward to meeting you properly tomorrow.'

Dolph bowed and watched her walk away. Miss Croome stirred then. 'I shall order the carriage. I will meet you in the hall, Leah.' And she, too, walked away.

Dolph scanned the crowd and became aware of the many pairs of eyes upon him. Mostly male, and somewhat disgruntled.

'Might I escort you to the door?' Dolph took Leah's hand and placed it upon his sleeve very deliberately—a non-verbal statement as to his intentions, aimed at every last one of those fortune hunters. 'Shall I call upon you at eleven? Will that be acceptable?'

'It will.'

Miss Croome, already wearing her mantle, was waiting in the entrance hall.

'Which is your coat?'

'The green pelisse.' Leah indicated the garment held by the waiting maid.

Dolph moved behind her, holding the pelisse as she slipped her arms into the sleeves. As he settled the coat across her shoulders, the tips of his fingers brushed first the satiny skin of her neck and then a silky curl of hair that had escaped its pin. His breath stirred the soft hairs at her nape, and he saw gooseflesh erupt and felt her quiver in response. His own pulse thrummed, and the blood surged to his groin, causing him to grow hard. He wanted her. *Ached* for her.

Such a simple action, to assist her with her coat, and yet his reaction stirred so many complex needs and worries and regrets and...*guilt*. His old friend guilt. Seizing on a sudden impulse, he bent his head and put his lips to her ear.

'Do not stop believing, my sweet Leah.'

Her shoulders tensed beneath his hands. Her chaperone chose that moment to bustle into the hall, and Dolph took advantage of the distraction to press a kiss to the side of Leah's neck.

'All will be well. I promise you.'

# Chapter Twenty-Three

'So,' hissed Aurelia, as she and Leah waited to climb into the carriage behind Mrs Butterby, 'you did not tell me your Dolph is as obsessed with you as you are with him.'

'Is he? Am I?' Leah raised one eyebrow, affecting nonchalance despite the blush heating her cheeks. 'That sounds singularly inappropriate given he was my employer.'

'Tosh. You don't fool me, sister. Or are you in the habit of allowing your employers to make love to you under the cover of assisting you with your pelisse?'

Another shiver racked Leah as she felt again the brush of Dolph's fingers over her sensitive nape, and the sweet, petal-soft touch of his lips upon her neck. She had hoped no one had noticed. Trust Aurelia—nothing much escaped those sharp blue eyes of hers.

'Can you trust him, though, Leah? Ask yourself what he is doing here in London.'

'He has come on business. Please, take care,' Leah whispered urgently. 'Mrs Butterby will hear you.'

A footman handed first her and then Aurelia into the carriage, which immediately set off. Leah resisted the urge to look back to see if Dolph was there, somewhere, watching her depart. What did it all mean? The carefully selected words; that kiss; the fire that smouldered in those grey eyes? He'd said there was something she needed to understand before they could discuss the future. She tingled with excitement. She had prayed he might realise he loved her when she was gone, and she now prayed he could convince her of it, for her resolve was as strong as ever. If she must accept a marriage of convenience—and she was by no means certain she would do so—she would rather it was to a man whose heart was at least free to grow to love her. She would not wed a man still in love with his first wife, for that way lay misery and heartache.

A sharp nudge from Aurelia's elbow brought Leah back to her surroundings. They were nearing home. Mrs Butterby was uncharacteristically quiet, staring out of the carriage window and nibbling absently at the finger of her glove. As the vehicle slowed, she jerked out of her reverie.

'How is your headache now, ma'am?' asked Leah.

'Oh. It is a little better, I believe.' Mrs Butterby massaged her temples as the carriage drew to a stop. 'The noise at the rout did not help, but I have also been thinking about Beatrice, after our conversation this afternoon. I know I said there is still time, and that is true, but... I honestly did think she would be here by now. I know dear Sarah was very worried when she found out how badly her brother treated her.'

She accepted Vardy's hand to help her down the carriage steps and walked into the house ahead of Leah and Aurelia, straight up to the drawing room, where she sat down. 'We shall discuss what we are to do in the morning when my head is clearer. However, I cannot retire to bed without first asking you about Lord Dolphinstone, Leah.'

'What about him?' Leah caught Aurelia's smirk out of the corner of her eye and glared at her.

'May we attach any significance to his calling upon you tomorrow? He is a fine figure of a man and I do know he is well respected in Society. And an earl!' She sighed. 'Quite the catch!'

'I do not know,' she said. 'I hope so. And yet...' She shrugged helplessly.

Aurelia sat beside her. 'Why do you not tell us the whole, Leah? I was right there was something between you when you worked for His Lordship, was I not?'

'You were. We grew close and we kissed.' She smiled, ruefully. 'And I did not mean to, but I fell in love with him, despite knowing he had vowed never to remarry because he still loved his late wife. When I decided I must leave before I fell any deeper for him, he asked me to marry him.'

'He asked you to *marry* him? And you love him?' Mrs Butterby shook her head. 'Why are you here? Why did you not snap his hand off, you foolish girl?'

Leah sighed. 'He only proposed to me for the children's sake, to stop me leaving. I overheard him tell his friend Lord Hinckley that he would do anything to stop me going, and L-Lord Hinckley suggested he marry me. It was not even Dolph's idea. And he made no attempt to hide that it was a practical solution, as far as he was concerned.'

'The scoundrel!' Aurelia patted Leah's arm. 'But he followed you. That is a good sign, is it not?'

'I hope so. And what he said tonight... I told him my reasons for refusing him have not changed, and he said that his reasons for making that offer *have* changed.'

'But...that is wonderful.' Mrs Butterby clasped her hands to her bosom. 'So-o-o-o romantic.'

'But then he said there is something I need to understand before we can speak of the future. And I have racked my brains, but I cannot think what he means. I so want to believe my dream will come true, but I have been fooled before and now I just feel confused.'

'Well…he had the *look* of a man who is enamoured,' said Aurelia, 'but is he to be trusted? You know him best, Leah.'

Leah frowned. She so desperately wanted to trust Dolph, but the memory of Peter and Usk loomed large. Could she really trust her own judgement? *But…this is Dolph. Has he ever given me reason not to trust him?* She felt guilty for even doubting him. She loved him, and surely trust must go hand in hand with love?

'You are right, Aurelia. I *do* know him. He was honest about the reason for his proposal at Dolphin Court and I trust him to be honest with me tomorrow.' She prayed she was right. 'I fear I have allowed conjecture and my emotions to distort my good sense.' She rose to her feet. 'I shall see you both in the morning. Goodnight.'

Despite her resolve to stop trying to guess what Dolph was to tell her, and to trust him, Leah still struggled to sleep. The following morning she awoke with a start as Faith bustled into her room.

'Miss Thame! Miss Thame!'

Leah blurrily focussed her eyes on her maid as she fought the desire to turn over and sink back into oblivion. But the urgency in Faith's voice roused her curiosity.

'What is it?' Leah propped herself up on one elbow.

'It's Miss Fothergill, miss. She has arrived, and…oh, miss, I knew you would want to know, so I hurried up here straight away.'

Leah frowned. *Beatrice? Here?* 'What time is it?'

'Almost nine, miss. Mr Vardy has put her in the morning parlour next to the fire. She's chilled to the bone, poor thing.'

Leah jumped out of bed and grabbed her shawl, thrusting her feet into her slippers before hurrying from her bedchamber. 'Have Mrs Butterby and Miss Croome been told?'

'Bet has gone to tell them, miss.'

The door to the morning parlour was ajar and, from within, Leah could hear the snap of the fire. She paused outside the door.

'Thank you, Faith. Please ask the kitchen to send up a warm drink and something to eat for Miss Fothergill.'

'Mrs Burnham is already seeing to it, miss.' Faith bobbed a curtsy and hurried away. Leah bit her lip and pushed the door open, wondering what she might find.

Beatrice was sitting on the chair nearest the fire, huddled over and seemingly talking to a wicker basket by her feet. Her head snapped up as Leah entered and her fearful expression changed to one of sheer relief. She leapt up and rushed across the room. For one moment, Leah thought Beatrice would hurl herself into her arms, but her half-sister abruptly halted when just a few feet away, her fingers plucking nervously at the skirts of her lilac gown.

'Leah! I cannot tell you how happy I am to see you again.'

Her attempt at a smile tugged on Leah's heartstrings. She cared not for societal norms of behaviour. Beatrice was her half-sister—her flesh and blood—and Leah's instinct was to touch...to offer comfort. She smiled warmly, opened her arms and drew Beatrice close in a hug. Her cheek, when Leah kissed it, was cold.

'And I,' she said, 'am delighted you have joined us at last. Come, sit by the fire again. You are shivering.'

She urged Beatrice to sit back down and then tugged another chair alongside so she could keep hold of her sister's icy hand. The basket rocked and an unearthly yowl sounded from within.

'What on earth is in there, Beatrice?'

'Oh, dear. I hope it is all right. It is Spartacus. My cat. I *could* not leave him behind.'

'Of course you could not. Is it time to let him out of there, do you think?'

'He is hungry. I—I asked Vardy to bring something for him from the kitchen. Is that all right?'

'Beatrice…my dear…this is your home. Yours and mine and Aurelia's. If you wish to bring your cat, and to give an order to the butler, you are perfectly entitled to do so.'

Leah was rewarded with a smile that revealed dimples in both Beatrice's cheeks. 'I am sorry. I worry… I—I do not wish to take advantage, or to upset anyone.'

'Trust me. You will not upset any of us. Everyone will just be happy you have arrived, I promise.'

Another furious and long-drawn-out yowl emerged from the basket as Mrs Burnham, the housekeeper, entered, carrying a tray laden with a pot of chocolate, two cups, a plate of fragrant, gently steaming fresh rolls, and two dishes, one of meat scraps and one of water.

'Thank you, Mrs Burnham.' Leah moved a side table to within Beatrice's reach. 'Place it here, if you please.'

Mrs Burnham poured the chocolate and then placed the two dishes on the floor, at the edge of the carpet square. 'For the cat,' she said.

'Thank you.' Beatrice knelt by the basket and unbuckled the straps. Before she could open the lid, a huge black cat pushed it up and squirmed through the opening. He hissed loudly, ears flat to his head, before streaking across the room and scrambling onto the windowsill where he glared malevolently at the three women. 'Oh, dear.'

Leah bit back a smile and judged it better to ignore Spartacus's antisocial behaviour for Beatrice's sake.

'Thank you, Mrs Burnham. And would you arrange for water to be heated for a bath for Miss Fothergill, please?' Leah smiled at Beatrice. 'A bath will warm you up, and we can eat a proper breakfast afterwards with Aurelia and Mrs Butterby, if you are still hungry.'

As soon as the door closed behind the housekeeper, Leah handed one of the cups to Beatrice, who wrapped her hands around it and sipped, her eyes closed. Leah took advantage of the moment to study her sister. She looked thinner than she remembered from their meeting in Bristol eight weeks ago, and some of her bloom had faded.

'I presume by your early arrival you travelled up on the mail coach, Beatrice? You must be exhausted. I...' Leah hesitated to pry, but she could not resist saying, 'I am surprised your brother allowed you to travel all this way unescorted.'

Beatrice slumped in her chair, closing her eyes as she rubbed the middle of her forehead, effectively shielding her expression from Leah.

'He did not know. I—I had to run away, you see. Percy...he's my brother...he found the will and he insisted he would bring me to London himself. Well, him and his wife, Fenella, and *her* b-brother...but, oh, Leah... I could not bear them to taint my new life, and so I *had* to leave when I got the chance but, the whole way, I was so scared he would catch me and spoil everything.'

She hung her head and heaved in a shuddering breath, and Leah recalled Beatrice's agitation when she had mentioned her brother after their first meeting in Bristol. She couldn't wait to hear the whole story of what had happened, but she curbed her curiosity.

'At least you are here now, and you are safe from him, Beatrice.'

Beatrice shook her head despondently. 'You do not know my brother. He will not give up so easily.' Then she fell silent, catching her lower lip between her teeth before releasing it and straightening in the chair. 'He is not my brother, though, is he? I ought not to feel guilty for running away. And I have another family now. He can no longer tell me what to do.' She turned a pair of huge blue eyes—so like Aurelia's but trusting rather than wary—to Leah. 'Can he?'

Leah squeezed Beatrice's hand. 'No, Beatrice. He cannot. You are a wealthy young lady now, and we—Aurelia and I—are your family.'

Beatrice set her cup down, picked up a plate and took a roll. She bit into it and chewed, her forehead creased in thought. Then she swallowed and sighed. 'But he knows this address, Leah. He will follow me here, I know it.'

'Let him come, then. You need never be alone with him—I, or Aurelia, will be with you.'

Beatrice smiled. 'Thank you.'

'There is no need to thank me. We are sisters. We will all look after one another. And, look…even Spartacus has made himself at home.'

She pointed at the cat—the biggest she had ever seen—who was crouching over the dish and wolfing down food as though he hadn't seen a feed in a fortnight.

'All will be well,' she added, and her heart leapt as she recalled Dolph saying the exact same words to her last night, and as she remembered he would be here at eleven o'clock.

## *Chapter Twenty-Four*

While Beatrice bathed, Leah returned to her bedchamber to wash and dress. Faith told her Aurelia and Mrs Butterby were both awake and would see her in the morning parlour for breakfast. When a knock sounded at Leah's door, it was Maria, Beatrice's maid, with Beatrice herself, her hair still damp and smelling of lemons, and dressed in an ill-fitting yellow-sprigged muslin gown and a threadbare shawl draped around her shoulders.

Leah frowned. 'Are you warm enough dressed so scantily, Beatrice?'

Beatrice turned pink. 'I did not bring many gowns with me. Only what I could carry.'

'Faith? Fetch my paisley shawl, will you, please?' Leah smiled at Beatrice. 'I could not forgive myself if you catch a chill with that damp hair. Please oblige me by borrowing one of my shawls—the weather is hardly warm enough for such lightweight clothing.'

Beatrice hung her head. 'I am sorry. I didn't think. My sister-in-law likes big fires at Pilcombe Grange, and it is often stifling indoors.'

'And do *not* keep apologising.' Leah tucked her arm through her half-sister's. 'My comment was not a criticism but concern for your comfort. You will soon have a new wardrobe, and then your clothes will be suitable for London and for this house, and you will forget all about that brother of yours. Now, come. Aurelia is impatient to see you again, and Mrs Butterby is longing to be introduced.'

Later, as the four women sat at the table in the morning parlour, breaking their fast, Leah had to bite her tongue on more than one occasion as Aurelia and Mrs Butterby questioned Beatrice. Really! She might as well not have wasted her time in trying to reassure Beatrice and ease her fears because, by the time they rose from the table, her sister was as anxious as ever. Mrs Butterby, talking non-stop as she tried to prepare poor Beatrice for her new life in the bosom of the *haut ton*, walked ahead with Beatrice to the drawing room while Leah and Aurelia followed behind.

'That brother!' Aurelia shook her head. 'I should like to meet him. I would soon send him packing, I can tell you.'

'I do not doubt it. But, Aurelia... I do think it will help reduce Beatrice's anxiety if we avoid talking about her brother too often.'

Aurelia stopped and frowned. 'What do you mean? I am trying to give her some backbone—she needs to stand up for herself.'

'I know. But her confidence needs building up first, and if we keep reminding her of her brother, it will take her much longer to accept she is safe from him.'

'You mean if *I* keep reminding her of him. But I want to know what he did to her to make her so...so...*meek*. I cannot wait for him to call here.' Aurelia's dainty hands balled into fists. 'How dare he turn a beautiful woman into this...this...*blancmange*?'

'Come…' Leah linked her arm through Aurelia's and continued towards the drawing room. 'You and I are not going to quarrel over this, are we? It is far too soon for Beatrice to cope with all these questions, let alone Mrs Butterby's warnings of disasters waiting to befall the unwary newcomer to Society. The poor thing must be exhausted.'

'You are right.' Aurelia shook her head. 'I do not admit this lightly, but even if Beatrice did not fear her brother, I would distrust him. I find it hard to trust the gentlemen of this world.'

'I had noticed,' said Leah, dryly. 'But at least now Beatrice is here we can finally discuss whether or not we publicly admit to our relationship.'

'You know my opinion on that. I think we should announce it and be damned.'

'As do I, but I can also understand why Mrs Butterby advises caution.'

'Caution?' Mrs Butterby queried from where she and Beatrice sat on the sofa. 'About what did I advise caution?'

'Whether or not to openly acknowledge the three of us are half-sisters,' said Leah. She sat on a vacant chair—Spartacus, busy grooming himself, having commandeered the seat closest to the fire—and smiled at Beatrice. 'We agreed to wait until your arrival, as the decision will affect you too.'

Beatrice straightened, frowning. 'Why should we not admit to our relationship?' Her gaze darted between the other three women. 'I am *proud* to have you as sisters and I care not who knows it.'

Aurelia—standing next to Leah's chair—nudged her. 'There. Beatrice agrees with me.'

'But…you do not understand, Beatrice,' said Mrs Butterby. 'By openly admitting you are the offspring of the late Lord Tregowan, you are exposing your mothers' morals to the censure of Society.'

'Speculation is already rife,' said Leah.

'Ah, but speculation is merely that. Once you acknowledge the truth, there will be no going back. And there will be suitors, and families, who will not even consider an alliance if there is a hint of a taint in your bloodlines.'

'If I am not good enough for a man to marry based upon my own merit, then *he* is not good enough for me to consider,' said Aurelia.

'And I, too, am proud to call you both my sisters,' said Leah. 'So I agree we should acknowledge our relationship, for, as Aurelia pointed out, to keep it secret would mean a lifetime of lies, and surely there can be nothing worse than starting out married life upon a lie.'

*And I shall start with telling Dolph the truth.* Her pulse quickened at the thought he would soon be there.

'Well. If you are all determined...' Mrs Butterby paused, heaved a sigh, shook her head, and then, unexpectedly, she smiled. 'May I say... I applaud your courage and your integrity. And I am also slightly envious you have one another. I hope you continue to support each other, and that you become lifelong friends as well as sisters.' Her voice faltered over the last few words, and she took out her handkerchief and blotted her eyes. 'There! I have turned all maudlin! Beatrice, my dear, you must be exhausted... Why do you not go upstairs to rest now? And—' She shot to her feet. 'Leah! In all the furore of Beatrice's arrival, I quite forgot! Lord Dolphinstone arrives shortly. Oh, my goodness.'

'Lord Dolphinstone?'

Leah blushed at Beatrice's quizzical look. 'I will tell

you all about it later. Mrs Butterby is right… You do look exhausted. Go and get some rest.'

Beatrice's expression changed to one of anxiety. 'Oh, no. I couldn't possibly… What if Percy comes here?'

'What if he does?' Aurelia went to Beatrice and hauled her to her feet. 'We are here to support you, and he no longer has any authority over you.' She hugged her, hard. 'You are safe, Beatrice. Come along, up the stairs with you. And perhaps you'd better take that monster with you.'

She indicated Spartacus, and Beatrice, blushing, scooped him into her arms, saying, 'Oh. Of course. I'm sorry.'

Spartacus put his ears back and grumbled, but he made no attempt to escape. Aurelia glanced back at Leah as she shepherded Beatrice out of the room.

'Be sure of what *you* want, Leah. Do not allow him to bamboozle you with sweet words that disguise an empty heart. You deserve to be happy and you need not answer him straight away if you are unsure. Trust your instincts… They will tell you if he is sincere.'

'She is right,' said Mrs Butterby when the others had gone. 'If His Lordship has truly discovered deeper feelings for you, he will be prepared to prove it and he will wait for your answer. *You* need to be certain. Aurelia never ceases to surprise me. Here was I, thinking she is as hard as nails with not a romantic bone in her body, but she clearly does believe in love.'

'For others, maybe,' said Leah, 'but I am not so sure she believes in it for herself. She appears to regard her marriage as a purely business transaction. I cannot see her ever surrendering her own heart to a man.'

'Well. Time will tell.'

'Thank you for supporting our decision, Mrs Butterby.

It means a lot. I know you are eager for us all to make the best matches we can.'

'I feel it is my duty to dear Sarah's memory, but I would not see any one of you marry unwisely, my dear. I want you all to be happy in your marriages.'

'As do I. Do you know, I always hoped that one day I would marry for love, just as my parents did.' Leah frowned. 'Or so I thought. It was a shock to discover their union was an arranged marriage. May I ask… I understand why my mother agreed to the marriage, but was my father's incentive a purely mercenary one?'

'Not entirely. All three of your fathers were paid handsomely, of course, but there was also promotion, in your father's case. He was a curate, and Lord Tregowan arranged for him to take over the living at the church in the village where you grew up.'

*So Papa wed Mama as a means to an end? He used her—and she used him, to give her respectability. But they still fell in love.*

Her understanding of the complexities of relationships shifted, and hope bloomed in her heart. Hope for her and for Dolph.

At that moment, Vardy entered the drawing room and bowed.

'Lord Dolphinstone has arrived, ma'am, and requests an audience with Miss Thame.'

Leah's stomach lurched.

'Thank you,' said Mrs Butterby. 'Please show him up. Leah, do you wish me to stay with you, or would you prefer privacy?'

'I should prefer to speak to His Lordship in private, I believe. Thank you.'

Mrs Butterby smiled and hurried out of the room.

\* \* \*

Dolph followed the butler upstairs to the drawing room, his stomach tied in knots. Last night, when he was with Leah, he'd been convinced she would forgive him and accept his proposal. But various conversations and comments by others at the rout had rocked his confidence—his simplistic view that her admirers consisted solely of fortune hunters had been shattered as it became clear he was not the only man who admired her for both her appearance and her character. How had he been so blinkered as to believe no other men would see her appeal? He'd lain awake half the night fretting he'd left it too late to win her.

Now he must not only confess the truth about Rebecca and his blame for her suicide, but he must also convince Leah that he truly loved her. Would she believe him— and forgive him—after he hurt her so badly with that clumsy proposal at the Court?

The butler showed him into the drawing room. Leah's expression gave away nothing of her feelings, no hint of what her answer might be, her lovely blue-green eyes guarded. He longed to fling himself at her feet and to beg her to forgive him and to accept his love and his heart, but he could not. First, he must tell her the truth.

'Good morning, my lord.'

Dolph drank in her willowy form, clad in a simple primrose and white striped gown. Her shining red hair was loosely pinned, and she glowed with health. How had he been so slow to realise how much love he held in his heart for this woman? Love that now filled every cell and permeated every thought. How could he bear to lose her now? He would move heaven and earth, mountains included, to make her happy. To keep her content. So much he wanted...*needed*...to say. He opened his mouth, tightly reining in all that emotion swirling through him.

'Good morning, Leah. I believe you are aware why I have sought an interview with you this morning?'

Dolph bowed, cringing at his own stiff formality. He sounded as though he were about to interview her for a job. But what else could he do but revert to the manners expected of a gentleman? He did not want to place too much pressure on her. He owed it to her to help her understand everything before he placed his heart and his future happiness in her hands.

'There is something I need to tell you first, however...'

He fell silent as Leah held up one hand.

'May we sit first?'

'Yes! Yes, of course.'

Dolph gestured towards the sofa. Leah glided across the room and sat down. About to move to a nearby chair, he changed his mind and sat next to her. She—almost imperceptibly—inched away from him, plaiting her fingers in her lap. His heart sank as she shot him a sideways glance.

'There is something *I* must tell *you* first,' she said. 'It might change your mind about your intentions.'

He bit back his instinctive denial that anything could change his intentions. She was deadly serious and he owed her the respect to listen to what she had to say first.

'Very well. I am listening.'

He could not tear his gaze from her restless fingers as they fidgeted in her lap.

'We spoke yesterday about my good fortune and about the third beneficiary of Lady Tregowan's will.'

'I recall.'

'She arrived this morning. Miss Beatrice Fothergill—'

'Fothergill? Any relation to Sir Percy Fothergill?'

'Yes. No.' She sighed. 'That is what I wish to explain. Aurelia, Beatrice and I have agreed to openly acknowledge the reason Lady Tregowan bequeathed us her entire estate.' She captured his gaze. 'You will be the first to know. We are sisters. Well, half-sisters, to be precise.'

'Half-sisters? You mean… Lady Tregowan was your mother?' How had *that* remained a secret in Somerset society, especially when Lady Tregowan had never given Tregowan a child?

'No. Lord Tregowan fathered all three of us. He arranged marriages for our mothers before any of us were born. M-my papa was not my father. I am illegitimate.'

He'd noticed that hitch in her voice before when she spoke of her father—the man who raised her. And now he understood.

'And this is what you discovered at that meeting in Bristol?'

'It is.' The look she sent him was frank. 'As you may imagine, it took time to take in all the implications.'

'Indeed.' No wonder she did not race off to London straight away, quite apart from the added complication of him arriving home the very same day. And no wonder she had appeared distracted.

'If you think this changes my mind about you, Leah… about wanting you as my wife…you are mistaken.'

'But… I am illegitimate.'

'Not in the eyes of the law or Society. Your parents were married when you were born; your father raised you as his own child. No one knows.'

'But they *will* know. We intend to acknowledge each other as sisters. Mrs Butterby has counselled us against it, but we are as one on it. It will cause a scandal.'

'A scandal?' Dolph laughed and shook his head. 'At first, maybe, but it will not endure. Society will absorb the news, gossip about it for a while and then move on to the next juicy titbit.

'Leah—' he took her hand and raised it to his lips, pressing them to her warm skin, breathing in her familiar fragrance of lavender-scented soap '—this sort of thing happens more often than you can ever know. The morality of many in the *haut ton* can be summed up by one phrase: *don't get caught.*'

'But we will be caught, by our own admission.'

'And your mothers' reputations will be picked over and some will visit your mother's sin upon you. But it truly makes no difference to me. Now...tell me about your new sister. What is she like? Does she look like you or more like Miss Croome?'

'She resembles Aurelia, but she is a gentler soul. Aurelia is a little...prickly...at times.'

'Really? I cannot say I noticed.'

Leah's eyes crinkled in amusement. 'Aurelia may be fierce but she has a good heart.'

'I shall take your word for it.' Dolph's pulse picked up speed and his mouth dried. The time had come... He could put it off no longer. 'Leah... I still have my own confession to make.'

She shifted so she was half facing him, her face serious. 'I am listening.'

'You know of my vow to never marry again.'

'I do.'

'I allowed you... George...*everyone*...to believe it was because my love for Rebecca was too strong to be replaced. That was never the reason. The shameful truth is that I did not love Rebecca. At least, not enough. Ours was an arranged marriage—I was fond of her, and we were not unhappy.' He stared at his hands, gripped together on his lap. 'I believed that, at least. After she died, however, I discovered exactly how unhappy she had been.' He raised his eyes, forcing himself to meet Leah's gaze. 'My neglect of Rebecca—my selfish complacency—caused her death.'

Leah frowned. 'But…her death was an accident. Are you telling me you were there when she died?'

'No. But if I had been there…maybe it would not have happened. Leah, what I am about to tell you is known to *nobody* else. Rebecca killed herself.'

# Chapter Twenty-Five

'She…? Oh, *no*. Poor, poor lady.' As her initial shock subsided, Leah's voice lowered. 'And poor you. What a dreadful thing to happen, and how hard it must have been to keep it to yourself.'

He searched her face, his brow wrinkled. 'You immediately express sympathy with no sense of shock when many would condemn her for committing a mortal sin. And you a vicar's daughter, too.'

'Papa—' again, she felt that dull ache when she spoke of him '—was the least judgemental man I have ever known. He understood that, at times, life becomes too hard to bear and, if a person is determined, there is little to stop them, short of locking them away for their own protection.'

Dolph bent his head, clenched fists pressed to his eyes. His back heaved. Leah laid her hand on his back, circling gently…soothing the only way she could, for she doubted she could conjure any words that might comfort him. But she could listen, and help him deal with the grief revived by speaking of what happened.

'I feel so guilty.' He mumbled slightly, his hands still covering his face. 'I should have noticed her mind was so disturbed, but I thought she was still recovering from Matilda's birth. I thought nothing more of it, other than trying to jolly her out of it. I had no idea…but that is no excuse! I should have known…should have realised. I should have *stopped* her.'

Leah's thoughts ranged into the past, to the years after Mama's death, and to the times when Papa would return from visiting parishioners in need of spiritual guidance. At times, he would unburden some of the weight of his own inadequacies, talking to Leah as though she were another adult instead of a girl.

'It might comfort you to know Papa had a theory that some mothers suffer greatly after childbirth.' She blushed at speaking boldly of such a subject to a man, but the urge to ease Dolph's distress outweighed her embarrassment. 'Papa noticed it in several new mothers, and he became convinced it was a biological occurrence. He told me he had seen too many suffer from abnormally low moods, and that status made no difference. A duchess was as likely as a peasant to succumb to that depressed state of nerves. For some it lasted but a few days and was quickly shrugged off. For others, though…' She paused, thinking back, picking her words carefully. 'He heard of young mothers who were committed to mental asylums for their own safety, and also of others who successfully hid the extent of their distress from their families. Sometimes for years.'

'I never made the connection before, but Rebecca's mood was also low for a month or so after both boys were born. And your father noticed the phenomenon several times, you say?'

'Yes. Papa felt keenly for all those poor souls—not only new mothers—who suffered and did his best to counsel them. Occasionally, though, there would be a person who could see no release other than to take that final, drastic step.'

Leah became aware Dolph was looking at her, hope in his eyes.

'Anyone's death by their own hand is hard to bear,' she said, 'but it must be particularly so when it is the mother of your children.'

'I longed to understand. She left a letter, but it did not explain why. That is what I found so difficult, and I felt so guilty that I let the children down by not realising how unhappy Rebecca had been. I swore to myself I would not put another woman through what she went through because I believed it was my neglect—my preoccupation with politics and government—that had made her so very unhappy. I returned to Dolphin Court determined to make it up to the children for losing their mother, and for my abandonment at the very time they needed me. I told myself my needs were unimportant…that I did not deserve happiness. I would get my satisfaction from making my children happy and running the estate.'

He sighed and gathered Leah's hands in his. 'I had no contingency plan for meeting a woman like you.'

'A *contingency* plan?'

He winced. 'That's not very romantic, is it? But it's the truth. You shattered my carefully constructed idea of what my life should be. Leah…my darling…'

Dolph hauled in a deep breath and leapt to his feet, tugging Leah upright to face him. The words burst from him.

'Dolphin Court is not the same without you. Our family is not the same without you. I know I am asking a great deal when you are the toast of Society but, please… come home with me. Tomorrow! Be my wife. I promise I'll make you happy. I'll get a licence. We can be married right away, here in London. Or we can wait until we get home if you prefer. All I know is that I cannot wait to take you home where you belong. I love you. I should have told you that the first time I proposed, but I made the most spectacular mull of it, didn't I?' He dragged in a fractured breath. 'Tell me I'm not too late.' Agony and hope warred in his expression. 'Please tell me you will trust me to make you happy.'

Leah gazed into his stricken eyes, and she dared to believe there could be a happy ending for them after all.

'Of course I trust you.' She caressed his cheek, marvelling that she could touch him whenever she wanted to from now on. 'And I know we will be happy.' Any doubts had evaporated and those painful experiences with Peter and Usk were now just distant memories. 'But... I did not tell you about the conditions attached to my inheritance, one of which is that all three of us must reside in London for the entirety of the Season and remain under Mrs Butterby's chaperonage until we marry. I did not think to ask if that condition means I must stay in London even if I do marry.'

'What happens if it does mean that and you do not stay in London?'

'I forfeit my share of the inheritance.'

Dolph frowned. 'What would then happen to your share?'

'It would be divided between Aurelia and Beatrice and, other than an annual allowance of two hundred pounds, I would lose everything.'

A smile spread across his features. He grabbed her hands and cradled them to his heart. 'You will not lose me, sweetheart. You will not lose the children. Marry me. Come home to Dolphin Court and allow your sisters to take your share. You will still have them, too. I don't *care* about the money. We won't need it. I will settle a sum on you so you are protected should anything happen to me. I just want you, and for us to go home together.

'Please, Leah. Say yes. Say you will marry me.'

'Oh, yes, my darling.' Leah pulled her hands free to cradle his face, and she kissed him thoroughly, joy cascading through her. 'Yes. Yes. Yes,' she whispered against his lips.

Then she pulled back. She had just found her sisters. She loved Dolph, so very much. But...

'What is it? What is wrong?'

'Oh, Dolph! I cannot leave. Not yet.'

She braced herself for a tirade of words aimed at persuading her she was wrong.

'Tell me why.'

And there, she realised, was another reason she loved him. He would listen to her doubts and not dismiss them because they did not suit him.

'It is Aurelia and Beatrice. We are still strangers— especially Beatrice—and I desperately want to get to know them better.'

'They can come and stay with us at Dolphin Court. Any time.'

She sighed. 'But...they might need me. Here. In London. Dolph... I did not tell you of the other conditions in the will.'

Dolph sat on the sofa and tugged her down next to him. 'Tell me now.'

'The most important one is that each of us must marry within a year if we wish to keep our inheritance. I... I am sorry, but I cannot abandon my sisters when they have such momentous decisions to make. I really do need to stay.' She searched his eyes.

'Then stay we shall. All of us, the children too. My

town house is in South Audley Street, just a five-minute walk from here.' He hugged Leah to him and then kissed her. Very thoroughly. 'We can marry, and you will still be here for your sisters. In fact, you will be in a better position to help them as Lady Dolphinstone.

'Now...enough talk, and kiss me again, my beautiful bride-to-be.'

A shiver of delight ran through Leah at his words. She had never considered herself beautiful, but Dolph thought her so, and his opinion was all that mattered to her. She surrendered to the magic of his lips, pressing close to his firm body, barely believing her good fortune. This man, whom she loved so very deeply, loved her in return, and she could not wait until they were man and wife. As their tongues entwined, however, a thought penetrated the sensual haze surrounding her. She eased her lips from his, ignoring his protesting groan.

'Can we tell the children? Today?'

Dolph's chest vibrated as he laughed, a delicious, deep rumble of a laugh. He pressed his lips to her hair.

'Yes, we can tell the children. We will go now. I insist upon it.' He leapt to his feet and pulled her up. 'In fact, we will tell the whole world, for only then will I fully believe this is real and not a fantasy conjured up by my mind to taunt me.

'I want the entire world to know how much I love you, my beautiful, kind and clever Leah. And the sooner, the better.'

*Two days later*

Glorious anticipation flooded Leah as she and Dolph climbed the stairs of his town house hand in hand.

It had been a perfect day, beginning with their wedding ceremony at St George's, Hanover Square. The children had been on their best behaviour while their father had exchanged vows with their former governess, whose new half-sisters and erstwhile chaperone had shed a tear or two. The wedding breakfast had been a celebration of their union and an opportunity for the two newly merged families to get to know one another better after two days spent on feverish wedding preparations.

Leah recalled, with a happy glow, the children's excitement when they were told she was to be their new mama. Stevie and Nicky had understood straight away and had flung themselves at her, jabbering nineteen to the dozen. And Tilly—although it was clear she didn't really understand—had been determined not to miss out and had squirmed her way into the middle of that group hug. Aurelia and Beatrice had been just as happy and excited for her, as had Mrs Butterby, and Leah prayed they, too, would marry the men of their dreams, just as she had.

After the wedding breakfast, a walk in Hyde Park for the entire clan had ended a memorable day in style. Now, finally, the newly-weds were alone.

Leah walked ahead of her new husband into his bedchamber and turned to him as he closed the door. He opened his arms, and she stepped into his embrace. He heaved a sigh.

'Happy?' she asked, although she knew the answer from the big smile that had adorned his face for most of the day.

'You do not know how happy, my darling.' He kissed the tip of her nose before leaning away to study her. 'Have I told you today how stunning you look?'

'Oh...' She gave him a playful smile, and her pulse

quickened as his gaze dropped to her mouth. 'Once, maybe…or, maybe, a thousand times.'

She tiptoed up and kissed him, rousing a hunger within her shocking in its intensity. She'd yearned for this moment for so long, and the taste of him…the thrust of his tongue…the feel of his arousal trapped between them sent shock waves through her entire body. She ached for him…craving the moment their bodies were joined as their hands and their hearts had earlier been joined in church.

Dolph trailed open-mouthed kisses across her jaw and neck as his fingers thrust into her hair. Before long, it tumbled over her shoulders and down her back, and he lifted a handful to his face, breathing in deeply.

'So beautiful. You smell divine,' he whispered, as he gently turned her, his fingers getting to work on the buttons down the back of her gown.

The gown slid from her shoulders, and gooseflesh rippled across her back as he untied the ribbon that held Mama's ring and kissed her nape.

'Have I ever told you I adore your freckles?'

His fingertips danced across her shoulders before his tongue traced a path from nape to shoulder as he unlaced her. She caught her breath as her corset fell away, her heart pounding in her chest. She turned to him, clad only in her shift, and searched his grey eyes.

'Leah?' His hands skimmed up her arms.

'Dolph?' she murmured, before allowing her lips to curve in a knowing smile. She reached for the buttons of his waistcoat.

Dolph's head tipped back, and he closed his eyes, his breathing harsh as she pushed his coat and waistcoat from his shoulders and unwound his neckcloth, exposing the strong column of his throat. She pressed her lips to his warm skin, breathing in his beloved scent as her fingers played among the curls of chest hair visible in the open neck of his shirt.

Dolph groaned, muttered something unintelligible, stepped back, and in one swift movement, he ripped his shirt over his head, flinging it aside before kicking off his shoes and reaching for his trouser buttons. Leah stepped back, her eyes raking his chest and lingering over the bulge in his trousers. Deliberately, she licked her lips.

Dolph paused. His eyes narrowed. 'You minx,' he growled.

Leah held his gaze and gave him a teasing smile as she gathered her shift, raising it. His chest heaved and another groan, tormented, shuddered from him. She stripped her shift over her head and felt her hair spill across her bare shoulders and breasts, and she stood naked beneath his gaze as he appraised her body. She felt no embarrassment; rather, she felt confident and powerful as never before at the effect she had on this magnificently virile man.

*And he is mine. All mine.*

She could feel the heat radiating from his body and his intoxicating musky scent filled her. Her body felt heavy and warm; her skin tingled; her breasts ached; and that wonderful and irresistible physical yearning filled her, urging her to act.

But she stayed still. Waiting. Until Dolph raised his eyes to hers. Their gazes locked, and something intense flared in his eyes and she felt her own involuntary response. In one swift movement, they came together, lips meeting and tongues tangling with a savage intensity that stole her breath. His trousers were discarded. He guided her hand to him, and she gasped into his mouth as her fingers wrapped around his hot, silken, solid length.

Dolph's entire body stilled, and then his head dipped. She gasped again as his mouth closed around her aching nipple. Fiery darts of need radiated through her and she felt that same tiny pleasurable pulse beat within the sensitive flesh between her thighs.

Too soon, Dolph raised his head.

'Now, my dazzling Countess,' he growled. He nipped her earlobe. Then he backed her towards the bed. 'Allow me to prove to you how much you mean to me.'

Later, as Leah—sated and complete—lay in her husband's arms, sprawled across his muscled, hair-roughened chest, Dolph heaved a sigh sounding of pure contentment. Leah raised her head and studied him sleepily.

'I love you, Lord Dolphinstone,' she said, simply.

He met her eyes and smiled lovingly before framing her face with gentle hands and kissing her—a slow, sweet, savouring kiss. She felt him slowly grow hard against her thigh.

'I love you too, my Lady Dolphinstone,' he whispered against her lips. 'So very, very much.'

She had nearly lost him—afraid to believe hope might ultimately triumph over experience. But it had, and now she meant to savour every minute of every day—and every night—of their life together.

Her hand stroked down his magnificent body and closed around his solid erection.

'Do you care to prove again how much I mean to you, my lord?'

In one swift movement, he flipped her over onto her back, pinning her to the mattress as he settled himself between her thighs. She relished the weight of him, her entire being throbbing with anticipation.

'You mean the world to me,' he avowed as he filled her. 'And I will never stop proving it to you.'

* * * * *